SOMETHING WAS
DIFFERENT ABOUT HIM

He kept his eyes on hers, his gaze holding a strange, dark intensity that made a flood of heat nearly consume her. *Oh, dear God.*

They danced without speaking, without smiling, and a casual observer might think they were a couple who was bored, with life, with each other. But someone who was watching intensely might have seen Maggie's parted lips, the way her breath was catching oddly in her chest, the way his arms pulled her subtly closer and closer until they were nearly fully embracing.

When the music stopped, Lord Hollings pulled her out of the ballroom and to the empty veranda. He didn't say a word. Neither did she.

Even when he pressed her against the cold stone of the mansion, even when he brought his mouth against hers, even when he pressed his body to hers, even then, they were silent.

BOOK YOUR PLACE ON OUR WEBSITE AND MAKE THE READING CONNECTION!

We've created a customized website just for our very special readers, where you can get the inside scoop on everything that's going on with Zebra, Pinnacle and Kensington books.

When you come online, you'll have the exciting opportunity to:

- View covers of upcoming books
- Read sample chapters
- Learn about our future publishing schedule (listed by publication month *and author*)
- Find out when your favorite authors will be visiting a city near you
- Search for and order backlist books from our online catalog
- Check out author bios and background information
- Send e-mail to your favorite authors
- Meet the Kensington staff online
- Join us in weekly chats with authors, readers and other guests
- Get writing guidelines
- AND MUCH MORE!

Visit our website at
http://www.kensingtonbooks.com

A
CHRISTMAS
SCANDAL

JANE GOODGER

ZEBRA BOOKS
Kensington Publishing Corp.
http://www.kensingtonbooks.com

ZEBRA BOOKS are published by

Kensington Publishing Corp.
119 West 40th Street
New York, NY 10018

All Kensington titles, imprints, and distributed lines are available at special quantity discounts for bulk purchases for sales promotion, premiums, fund-raising, educational, or institutional use.

Special book excerpts or customized printings can also be created to fit specific needs. For details, write or phone the office of the Kensington Special Sales Manager: Attn. Special Sales Department. Kensington Publishing Corp., 119 West 40th Street, New York, NY 10018. Phone: 1-800-221-2647.

Zebra and the Z logo Reg. U.S. Pat. & TM Off.

ISBN-13: 978-1-4201-0379-3
ISBN-10: 1-4201-0379-2

First Printing: October 2009
10 9 8 7 6 5 4 3 2 1

Printed in the United States of America

Chapter 1

New York, 1893

Margaret Pierce sat in the pink parlor, a whimsical room her whimsical mother loved, hoping it would somehow calm her. She rocked back and forth, her hands clutched together, as she prayed fervently for her father.

She heard the front door open, the murmurings of her mother talking to one of their few remaining servants, and listened as her footsteps sounded, tap-tapping, on the marble floor. Her heart beat a slow, sickening beat in her chest.

"There you are, Maggie," Harriet Pierce said, looking unusually drawn. "It's done with now."

Maggie looked at her mother, afraid to ask what had happened to her father, a gentle, wonderful man who was going to prison. She could not bring herself to go to the hearing, unable to bear the weight of all that had happened, unable to look in the eyes of the man who held her father's fate in his filthy hands.

She was afraid to ask her mother how long her father would be in prison, even though she knew what the answer would be. She'd made sure of that.

"Oh, my dear," her mother said, rushing over to sit by her daughter, embracing her tightly, and Maggie realized she hadn't been trying quite hard enough to hide her feelings. "This has been difficult for you, I know. The two of you are so close. I think that is what is so upsetting to him, not being with you on your wedding day. For your children when they are born."

Maggie pushed her mother gently away, staring at her with the beginnings of terror gripping her. "It's only a year. He'll be home with us for the wedding and certainly in time to see his grandchildren."

Her mother's eyes welled up and she shook her head. "Whatever gave you that idea? Oh, Maggie, it's to be five years. Five years was always what we thought. What on earth made you think otherwise?" Her mother straightened her spine. "But we'll get through it. Your father is a relatively young man. He'll still be in his early fifties by the time he's home with us. Not so old."

"No," Maggie whispered, feeling as if she might faint, feeling as if the world were tilting crazily around her. "One year. It's to be *one* year," she said, her voice taking on the edge of desperation.

"Oh, darling," her mother said, trying to pull her into another comforting embrace. "The years will fly by. You'll see."

Maggie stood up, agitated beyond bearing. "It's impossible. He promised."

Her mother smiled up at her. "Who promised? No one promised any such thing. Certainly not

Papa. Oh, he didn't, did he? I do declare that man would say anything to make you feel better."

Maggie looked at her mother, her eyes wild, her breathing erratic.

"Maggie, what are you doing?" her mother asked sharply, looking at her wrist.

She looked down to see a row of neat little red crescents on her wrist where she'd been digging her thumbnail into her skin. Distractedly, she pulled down her sleeve, then took a bracing breath. She'd nearly lost control, which would have upset her mother terribly. Sitting down, she grasped her mother's hand and smiled shakily. "I'm sorry. I had this crazy hope is all. I'm just so worried about Papa. About everything, I suppose."

Her mother visibly calmed when she saw her daughter's smile, and Maggie vowed to never let her mother see how terrified, how very distraught she was. Harriet had always been an emotionally fragile person, and Maggie had always tried to keep her life as calm as possible. With all that was happening around them, keeping calm was hopeless, but she did not want to add to her mother's torment. It was almost as if the devil, having decided to pick out one poor family to have fun with, had picked Maggie's and was enjoying himself immensely watching them all suffer. For never had a family's life gone from idyllic to nightmarish in the space that Maggie's had. Indeed, it was difficult to believe that just three months before she had had everything a young woman of twenty could ask for: friends, loving parents, two protective brothers, a beautiful home, and a brilliant future.

When news of her father's arrest for embezzlement hit the *New York Times*, friends disappeared, invitations dried up, servants quit. Once on the fringes of the elite New York Four Hundred, now the Pierces were shunned at best. For the worst of it was that her banker father had embezzled money from the very people they depended upon for the social status they had so enjoyed. One brother, an attorney in one of the most prestigious law firms in New York, was fired and was now working in a tiny firm in Richmond, where no one had heard of Reginald Pierce. Thankfully, her oldest brother was in San Francisco, far removed from the scandal.

After her father's arrest, creditors immediately began knocking on their door and the state demanded repayment of an impossible sum. Everything was gone, including their fashionable home on Fifth Avenue. They were to be out in three days, leaving behind a lifetime's accumulation of wealth. Everything would be auctioned.

Arthur Wright was their last hope. How many times had Harriet thanked God for him? Thank God, thank God. Arthur Wright, who bored Maggie to tears, whom she didn't love, but who loved her. "I suppose it won't do for Arthur to see me tonight with a red nose and watery eyes," Maggie said in an attempt at levity.

"Do you think he's going to ask today? That would be a wonderful ending to an absolutely horrid day," her mother said, fretting her hands in her lap. Her mother, never the calm and collected one, had lately looked rather like a harried wash maid, her hair a mass of messy curls, her clothing always slightly askew. Once they'd let go of almost all of their servants, poor Mama could not handle the daily ablutions required of her. She was clean but looked as if she'd just come in from a violent windstorm. And her eyes always darted about a room, as if the miseries that had struck this family were tangible things she could duck away from.

"I'm almost certain that is why Arthur is coming over tonight," Maggie said, smiling. This, at least, was a genuine smile, for Arthur had more than hinted that tonight was the night they would formalize their engagement. She knew her mother would worry until she was safely settled, just as she knew their worries were over. She and Arthur were already unofficially engaged; she was awaiting only the ring and a formal announcement in the *Times*. She should be ecstatic, but the truth was, Maggie didn't want to marry anyone. At least not anyone in New York.

"I'm so glad," Harriet said. "We really shouldn't hold out hope any longer."

"Hold out hope for what?"

"Oh. I meant about the earl, dear. I was holding out hope that he'd return or write. *Something*. A title would have been so very nice."

Maggie let out a laugh even as her heart gave a painful wrench. She had met Lord Hollings over the summer in Newport. He'd been friends with the Duke of Bellingham, who'd married her best friend, then taken her away to England, away from her. Maggie had been stupid and naive enough to fall in love with the earl, though thankfully she hadn't been foolish enough to let anyone know, including him. "The earl was just being kind to me because I am Elizabeth's friend. You know that."

"But those dances," Harriet said, letting her voice trail off.

"It was great fun but nothing more than an innocent flirtation. What Arthur and I share is far deeper. Far more meaningful." Goodness, she was getting so good at doing anything to make her mother feel better—which apparently included marrying a man she did not love.

As she thought back, it seemed as if her life took a sudden and desperate turn for the worse when Elizabeth married her duke. Maggie was left with a world crumbling around her, with her flailing and trying with all her might to stop it.

"I should probably get ready," she said, attempting to sound like her old, perky self. "Arthur is coming for supper and he'll be here within the hour. Could you help me with my dress?"

Only the most loyal servants had stuck with the Pierces after it became clear there would be no more money forthcoming. It was something they would all have to get used to, fending for themselves, dressing themselves, cooking their own food. Maggie had always thought of herself as a modern independent woman until the day she realized she could not dress herself without help. Without Arthur there would be no balls, no new dresses every season, no French chef in a grand kitchen. Her mother was far more upset about their change in fortune than Maggie was, though she was greatly affected by her mother's despondency.

Without Arthur, her mother would have had to move to her sister's home in Savannah, Georgia. It was a dreaded alternative, for neither wanted to live in Savannah.

Once she was dressed for supper, Maggie glanced at the mirror, noting absently that it needed a good polishing. She looked exactly the same. Exactly. No one could know what was inside her, the secrets, the shame. She smiled brilliantly, her teeth white and straight, her eyes sparkling.

"Of course I'll marry you, Arthur," she gushed to her reflection. Then she let out a sigh and for just a moment almost gave in to the tears that had threatened for weeks, that left her throat feeling perpetually raw. Arthur did not deserve what he was getting. He deserved the girl she used to be, carefree and innocent and full of hope, not the girl she'd become. Guilt assaulted her and she pushed it brutally away, knowing Arthur would be much happier to marry the girl he thought she was than be told the truth. With a start, she realized she was digging her thumbnail into her wrist again and she looked at the crescents with a bit of vexation. She'd ruined the sleeves of two blouses already with tiny spots of blood that would not wash away no matter what she tried.

She heard the rustling of skirts and her mother, her hair in wild disarray, peeked into her room. "He's here," she hissed delightedly. Maggie shook her head fondly at her mother's complete glee.

"Arthur comes to dinner every Tuesday night, Mama. I don't know why you have it in your head that tonight is the night he will propose."

"Because if he doesn't, we'll both be on a train to Savannah," she pointed out. "Not that it wouldn't be wonderful to see my sister, but Catherine's house is so small, especially with her children and that huge husband or hers. She's still got two at home, you know. Children, not husbands." Maggie wrinkled her nose, making Harriet laugh. "It's not Catherine I worry about." Harriet had often commented on the fact that she didn't like her sister's husband, found him coarse and far too opinionated. "And I may have hinted that you would be safely married soon. It's not that she wouldn't welcome us both. It's simply that she's not expecting two more females for an extended time."

Maggie lifted her hand to stop her mother's guilt-ridden monologue. "I understand completely. Besides, we don't have to worry about Aunt Catherine or her children or Uncle Bert because we have Arthur. Now. How do I look?" she asked, swishing her yellow skirts back and forth. With her dark hair and flashing brown eyes, yellow had always been a good color for Maggie.

"You look like a girl who's about to get engaged," Harriet said, her eyes misting a bit. "Now hurry before he changes his mind. He's in the pink parlor."

"Oh, Mama, you didn't. You know that men loathe that room. He'll feel positively uncomfortable." She followed her mother down the stairs, motioning to her silently to stay put and not eavesdrop at the door even though she knew her mother would.

"Hello, Arthur," she said, closing the door firmly and walking toward the tall man sitting awkwardly in a delicate Queen Anne chair. He was all knees and elbows, her Arthur. He stood abruptly, almost as if surprised to find Maggie here in her own home.

"Good evening."

He didn't smile. Perhaps he was nervous, Maggie thought. Or perhaps he'd decided that a buoyant greeting would be inappropriate given that her father had just been sentenced to prison.

"I'm so sorry about your father," he blurted out. Arthur Wright was a man who did not feel comfortable in the company of women, for he came from a family of five boys. He got on well with Maggie because she had older brothers and so knew how men ticked. He'd once told her that she was the only pretty girl he knew that he could spend more than a minute with. Maggie took that as the compliment it was intended to be.

Maggie swallowed heavily at the mention of her father. She had not allowed herself to think of him locked away in prison with all sorts of rough men. Her father, who loved the ballet and a fine port and cigar after supper, was not at all the kind of man who would thrive in such a place. "I miss him already," she said, her throat closing on the last word. She cleared his throat. "But we shall all be fine. Mama says the time will fly."

"Yes. Five years, I heard."

It was supposed to be one. One year. He could have endured one year. "Five years will go by so swiftly," she repeated, her smile brittle.

"Yes. But there will always be the taint," he said, and Maggie stiffened. It was so unlike Arthur to say such a thing, for if he was anything, he was kind to a fault.

"I suppose there will be."

"And that's the thing. That's it, you see," he said, sounding muddled.

Maggie didn't understand until she looked at his face, filled with torment and real despair. And she knew, without a doubt, that Arthur Wright had not come that night to propose. He had come to break it off.

His face crumpled briefly, but he regained control of his features and stood there, making her say it because no doubt he could not bring himself to.

"You are breaking it off," Maggie said dully.

He nodded, his eyes filling with tears, for Arthur did love her. She'd always known it, believed it.

"It's our business. I know how that sounds. You cannot know how hard this is for me. How I fought . . ." He broke off, shaking his head miserably. "But my father can't take the chance for his name to be associated with . . . with . . ."

"Mine."

"Oh, Maggie, not yours. Your father's. This is the worst thing that's ever happened to me," he said, trying desperately to hold it together and failing miserably. "I love you," he cried, then pulled her to him and embraced her, kissing her hair in an almost frenzied way.

Maggie stiffened, then pushed him gently, but firmly away. "It's just as well, Arthur. I do believe that you love me, but you obviously don't love me enough. And I don't love you at all." She shouldn't have hurt him, she should not have lowered herself to such cruelty. But then, he didn't know anything of what she'd gone through, of what she was going through. If losing her was the worst thing that had ever happened to him, then he had led a pathetically easy life. She should tell him just how awful life could get.

"You don't mean that," he said, stricken.

"It doesn't matter," she said dully. "Could you please go?"

"How could you say such a thing? How?"

"You hurt me. And I hurt you back. I'm sorry," she said, sounding more like some sort of automaton than an anguished woman. "Please go," she repeated.

He bowed his head. "Of course."

He left the parlor, that ridiculous pink parlor, and Maggie was glad that the last thing he would remember was where she stood when she delivered the final blow to her already miserable life.

Chapter 2

Maggie sat at the dining table, waving a fan frantically at her face thinking that if she was wilting from the heat in New York, how would she feel in Savannah?

"The heat never really bothered me," Harriet said, lying through her teeth, Maggie suspected, for her cheeks were brightly flushed and her hairline damp from sweat.

"I suppose one gets used to it," she said, stopping the fan for a moment because her wrist was beginning to ache.

"I don't remember ever being hot as a child," her mother said, slipping into her gentile southern drawl for affect, and Maggie smiled. Her mother had visited her sister several times over the years, but those visits were always carefully timed to miss the worst of the Northeast's winters. "I daresay I won't miss those horrid winters here. Your father would joke and tell me I'd never quite got rid of my southern blood." Harriet frowned, then gave a little shudder, as if shaking away any sad thoughts.

Maggie always liked winter, or at least the change of seasons. She could not imagine a Christmas without the biting cold or threat of snow. She adored her winter muffs, the way her cheeks would bloom with color. The taste of snow. And she would miss her brother and friends and the hope she'd had of ever having a normal life. Savannah meant more than heat, it meant she would either have to live off her relatives for life, find a husband quickly, or get a job. Though she hadn't dared tell her mother yet, Maggie's plan was to become a governess to some wealthy southern family. It would be a fair tragedy to her mother to have Maggie out working, but what other choice did she have? And being a governess was respectable.

If she were a governess she could have the pleasure of being with children even though she would never have her own. It would be a wonderful compromise. She'd find a nice family, one with clean, polite children, hopefully in Savannah so she could be close to her mother, and she would teach those little scrubbed faces. She could become like a second mother to them. And she would have everything any woman could ever want.

She would be old spinster Pierce, whom the children loved.

And everyone else felt sorry for.

Maggie gave herself a mental shake to rid herself of any thought that was the least bit upsetting. "Mama, I have made a decision."

Harriet gave her daughter an uncertain smile.

"When we reach Savannah, I am going to find a position as a governess. I do not want to be dependent

on Aunt Catherine and that would give me a bit of
independence."

"You don't even like children," her mother pointed out.

It was true. Maggie had never liked to be with
them. She'd never actually spent more than a few
minutes with a child, but simply accepted the fact
that someday she would have one or two of them
running about. Still, she decided to argue anyway.
"What kind of person does not like children? Of
course I like children."

"You find them messy and loud and rather silly.
And I completely agree."

"Mother!"

Harriet laughed. "The only children I have ever
been able to tolerate were you and your brothers.
You were always so quiet and well behaved. Most
children are not like that. It is completely out of the
question at any rate. I don't believe I could stand any
further humiliation."

"But what am I to do? I cannot live on the good
charity of your sister forever. I must be independent."

"Why not simply work as a shop girl? Or better
yet out in the cotton fields?" her mother asked
with uncharacteristic sarcasm. "Haven't I been
through enough without having a daughter as a governess? My goodness, Maggie, it's almost as if you
are contriving to make me more miserable than
I am."

Maggie looked down at her plate, hating to make
her mother, who had been through so much, even
more unhappy. "I'm sorry, Mama, it's just that I don't
know what to do."

"You will get married, of course," her mother said, instantly happy.

Maggie only felt her dread grow. She could not marry, though she couldn't tell her mother that. She told herself she would not allow her mother to win this fight, and had had her arguments for independence dancing in her head since the moment Arthur had left the house. Her first thought had been: what do I do now? Her options were woefully limited. She knew only one thing: children, whether she liked them or not, were safe.

"I will not marry."

Her mother let out a long sigh. "I know right now your heart is broken and you feel as if you will never find another man to love, but you will."

"But I don't want to get married. The only reason I was marrying Arthur was to protect us. But your sister . . ."

"Do you think I want to live under my sister's roof? To lie to her about your father? To come up with more lies and more lies to explain why we have no funds? As soon as you find a husband, our problems will be solved. Unless you believe a governess's wages can house and clothe both of us."

Maggie felt her cheeks flush. Her mother had never spoken to her this way. In fact, she could hardly remember her ever raising her voice. "Of course I don't believe that. I only wanted to relieve you of some of the burden."

"How on earth would I explain to my sister why you've become a governess?"

Maggie lifted her chin. "You could tell her the truth."

Maggie watched as her mother's face, already

flushed from the heat of the day, turned livid. "I could *never*," she said. "You don't know your aunt as I do. She would pretend to be saddened by our circumstances, but I know she'd be secretly happy. I'm the one who made a good marriage. Your uncle is little more than a laborer. I have never made her feel bad about her decision to marry him, but I know she resents the life I've had. Nothing would make her happier than to see how far we've fallen. Oh, sometimes I wish your father were here so I could strangle him."

It was the first time in Maggie's life that she'd ever heard her mother utter even a hint of criticism against her aunt or her father. Obviously the strain of these last few weeks was wearing on her.

Maggie stood and went to her mother, giving her an awkward hug. "We'll be fine, you'll see," she said, not believing for an instant that she was telling the truth. "I'm sorry, Mama. Everything's just been so upsetting lately," she said, giving her mother another squeeze. "I'm not feeling well. Perhaps that's why I feel so out of sorts. I think it's the heat."

"Why don't you go lie down?" her mother said gently. "Try not to think about anything."

Maggie left their dining room thinking that she simply could not bear another bad thing happening to her. She wished she could simply disappear, dissolve into the air forever. It wasn't death she wanted, for she'd never contemplate anything so final. She simply wanted to cease to feel for a while, to lie on a cloud in a crystal-blue sky and stare into space for, perhaps, three years.

"The post, Miss Pierce."

She looked up to see the sad face of her beloved

butler. While she was growing up, Willoughby had been more like a gruff old grandfather than a butler. His wife, the housekeeper, and he were the only servants left in the house. "Thank you, Willoughby," she said, feeling ridiculously close to tears. They were leaving this house in two days, never to return, and she likely would never see Willoughby again. She took the post without looking at it closely. "I know Mama already thanked you and Mrs. Willoughby for staying on 'til the end," she said, forcing a small smile. "But I wanted you to know that I will miss you terribly. No house I ever live in will be quite the same without you."

"Thank you, miss," he said gruffly, then gave a little bow and walked down the long hall to where his wife was no doubt working to pack their things.

Then she looked down at her letter and smiled genuinely for the first time in weeks. It was from England, no doubt from her friend Elizabeth, the new Duchess of Bellingham. These frequent missives from her were the only normal thing in her life, she realized. Elizabeth wrote to her as if everything were the same, as if they still lived a few blocks apart, as if they were planning to go together to the country dinners she described. Indeed, her letters were so filled with details of her happy life, it was almost as if Maggie were there.

Maggie walked to her room, holding the letter against her chest, hesitating to open it in order to savor it. But when she opened it, she immediately knew it was not from her friend, but from the Duke of Bellingham, her husband.

June 3, 1893

Dear Miss Pierce:

As you know, my wife and your friend is expecting to deliver a baby on or around Christmas. It would be my fondest wish to give my wife the gift of her closest friend being nearby during this time. Elizabeth's mother will be unable to journey here for the birth, and I feel it is necessary for her to have some sort of female companionship at this time. I pray it will not be a large inconvenience to you. Elizabeth speaks of you often and with great fondness. Please let me know whether you can come, and address any correspondence to me. If, indeed, you can travel to Bellewood, as is my fondest wish, I would like this to be a surprise for my wife.

Sincerely,
Randall Blackmore,
Duke of Bellingham

Maggie looked down at the letter, her eyes watering, the finely scrawled letters mere blurs before her. The duke would never know what he had done, how those few words he'd so casually written would completely change her life. She had thought so many, many times in the past few months that she needed something good to happen. How often had she wished for just one thing good among all the bad and horrid things that had happened to her since Elizabeth had gone away? Maggie Pierce, whose life had taken a decidedly desperate turn, knew she held in her hand her only salvation.

Chapter 3

England, one month later

Edward Hollings was trying, rather desperately, to think of a single reason why he should not bring his step-aunt and her brood of children to visit Belle-wood. Finding reasons to avoid his best friend's estate had not been an issue until he'd received a happily worded note from the duchess gushing about the imminent arrival of one Miss Pierce.

He'd held that note in his hand and crushed it with a curse. Damnation. His life had been wonderfully bland, filled with the normal pleasures, willing married women, balls, gambling, and overseeing his late uncle's vast and remarkably astute investments. Unlike many of the peerage, Lord Hollings was fortunate to have inherited a title that was once held by a financial genius. The former earl had been unsuccessful in only one aspect of his life: bearing children. So, finding himself a widower rather late in life, he'd married a woman who had more than proved her fertility by bearing six children in quick succession. Step-aunt Matilda's fertility ground to a halt the moment her first husband died and she married his now-deceased uncle. And so when Edward's uncle died, without an heir, he inherited the estate, as well as his step-aunt and her children. A few men had wondered aloud why he was continuing to support an entire family when he had no legal responsibility to do so, but what was he to do? Send a poor family packing to live in some moldering estate in the middle of nowhere? No.

And so his step-aunt and her six children had become part of his bachelor family, which already included a sister who refused to marry. Refuse was likely an exaggeration, for no one had actually asked her yet. But Edward was quite convinced no one had asked her because she had purposefully made herself completely unappealing to every male in all of Britain. He'd threatened to ship her off to America if she persisted in being so absolutely obstinate, something she'd enthusiastically agreed to, much to his frustration. The duchess was no help in that regard, insisting that, even though her own forced marriage had ended wonderfully, no woman should be asked to marry someone she wasn't completely in love with.

What utter rot.

His sister, Amelia, would point out with sharp-shooter precision that she should not be asked to be married when her brother was so apparently opposed to that particular life state. She would also point out, rather gleefully, that he needed an heir and so should be required to marry sooner than she. As far as marriage went, he'd only been tempted once, and had found that particular time so horribly trying he'd vowed to avoid any sort of emotion that could be construed as love.

And now *she* was coming to visit.

Surely, he was being tested by God or played with by the devil.

"So," his sister Amelia said, waltzing into his study as if she had every right to be there, which she didn't. It really was as if his sour thoughts had conjured her from nothing. "Are we all going to Bellingham?" she asked, waving a piece of vellum in front of her that looked suspiciously like the one the duchess had sent to him. "It's always so much fun there. I absolutely adore the duchess and the children do, too." She lifted the letter up with a flourish and read, "My dearest friend, Maggie Pierce, is arriving within the fortnight, and as Miss Pierce is already well acquainted with your brother, it will be a homecoming of sorts for her." She lowered the letter, an evil little twinkle in her eye. "You are *well acquainted* with Miss Pierce?"

Edward pretended to look over his own letter, silently cursing the duchess for also writing to his sister. "Yes. We met in Newport. I thought she mentioned it."

"How well are you acquainted? I only wonder that Her Grace would mention someone so specifically if it would have little or no meaning to you." In a flash, she changed tactics and jumped down onto his favorite leather chair, her skirts billowing up in her exuberance. "Oh, do tell. Is she *the one*?"

"There is no 'the one,'" he said darkly.

"But I'm quite certain I overheard His Grace and you discuss someone of importance. And you were an absolute ogre when you first returned from

America," she pointed out rather happily. "Everyone thought there could be only one reason for a man to be in such a mood. Love." She was fairly giddy with her teasing.

Edward let out a beleaguered sigh. "I am so sorry to disappoint you, Amelia, but I have no tragic love story to impart to you. Miss Pierce is Her Grace's best friend. I am the duke's best friend. We were thrown together quite a bit, something we both tolerated for the sake of the happy couple."

Amelia pouted. "And here I was hoping she was something special. You are getting rather old. One never knows when one will meet one's maker. It's almost as if you want Frederick to inherit the title." It was something Amelia often talked about, or threatened, depending on their conversation. His cousin Frederick was, politely put, an idiot, a dandy who spent more money a year on the proper buttons than most gentlemen spent on a good port. Edward had never liked him, something Amelia was well aware of, and so the threat that Frederick would inherit the title should he die prematurely always hit its intended mark—even when Edward pretended it did not.

"Unless you are planning to do me in yourself, I fear I will live a long and healthy life. Certainly long enough to marry and guarantee an heir."

"As Uncle did?" she asked, suddenly serious.

"Please do not worry about me and my heart, Amelia. We are both doing famously well."

"I do worry. And I don't care what you say, you've changed since returning from America. If it wasn't this Miss Pierce, who was it, then?"

"The duties of the earldom weigh heavily," he said, and nearly chuckled aloud when his sister rolled her eyes. But she accepted his answer, content to wait until he was honest with her, which he would never be. The tragic truth was, he'd very nearly succumbed to Miss Pierce's charms, finding himself so ridiculously enraptured it was unmanning. He could only congratulate himself that no one, not even Miss Pierce, had ever known quite how far he'd fallen. It would have been a damned embarrassing thing to admit given that their entire relationship had been based on mutual pretense. He had been trying to avoid all those American mamas looking for a title, and she had been trying to avoid marrying a particular someone. Last he'd heard, though, she'd been expecting a proposal any day from the very man she'd said she'd been trying to avoid. Odd, that. Maybe the entire time she'd been pretending to like him merely to make the other gentleman jealous. That thought rankled and he frowned, something Amelia immediately picked up on.

"I am trying to work," he said, pointedly looking down at a pile of estate papers laid out in front of him.

"You should hire someone to worry about the estate," she said, becoming bored with him.

"Perhaps I should hire someone to keep you entertained and out of my hair. If you care to stay, I could use someone to look over these rents for me—"

"I'm off," she said immediately. "I have to help Aunt Matilda get ready for our visit. We are going, are we not?"

Edward let out a sigh. "We are."

Amelia beamed him a smile, leaving him alone to dread his visit to Bellewood, where he would certainly see Maggie. Perhaps she was traveling to England to gather her trousseau together. Well, good for her. She should find a good man to marry her, someone from her own country. Someone who didn't find everything she did so completely charming he turned into an absolute fool.

Eyeing the door to make certain his sister was truly gone, he slowly opened the middle drawer of his desk, reaching back so that his fingers touched a small bundle of papers. Usually, it was enough simply to reach inside and touch them. He chose not to think about why he felt the need for this concrete evidence of her. But he didn't have a photograph or a lock of hair, and for some reason, thinking about the letters, touching them, made her real again. Slowly, he pulled them out, opening one and smiling. Maggie was suddenly there before him, grinning, lively, her brown eyes alight with some secret, probably nonsense.

> *It is dreadfully boring in New York right now. Poor Elizabeth has been locked in her house since we returned from Newport. Please do not tell the duke, as I believe his tender feelings would be greatly damaged by the knowledge that even at this moment Elizabeth is bound and gagged in their Fifth Avenue home in fear she will somehow escape matrimony.*

He chuckled softly, hearing her lilting voice in his head. Without reading further, he refolded the letter and placed it with the others, tying the wellworn ribbon as he had done perhaps a dozen times. With an impatient inward breath, he put them back in the drawer, telling himself he was an idiot.

Chapter 4

London, late October

"Mother, I am ready to go," Maggie said, tugging on her kidskin gloves. Not two minutes before, an excited girl had knocked on their hotel door and gushed about a fine coach that was waiting for them. At least they would ride in style, she thought, frowning at the fray marks on the tips of the fingers, a sure sign she came from a family of former means. They had been expensive gloves and now they were simply old gloves, but, she supposed, they were better than no gloves at all.

"How long a drive is it?" Harriet asked, giving her hair one final inspection, then shrugging. The two women could have taken a train, for it would have brought them to Bellingham far faster, but were grateful the duke had sent his coach. In truth, their funds were so far depleted from hotels in New York and passage to England, they'd hardly been able to pay for a respectable hotel. As it was, they had only the fare to return home in their pockets. The two women had become exceedingly thrifty in the past weeks, counting their coins and carefully devising a budget.

They could not afford to bring a lady's maid with them, so the two of them had muddled through the best they could in the past few weeks. Maggie, especially, had become quite proficient at her own grooming, but not so successful with her mother's dandelion fluff hair. Her own springing black curls were quite forgiving and Maggie could gain a rather charming affect by pulling them back loosely in a single ribbon.

"It's a two- to three-hour trip if we do not stop," Maggie said pointedly, as her mother almost always found it necessary to stop.

"And they are expecting us."

Watching her mother tuck a wayward strand of hair behind her ear gave Maggie a sudden jolt of tenderness for the woman who could drive her quite mad sometimes. She realized Harriet was nervous, more nervous than she herself was. No matter how many times her mother had told her she actually preferred traveling to England with her rather than going immediately to live with her sister in Savannah, Maggie still did not quite believe her.

"They are expecting us," she said with an indulgent smile, and held up a missive she'd received just yesterday from Elizabeth gushing about how she couldn't wait to see her friend.

"Oh, don't look at me as if I'm daft," her mother said with good humor.

Maggie came up behind her mother and helped her with her hat. "There," she said, pushing it forward a bit. "You look quite dashing with it cocked this way." The ostrich feather was looking a bit battered, but there was nothing to do for it. She kissed her mother's cheek.

"It's not the latest style," Harriet said, eying herself critically.

"Oh, what do they know about style so far out in the country? And really, Mama, you know Elizabeth won't care."

Maggie beamed a smile at her mother hoping to ease her worry. She'd decided the day she received that invitation from the duke that this was the chance of a lifetime, a chance to begin a new life, a life that did not include a father in prison and one that certainly did not include all the horrible sordid things that she had done. She was Maggie Pierce, the indomitably happy, buoyantly joyful woman she always was. Fooling people was remarkably easy, including her own mother.

Maggie had not told Elizabeth of their woes in her letter accepting the duke's invitation, though she had attempted several times. Somehow, writing it down made it all seem so sordid, and what her father had done to his friends was so absolutely unforgivable. Which, of course, it had been.

Her mother walked toward the door, then stopped and clutched her hands to her middle. "We had a maid, but she became violently ill before we departed and so refused to go aboard the ship."

That was the story Harriet insisted on telling when the two women showed up without a personal maid.

"You know I do not feel comfortable lying to Elizabeth. They'll have to know the truth eventually, Mama."

"She refused to go aboard the ship," she repeated, almost as if it were true.

"Fine. She refused to go aboard the ship. We had a boatload of servants who all refused to go with us. Does that make you happy, Mama?"

"Excessively so," she said, smiling rather coyly for a woman in her forties.

"They are here," Elizabeth said, hurrying as fast as her growing belly would allow to her husband's study. "How do I look?" she asked, standing in front of the Duke of Bellingham and smiling.

"Like a cow," Randall said dryly, standing immediately when she entered the room.

"Better a cow than a peacock," Elizabeth said pertly, eying his jewel-toned vest with mock horror.

"You said you liked this." He looked down at his rich-looking vest with doubt.

"And you," Elizabeth said, edging around his desk and coming up to him to kiss his freshly shaved jaw, "told me I was beautiful just this morning."

"You are and you know it," he said, drawing her close. "I've noticed you getting a bit full of yourself lately. It's decidedly unfashionable for a woman about to give birth to look so beautiful."

Another kiss. "You just said I looked like a cow."

"A lovely Hereford."

She gave him a gentle smack on his shoulder as he continued to smile down at her.

"Excuse me, Your Graces," Tisbury, their butler, said after clearing his throat. "Miss Pierce and Mrs. Pierce have arrived."

Elizabeth clapped her hands, completely overjoyed

at the prospect of having her greatest friend with her. How she had missed Maggie. No one knew her better, was a greater champion—except, perhaps, her new husband. Joy bubbled up her throat and came out as laughter. Maggie had always been the one to cheer her up, but she was undoubtedly more happy than she'd ever been and didn't need her friend's effervescent personality about now. Perhaps when she was in the throes of labor she would need Maggie's incessant happy chatter.

"Where are Lord Hollings and Lady Matilda? And the children? They should be here," Elizabeth said, dragging her smiling husband along. "Tisbury. Are Lord Hollings and Lady Matilda coming? And the children?"

Tisbury, one of the most efficient of men, was not affronted by the question. He simply nodded and said, "They are all in the grand hall, Your Grace."

"The flowers. Did the maids check the flowers? They were looking a bit droopy and—"

Suddenly, Elizabeth found herself being kissed soundly. "Stop. Everything is perfect. And if it is not, I hardly think your Miss Pierce will notice. Your stomach will block out any view of the flowers."

Elizabeth laughed, then scowled. "I don't know why I laugh at you when you are perfectly horrid to me." He bussed her cheek and looked down at her with such utter love, Elizabeth could not maintain her scowl for more than a few seconds. "It's just that Maggie is not used to all this. I'm not used to all this yet. I still cannot believe this is where I shall live for the rest of my life."

"She'll be fine, Your Grace," he said, tucking her arm against him.

* * *

"You'll be fine, Mama," Maggie whispered harshly to her mother, who hadn't stopped her panicky monologue since the moment they'd peeked out of the carriage window and seen their first glimpse of Bellewood.

"We're pretenders," Harriet whispered in her ear as they walked up the shallow steps that led to the grand entrance of the enormous palace. Elizabeth's descriptions had not done the place justice. It was far grander than any private home Maggie had ever seen. One could hardly call it a home at all. "We don't belong here. We were always pretenders. How do you think your poor father ended up where he is today? Because we were trying to be something we are not. Oh, my goodness, I do believe I'm going to faint," her mother said, waving a hand in front of her face.

"You are not going to faint," Maggie said sternly, as if saying it in such a tone would prevent her mother from keeling over. Harriet's face was quite flushed, Maggie had to acknowledge, but just now her mother's chatter was more irritating than anything else. She knew, more than anyone, what being a pretender meant.

Before they reached the top step, Maggie looked up to see Elizabeth breaking away from her husband and rushing toward her, completely unmindful that she was a pregnant woman rushing headlong toward a set of hard marble stairs. The two friends embraced, and it was so strange to feel Elizabeth's belly protruding. Elizabeth had always been so painfully thin, thanks to her mother's strict diet and stricter control. Both woman were laughing and crying and clinging together as if it had been years and years they'd been apart instead of just a few long months.

"You look absolutely stunning," Maggie gushed, meaning every syllable. Elizabeth, who had always been a beauty, had gained some much-needed weight. She had about her an air of exuberant health, the quintessential glow of pregnancy.

Elizabeth stepped back, wiped the tears from her eyes using a handkerchief instantly produced by her husband, and placed her hands upon her belly. "Randall says I am a cow."

"A lovely Hereford, if I recall," His Grace interjected.

Maggie watched the miracle of two people who'd hardly known each other on their wedding day look at each other with such unabashed love it was almost painful to witness. Especially painful for a woman who knew she would never know such love.

Just beyond the duke and duchess, a small commotion was growing, and it seemed as if a crowd was forming in Bellewood's grand entrance. Maggie was vaguely aware of the sound of children, which didn't quite make sense since there were no children at Bellewood, as well as a man and woman. Elizabeth was saying something to her, something about visitors and how she was certain she would be happy to have a familiar face here in England.

That's when she saw him, her very own earl, and realized with heartbreaking surety that she loved him still.

Chapter 5

It felt stunningly like being hit with a large and unexpected wave, slamming into her with such force Maggie literally stepped back from it. Lord Hollings was here. And he was standing next to a very pretty older woman with shockingly red hair. The two were surrounded by what appeared to be a brood of children.

"You remember Lord Hollings," Elizabeth said, stepping aside so she might get a better view of him. "And this is Lady Matilda, Lord Hollings' step-aunt. And four of her children, Mary, Janice, Robert, and Nathan."

"Two others are all grown up and on their own," Lady Matilda said with a musical laugh. "So glad to finally meet you."

Maggie concentrated on her, on the woman with her hand extended, on her pretty navy blue dress, that looked so lovely with her dark blue eyes and red hair. *Don't look at him, don't.*

"Miss Pierce." He said her name and it sounded

exactly as in her dreams, deep and slightly rough, a sound that made her chest ache.

Instead of immediately acknowledging Lord Hollings, Maggie grasped the woman's hand. "So pleased to meet you, Lady Matilda," she said, calling forth every ounce of social graces she possessed. She truly wanted to lift her skirts and run from the room, screaming like a banshee.

Why hadn't Elizabeth warned her? Why? Then again, why should she? No one had known, especially not Lord Hollings, how desperately she had fallen in love. But perhaps he had known and that is why he'd managed to leave New York on the first available ship, a man escaping a desperate spinster.

Finally, she gathered the courage to turn to him. "Lord Hollings," she said, proud that her acting skills were so intact. She gave him her warmest smile and grasped his hand briefly in greeting, glad she still wore her gloves and couldn't feel the intimacy of his warm touch. "It's so lovely to see you again."

"Likewise," he said.

Maggie turned immediately to Elizabeth, giving her a chastising look, but she could tell Lord Hollings stared at her or at least she imagined he did. "Elizabeth, you did not tell me you were living in a palace. Or should I call you Your Grace? Your Graces?" She let out a bit of laughter, feeling quite like she was about to lose the very tenuous grip she had on her emotions. She forged ahead.

"Your last letter to me had me believing you were living in a shambles, in a deteriorating old castle that was falling down upon your head. Mama, isn't this the most beautiful home you've ever seen?"

Elizabeth laughed, then pulled her friend in for

another embrace. "I've missed you so much, Maggie," she said, tears making her eyes shine brightly. "You must bring Arthur here to live for I shall not let you go."

At the mention of Arthur's name, Maggie almost lost her smile. Of course, Elizabeth wouldn't know about Arthur. She wouldn't know about anything. She wouldn't know they were destitute, that her father was in prison, that Arthur had jilted her, that she was completely ruined beyond redemption. That every time she smiled she felt as if something inside her was bending and would surely snap in two if she were forced to smile too much. She wouldn't know anything.

"That's a splendid idea. I do believe Maggie could convince Arthur of anything," her mother said in a frenetically joyous way that left Maggie with no other choice but to lie or else make a fool of her mother. She wished her mother had given her some sort of warning that, in addition to pretending their maids had abandoned them, she would have to pretend she was still engaged.

"I shall write Arthur this very day and tell him to book passage," Maggie said brightly, after giving her mother a telling look. "Do you think there's room enough here for us both?" Her mother was so visibly relieved by her daughter's fabrications, Maggie felt slightly less guilty for lying to her friend. She had plenty of time to tell the truth.

The small gathering laughed and Maggie was quite certain she had fooled them all, though she didn't dare look at Lord Hollings. He'd always had an uncanny way of seeing right through her. When she finally gathered the courage to look his way, she realized how foolish she was being for thinking whatever she said even mattered to him. He was engaged in a conversation with one of the children and apparently not even paying attention to her.

"You must be exhausted," Elizabeth said. "Your things should be in your rooms by now." She turned to a plainly dressed woman standing sedately off to one side. "Mrs. Stevens, would you please have someone escort Miss Pierce and Mrs. Pierce to their rooms? Dinner is at eight, but we often meet in the library before if you're up to it."

"You sound much too much like your mother," Maggie joked, then laughed at the look of pure horror on her friend's face. Then the two women dissolved into laughter.

"You are just what my wife needed," the duke said. "She thinks I'm entirely too stodgy. This house needs a bit more laughter."

Maggie and her mother made their escape to their rooms, following behind a crisply dressed upstairs maid. Her mother chatted beside her, completely unaware that her daughter was on the edge of losing herself. Her entire body felt numb and she was shaking uncontrollably. Only by grasping her hands tightly together could she mask the trembling.

The maid led them to a three-room apartment that contained a small sitting room bookended by two of the loveliest bedrooms Maggie had ever seen. Hers was done up in butter yellow with pure white trimmings and deep red accents. Every bit of furniture, every carpet on the floor looked as if no one had ever used it before. It was likely true that no one had, she realized, recalling Elizabeth's detailed letters about the home's disrepairs. Walking across a blue sitting room, Maggie peeked into her mother's room finding a similar color scheme, but this room was primarily deep red with white trim and yellow accents.

"Lovely, isn't it?" Maggie asked from the door.

"Oh, Maggie, I am so glad we've come," her mother said, with a rather unexpected gleam in her eye. It did not take long before Maggie found out what that gleam was about. "When I first saw Lady Matilda I had the horrible feeling that he'd gotten quickly married since the last time we'd seen him. But it is clear Lord Hollings is still available and still very much interested in you, my dear." Her mother was positively giddy.

Just last summer, her mother had had high hopes that Lord Hollings would propose to her. Maggie never did confide to anyone that the earl had been paying special attention to her only to dissuade other marriage-minded mamas from hounding him. At the time, Maggie welcomed a way to thwart the Wright brothers from a similar matrimonial pursuit. In all of her life she would remember that Newport summer as the happiest of times.

And what followed as the worst.

For Lord Hollings had left her without saying good-bye, without promises. Without hope. Now he was here, in what she'd thought would be a safe haven for her heart.

"Lord Hollings is not interested in me," Maggie said, suddenly weary.

"Of course he is," her mother said. "He couldn't keep his eyes off of you."

"Your imagination."

"Oh, no." Her mother clasped her hands together, much as a child does before a tray full of sweets. "This is an opportunity we cannot let go."

"Mother, please," Maggie said, bringing her hands to her temples in a futile effort to stem her growing headache.

Harriet looked shocked, then repentant. "I'm sorry, dear. You know how badly I feel about Arthur. None of this would have happened had your father not gotten us into this situation and I feel partly responsible for that. I only want the best for you."

"I know, Mama," she said, softening her voice. "What's best for me is to stay with you and Papa forever. I truly have no desire to marry." Maggie looked out the window and watched a crew of gardeners as they worked to cut the overgrown hedges of the garden below into something that resembled a straight line. "I have a confession to make," she said. "I never truly wanted to marry Arthur. I never loved him. I never wanted to marry at all, but I knew how much you wanted me to, so . . ."

"But every woman wants to marry. I don't understand."

No. Her mother wouldn't. Couldn't.

"Would it be so horrible if I were to spend my life with you?"

Her mother looked at her with an almost blank expression, as if what she was telling her was so far beyond her experience it was as if she were speaking a foreign tongue. "Of course it would. Do you remember how very miserable Elizabeth was when her mother was pushing her toward the duke?"

"I'd hardly call forcing your daughter to marry someone she doesn't love 'pushing.'"

Harriet pursed her lips, obviously not liking what her daughter was saying. "But it all ended up well, did it not? I would never be quite so adamant. However, I'm certainly not foolish enough to ignore the fact that my daughter is in close proximity to a very eligible earl." Maggie started to protest, but her mother would have none of it. "You must at least try."

Maggie stood abruptly, her anger returning as quickly as her mother's tears had doused it. "I thought we were going on with the ruse that I am still engaged," Maggie said. "If that's the case, I certainly cannot go out looking for a husband, can I?"

Her mother put a shaky hand to her temple. "I hadn't thought of that. I only wanted to protect you from humiliation."

Maggie didn't bother to point out she didn't feel humiliation as much as a bit of disappointment and a large dose of relief. "It's of no consequence anyway. Why can't you just let me be?"

"Why are you being so cross with me? Honestly, Maggie, you are talking in circles. First you are angry with me that I am lying about Arthur, and then you are angry for pushing you toward the earl. I don't know what I should say anymore."

Maggie's nostrils flared. "I told you I do not want to marry. I cannot marry, Mama."

"But the earl is here and I know he is interested. A mother knows these things. We can say Arthur has begged off. It's not unheard of. I do wish I'd thought of that before I mentioned him. But it's of no matter. And then you'll be free to marry the—"

"Mama, *stop*. I cannot marry anyone, most especially not the earl." God, if he knew what she'd done, he'd never forgive her.

Her mother stood, her face red with sudden anger. "I will not have a daughter as a spinster. And so that means you must marry. And you must find a husband now. Here. It is providence that we are here. You cannot throw this opportunity away as you threw away Arthur."

Maggie gasped. These uncharacteristic outbursts from her mother were getting more frequent of late. "What?"

Her mother pressed her fingers against her temples. "This is all too much. Too much. I don't understand you. You are a girl from a good family. A beautiful girl that any man would be proud to call a wife."

"No, Mama."

"How can you say that? Your father's taint will not reach you here."

"Please leave it be," Maggie begged.

"Make me understand. I don't understand."

"Oh, Mama, *please*. Why won't you listen to me when I tell you I cannot, *cannot* marry?" she said, beseeching her to stop or understand, she wasn't sure which.

She watched as her mother's expression changed subtlety, the slow dawning, the horror and disbelief. "It cannot be true," she said, staring at her daughter. When Maggie looked away, so ashamed she couldn't bear to look at her mother, Harriet let out a sound of distress. "Oh, no, Maggie. With Arthur? You let him touch you?"

Tears flooded Maggie's eyes. She was so sick of lying, so sick of it. But she told one more lie, one more because she knew her mother could never bear the truth. "Yes, Mama."

"And still he broke it off?"

"It was because of Papa," she said, telling the truth for the first time.

"When?" her mother asked, her eyes drifting to her stomach.

"Many weeks ago. And I . . . I am fine." It was the one thing she'd been grateful for, that he hadn't planted his foul seed in her.

Her mother's face turned a mottled red. Harriet was not a woman who got angry, who showed strong emotion of any sort. Indeed, Maggie hardly recognized her. "You have disgraced yourself," she said. "And this will be rectified. We shall return to New York immediately and force him to marry you. He should do the right thing. You are a girl from a good family and it is unconscionable that he used you, then refused to marry you. He will marry you."

"I don't want to marry him. I don't love him."

"Do you think that matters at this point?" her mother asked. "Oh, dear, did he force you?"

"No. It was all me." Again, the truth.

"I'm writing a letter today," she said, rushing to a small desk. She began pulling out pieces of their precious stationery. "This minute, to demand he marry you. Do you have any idea what you have done? Do you? How could you let us leave New York without telling me this? How, Maggie?" Her mother sat down heavily in the desk chair as if her legs could no longer hold her. She stared blindly for a moment before pressing her face into her hands to begin a soft keening cry that tore at Maggie's heart. When she dropped her hands, Maggie found herself looking into the eyes of a woman completely defeated. "It's too late," she said. "This cannot be rectified. I cannot think of anything worse. We must go on pretending you are engaged, of course. Unless . . ."

"Unless what, Mama?" Maggie said, too weary to even care what her mother was thinking.

"Unless we don't say a word. Once you are well married, it will be too late for any objections. The earl—" She began warming up to her plan of deceit.

"No, Mama. Absolutely not," Maggie said, even though she'd been thinking the very same thing when she'd thought Arthur would propose. At the time it had been so lovely to pretend none of it had ever happened, but she would never perpetuate such a lie to someone she loved. "I hate lying, but I don't want to encourage anyone's suit and most particularly not the earl, even if he should do such a far-fetched thing. I have accepted what I have done and you should, too."

Her mother's face crumpled in grief. "You are ruined. What shall we do with you now? Oh, how could you do this thing? After your upbringing, after all the sacrifices we made to make you a better life, to make you attractive to men like Arthur. And to throw it all away. I just don't understand you," she said. "My God, Maggie, what shall we do?"

"Let me think on it, Mama. I cannot think of that now," Maggie answered dully. "I'm going to lie down, if you don't mind." When her mother called her name, she kept walking, shutting out her cries, her disappointment, her anger.

When Maggie went into her room she lay dry-eyed staring up at the ceiling trying to stop herself from thinking about anything, but the images she'd been fighting for weeks kept assaulting her. Flashes of what had happened, bits of that terrible conversation flew at her, like some unstoppable pestilence.

"Bend over, my dear. Grab the desk."

He always seemed to have too much saliva in his mouth and would noisily slurp at it, swallowing audibly. His hands dug into her hips, pressing, leaving marks that remained for weeks. She'd feared at first they would never go away, a brand that would never fade.

Charles Barnes had been one of her father's business associates. She'd known him for years, and had instinctively, even as a child, stayed away from him. She'd never liked the way he looked at her, the way on those few occasions when she'd been forced to offer him her hand, he'd grasp it and hold, pressing her flesh in a way that made her want to go bathe. He had a way of sweeping his gaze up and down her body that was slightly repugnant. But he was one of her father's good friends and Maggie had always tried to be polite.

Mr. Barnes was a soft man, not overly fat, but simply soft, like a blob of melting butter. His features looked like so much moist dough plopped together with two small raisins pressed in for eyes. And his mouth, Maggie had always thought his mouth too full, too red.

This was the man who took her virginity. This was the man she bent over for. This was the man who put his penis inside her, who jerked in and out, grunting like a pig behind her, smearing her blood on her buttocks, who laughed when he was done as she'd cried.

This was the man who promised if she did this thing, this disgusting mating, that he would guarantee her father would only serve one year. He'd said he knew the prosecutor, that he would make a deal. He'd told her, even as he painfully squeezed her breasts, that her father would be so proud of what she was doing, the sacrifice she was making, and he laughed when she begged him to never tell.

As if he would. That is how stupid she'd been. How stupid and willing. She'd bent over that desk, felt the cool air on her legs, felt him drag down her bloomers, felt him separate her, felt him, felt him, felt him.

Maggie pressed the heels of her hands against her eyes, trying in vain to press the images away.

It had been her idea. Certainly, he had hinted at it. He'd told her he had the power to lessen her father's sentence, but why should he? What would he get out of it? There was no money left to give him. What would be worth such valuable information? What could anyone give him? What?

"Myself," Maggie had said. "You can have me. Once."

A slow, horrible smile had appeared on those too-thick, too-red lips. "Do you think you are worth it, my dear?" he asked as he moved one thick finger across his lips.

She'd swallowed down the bile and lifted her chin. "More than worth it."

"All right, then. I agree."

Maggie stood before him, her body suddenly bathed in a cold sweat, and she'd nodded. "But you must promise me my father will not be in prison for more than a year."

"Yes. I promise. Now. Bend over, my dear. Grab the desk."

Chapter 6

Edward was at the moment feeling rather put out. He'd gotten himself so worked up at the thought of seeing Miss Pierce again, he'd barely been able to stomach breakfast, and she'd nearly dismissed him. No, it was worse than that. It was as if he were an acquaintance, and not a very well known one at that. While he'd been pining away, pathetically reliving every moment of their time together in Newport and New York, she'd been getting on with her life. He'd already become a small speck in her long and happy life, a distraction on a long-ago summer season. Perhaps even—humiliating as it was to think—simply a means to make another man jealous. All that rot about how she wanted to dissuade the Wright brothers from matrimonial pursuit when what she'd truly wanted was to make herself more desirable.

How nice to see you again, Lord Hollings, she'd gushed, then turned immediately away to exclaim in the same tone how wonderful Rand's home was. What had he expected? That she'd throw herself into his arms? Perhaps not so much as that, but a warm look, a smile that said something other than "how nice to see you." Or a blush that told him she'd been uncomfortable, something, *anything* that meant she remembered him.

He felt his entire body heat with mortification when he recalled how he'd taken her letters out and read them. And if her fiancé dared show his face here, why, he'd . . . he'd . . . Ah, hell. He'd probably act the gentleman and welcome the chap.

"May I come in?" his sister said, walking into his private sitting room without so much as a knock.

"No."

She didn't even pause as she sat down upon his favorite chair, perching herself on its edge so that she couldn't begin to appreciate the comfort of the item. "I'm very disappointed," she said. "Here I was thinking Miss Pierce was some lost love when it was clear that she is not."

"I told you she was nothing," he said rather shortly, and immediately wished he had not. His sister pounced on him like a cat pouncing on an injured mouse.

"But she is something to you, isn't she?" This last was said with true tragedy.

"Amelia," he said as a warning. "If you persist on this ridiculous fantasy I am going to have to closely monitor your reading material. Again."

Amelia let out a huff of impatience. "You don't understand what it has been like living with you these past months. Were you always this bleak? I remember you as a much happier person."

Edward smiled gently at his pouting sister. Sometimes she seemed far younger than her nineteen years. It was hard to believe that Amelia and the duchess were nearly the same age. "The last time you spent any time at all with me was when you were eight and I was seventeen. That, as I recall, was a lovely summer."

She put her chin on her fist and looked as if she were trying to remember that far back. She straightened abruptly. "That was the summer of Giselle."

If Edward was shocked that his little sister remembered the daughter of one of his father's friends, he tried valiantly not to show it. She'd been nothing more than a baby then, a lonely little girl with no one to play with, one who desperately missed her older sister. God, he hadn't thought about his younger sister in months. She'd died when she was twelve, and Amelia had been inconsolable for months afterward. Certainly, Giselle and her extremely loose morals had helped him to forget his grief, a thought that filled him with a bit of guilt even now. No doubt following them around helped Amelia through the pain of missing Caroline.

"Giselle was very pleasant," he said.

"You used to laugh all the time. It was as if everything she said was supremely funny. I never did like her very much."

"I think I liked her rather well," Edward said with a crooked smile.

"Which is why it is so important for you to fall in love."

Edward let out a beleaguered sigh, then gave a small bow to his sister. "I vow I will make it my priority in the coming seasons to secure a proper wife," he said, hoping his wily little sister wouldn't notice his use of a plural in the word "seasons." Of course, that was too much to ask for.

"Season," Amelia said. "One that I should be participating in. I am nineteen, after all. If only I had a proper chaperone, an older, married woman who isn't encumbered with a husband hanging about. One who, perhaps, would adore a chance to see—"

"Stop right there, you devious little schemer. Mrs. Pierce cannot be your chaperone. At the moment, she is Miss Pierce's chaperone. Besides, I don't believe they will be staying in England as long as all that. It's only October now. The season doesn't get into full swing until April or May. You know that." Edward thought that would settle things directly, but he should have known better.

"We could ask. Perhaps they would enjoy extending their stay if it meant participating in the season. She can chaperone us both," Amelia said, her face alighting with the knowledge that she'd solved a major problem.

"Both?"

"Why, don't you think Miss Pierce would appreciate a London season?" She held up her hand to stem his objection. "I know she is here for the duchess. But once the baby is born, perhaps she would enjoy seeing London. No one likes to travel during the winter months. Just ask the duchess what she thinks of that idea. You recall how horrid her trip was on that awful cargo ship. Is that what you would wish for Miss and Mrs. Pierce? An ocean voyage on a dilapidated old cargo ship? And you can escort us everywhere. Steer her clear of the bad apples."

Edward had, throughout Amelia's monologue,

tried to interrupt her torrent of ideas, but he was pointedly ignored. Just as he knew whatever he said to her now would be pointedly ignored. But he decided to try anyway, for the thought of steering Miss Pierce away from ardent suitors was about as palatable as eating a pile of rotting, steaming fish. "Absolutely not. I would never impose on Mrs. Pierce to do such a thing. Besides, Miss Pierce is engaged to be married. A season for her would be pointless."

"Now you are simply being mean," Amelia announced with assurance. "Think on it, will you? And don't be such a poor sport. Just because Miss Pierce isn't interested in you doesn't mean you shouldn't look yourself. Perhaps she could help you find someone."

"Are you trying to make me angry?"

Amelia looked suitably shocked.

"Because I can tell you right now it is not working," Edward said pleasantly, lying through his teeth.

Amelia stood. "Just think on it, Edward. After all, until you find someone of your own, you'll have to dance with someone. Why not her?"

"Good-bye, Amelia," he said, smiling in an effort to disguise his growing anger. His sister was about as transparent as a new plate-glass window, but he had to admire her tenacity.

"I truly would like a season, Edward. Even if it is just for a little while. Next year I'll be twenty and have absolutely no prospects. I know how tedious it is for you. And I also know that Auntie cannot escort me this year. Not with Janice being so sick lately. Please think on it."

The only thing worse than his sister's needling was her sincerity—and she was being excruciatingly sincere at the moment. Janice reminded them both too much of Caroline, who seemed to simply fade away before their eyes before finally dying. "All right. I'll think on it."

Amelia brightened and Edward watched her walk in her singularly bouncing way with a feeling of pure inevitability. He owed a season to his sister, and damned if Mrs. Pierce wouldn't be the absolutely perfect chaperone for her. His list of suitable female chaperones was woefully short, especially with his step-aunt being unavailable. And if Mrs. Pierce was chaperone, Miss Pierce would certainly tag along. And he'd end up escorting her to balls and the opera and watching other men fawn over her, perhaps even fall in love with her. He almost thanked God she was engaged, because he didn't think he could bear watching her fall in love with someone else.

Chapter 7

Maggie sat on the southern veranda, feeling content and snug, with a warm cup of tea in her hands and her best friend sitting next to her. The two were silent, enjoying the rare warmth of a late October morning and the knowledge that for the next few weeks at least, there would be many mornings like this one. Across an expanse of green grass were the brilliant reds, golds, and burnished browns of fall foliage. It looked so much like home that for one fierce moment Maggie wished she were back in New York. But such a thought immediately brought with it the reason why they were not in New York.

Maggie decided at that moment to ruin their peace, because the lie she held in her heart was beginning to invade her feeling of pure contentment.

"I have some news to tell you," she said, and something in her tone made Elizabeth straighten suddenly even though she'd tried to keep her voice even.

Maggie laughed. "It's not as bad as all that." Then

she laughed again. "Actually, it is." She shook her head, still in a bit of disbelief that her life could have changed so drastically in the few months that the two women hadn't seen each other.

"I might as well just tell you right out. My father is in prison for embezzlement and we are destitute. There. I've told you. I feel so much better." She took a sip from her tea as if all was now well in the world.

Elizabeth looked at her for a stunned moment, then burst out laughing, only to sober moments later when she realized Maggie was not joking. "You're serious."

"Utterly," Maggie said dryly. For some reason, her troubles seemed far less serious here on this veranda with a cup of tea in her hands. "Poor Papa was sentenced for five years. Our house is sold, nearly all our belongings gone. The jewels, the horses, the books. Everything. Sam lost his job at Munroe and Phillips. He's in Richmond working at a much smaller firm with an old school chum."

Maggie thought she was fine, truly thought the pain of what her family had endured these last months was dulled by time, until she looked at Elizabeth and saw her friend was crying. Still, she tried valiantly to smile as she looked into her cooling tea. "Please don't, Elizabeth. I've cried enough for both of us." She swallowed heavily, willing the burning in her throat to dissipate.

"I'm sorry. It's just that . . . your father. Your mother! Everyone. It must have been awful," she said, losing the tenuous control she had.

"It was awful," she said, giving her friend a shaky smile. "But we're here now. And all that seems very far away."

"You don't have to be brave, Maggie. You don't have to pretend all is well. Not with me."

Maggie's eyes flooded with tears. "If I start crying, I fear I might never stop. Truly." She squeezed her eyes shut, then quickly dashed away the tears that fell. "So maybe another day I can tell you more. The awful details. But for now, I just wanted you to know. Only you," she stressed.

"Rand is a very understanding man, Maggie. You should not worry that he would think badly of you or your family."

Maggie held a little private debate inside her head. She knew if Elizabeth told Rand, Rand would tell Lord Hollings and then she would never be able to behave normally before either one. It was humiliating enough that everyone in New York knew their shame; she did not want every one in England to as well.

"I'd rather you not tell anyone. Is it terrible to ask that of you?"

Elizabeth thought a moment. "I will not lie outright."

Maggie, feeling awful to ask such a thing, waved a hand as if erasing her request. "No. I should not have asked that of you. But do you think you could ask His Grace to keep it between the two of you? I would never ask such a thing, but living in New York these past months has been difficult."

Elizabeth, who had full knowledge of how powerful New York's social elite could be, knew immediately what her friend meant. "It must have been horrid," she said.

"It wasn't fun. Though I must say that after you left, our social calendars were not quite as full as before.

So when word about Papa's indictment was in the newspapers, it was hardly a sudden drop in invitations." Maggie was putting it more than kindly. Night after night she'd sat with her mother before the fire reading or playing her beloved piano. They were long dreary nights, made more dreary with the knowledge that everyone else they knew in the city was out enjoying themselves. They'd gone to the New York Philharmonic once and never again. It was excruciatingly obvious that people who had been their friends were going out of their way to pretend they did not see them. Her mother left at intermission in tears, her father walking stoically next to her.

"I'm so glad to be away from all that pettiness," Elizabeth said fiercely. "No doubt my mother led the brigade."

Maggie laughed. "I never heard a word. But I do believe my star wasn't shining quite as brightly without you by my side." In fact, they had been written off nearly every social list, but Elizabeth needn't know that.

"I'm glad you're here to escape from all that."

Maggie looked down to her tea and frowned, and started to move to add to her cooling drink some hot tea sitting on the table before them when a footman was immediately on hand to replenish it for her. When he'd gone back to his station near the door, Maggie said, "Mama and I have become quite independent. We can tie our own stays, dress each other's hair and our own, serve ourselves food. It's quite liberating," she said with a hint of self-deprecation.

"Is everything gone? Not your piano."

"That piano paid for our passage here and back," Maggie said. "And thank God for it."

"But your *piano*," Elizabeth moaned. "You must have been devastated."

"It just became one more thing to deal with," Maggie said matter-of-factly. "Our lives have changed so much. We're officially homeless." She said it with so much pride, Elizabeth laughed.

"Until you marry Arthur," Elizabeth said.

Maggie felt her cheeks flush and she prayed her friend thought it was bashfulness and not shame. "Yes."

"When are you getting married?"

"We haven't set a date yet," Maggie said.

"Until you do, this is your home for as long as you want to stay," Elizabeth said.

"Mother had her heart set on living with her sister in Savannah." Goodness, the lies were building. "I cannot impose on you too long. I feel rather guilty dragging her halfway around the world simply so I could have a chaperone that I don't even need."

"Savannah? Georgia?"

"Mama grew up there and says it's quite lovely."

"I'm sure it is," Elizabeth said doubtfully.

"Oh, you needn't act as if we are being banished to somewhere terrible."

"I do wish you could stay here until your wedding. I've missed you terribly," Elizabeth said, and Maggie knew she meant every word. For a moment she allowed herself to think that it was possible, that she could stay in this palace forever. She'd have to tell the truth about Arthur eventually and then what would she do all day? Entertain Elizabeth? Watch their children when they came? Become like an impoverished relation who had to depend upon them for everything? Maggie knew she could never allow that, even though it was wonderfully safe and intoxicatingly tempting . . . if only for a little while.

"I've missed you, too," Maggie said. "It's been so dreary in New York without you. Not that I got to see you much when you were there last."

The two women laughed, remembering how strict Elizabeth's mother was, and how very afraid she was that Elizabeth would run off with another man and jilt the duke.

"I've much more freedom now," Elizabeth said. "But not for long, I fear." She looked down at her stomach and Maggie felt an unfamiliar twinge of jealousy. Elizabeth could never know how lucky she was—indeed how lucky she'd been her entire life. Maggie refused to blame her friend for being completely unaware of what real heartache felt like. No one, not even her own mother, knew the demons that plagued Maggie, the nightmares that visited her far too frequently, the dreams she still held even though there was no chance, none at all, that her dreams could come true.

"What on earth do you have to be afraid of?" Lady Matilda asked, coming onto the veranda.

Maggie turned, smiling, until she saw Lord Hollings following behind in her wake.

"Losing my freedom," Elizabeth explained. "When the baby comes. I think you have inspired me to be a more attentive mother, Lady Matilda."

Lady Matilda put on a look of horror. "My dear girl, please, I beg you, do not use me as a model of motherhood. It was frugality more than anything else, at least when I was younger, that had me forgo more conventional methods of child-rearing. Horace and I tried governesses," she said with a laugh. "And tried and tried. Governesses are miserable creatures, you know, poor things. I don't think most of them even like children."

Maggie flushed, because she'd been thinking that being a governess was one of her few options. *Miserable creatures.* Yes, that was about it, she thought. If she ever left here, being a governess was one of the few respectable options left to her. And did she like children? She truly didn't know. She'd never been around any, not for any extended time anyway. What if she didn't like children? Would she become one of those bitter, onerous creatures that she'd seen sometimes in Central Park walking about with their charges? Those unfortunate women from fallen families who would look at the privileged few around them with jealousy and longing?

"I had a wonderful governess," Elizabeth said. "Though I must say, I would never say she was a jolly person," she added thoughtfully.

"I expect when you have no choices, it is difficult to be happy," Maggie said softly.

"I'm certain it is the option of last resort," Elizabeth said, and Maggie forced a laugh.

"Oh, there are far worse things for a woman than to be a governess," she said, sounding, she suddenly realized, like a bitter, hardened woman.

"That is true," Lady Matilda said with a light laugh. "But certainly not for us, thank God."

For a moment, the roaring in Maggie's ears blocked out all sound as memories assaulted her. Only the piercing pain of her nail on her wrist saved her. That small discomfort allowed her to join in on the light laughter, to laugh at the joke that no woman of her class could think of a worse condition than that of being a governess.

"Miss Pierce."

Despite her resolve to remain unaffected by the earl, Maggie stiffened when he said her name. "Yes, Lord Hollings?"

"I wonder if you would care to walk the grounds with me."

Edward watched as Maggie stiffened and he wondered why she suddenly was so uncomfortable around him. Perhaps it was that he was nearly a stranger to her, a man she'd danced with, had kissed once, and was now embarrassed to be confronted by such memories. Despite her rather cool reaction to him, some mad part of his brain was making him walk with her, forcing him to fertilize the humiliating seeds of hope he'd planted when he'd heard she was coming to England.

"Of course," she said, putting down her teacup with what he thought was reluctance. "Lady Matilda, would you care to join us? I would love to hear about your travels in France. I do hope that Mama and I can go to Paris before we go home and I would like your advice on where to go and what to see."

Edward watched with disbelief as Maggie deftly brought up the one subject Matilda could talk with joy about for hours.

"If you don't mind, Edward," she said.

"Of course not," he said, even though he very much minded.

And so he was relegated to trailing behind his step-aunt and the woman he was quite certain he still loved but who most certainly did not love him.

He tried not to let his thoughts wander to her, but it was impossible not to take advantage of staring at her when she was so completely unaware that he did so. He let his eyes sweep down her back, from her curling black hair, to the tiny bit of skin that showed at her neckline above her shawl, to her waist, to her enticing backside. She was just as he remembered. Perhaps a bit paler without the summer sun to give her color. Her laugh was as musical as he remembered, the way she'd toss her curls from her forehead, the sure way she had of walking, long boyish strides that for some reason he found incredibly intoxicating.

He stared at her as they chatted seemingly nonstop, Maggie barraging his aunt with question after question, oohing and aahing over the minutiae of the glories of Paris and the French countryside. His aunt had lived in Paris for five years, so she had a great many stories to tell, and Maggie was very adept at ferreting them out. Clearly, Maggie had not wanted to be alone with him and he wasn't certain whether he was amused, angry, or hurt, the last of which was completely unacceptable.

Just when he was about to excuse himself from what had become a tedious and frustrating experience, one of his aunt's children, Mary, ran up to her mother. "Janice just got sick," she said. "It was the most horrid thing, Mama. She ruined the duchess's settee, I'm sure she did. It went everywhere and smells simply awful."

"Yes, Mary, you may spare me the details. All right, then." Matilda looked up apologetically to Maggie. "I'm afraid I'll have to cut my walk short, if you'll excuse me."

"Of course," Maggie said, smiling down at Mary, who was being particularly precocious at the moment filled with the gory details of her sister's sickness. "I think I've gotten enough exercise in this morning at any rate."

Edward watched as Matilda hurried off with Mary, leaving Maggie behind looking a bit bewildered as it dawned on her that she had absolutely no reason to hurry back to the palace the way the other two had.

"Your plans have been foiled," he said dryly.

Maggie looked at him with pique, not even trying to pretend she didn't know what he was implying?

"I thought it rather dangerous to be with you even under the watchful eye of Elizabeth. Now that we have lost our chaperone, I fear we must return. For your sake, that is," she said pertly, but with a mischievous gleam. "I am certain I am much too great a temptation for you. Though you have tried to hide it, it is very clear to me that you are still overwhelmingly smitten with me. While tragic, you can hardly blame me for your sad condition."

The relief that swept over him was so ridiculously intense, Edward nearly forgot to smile. This was the woman he remembered, the witty, chatty, confidence-filled charmer he'd known in Newport. He couldn't put his finger on it, but something had seemed a bit off with her, like a cake missing its secret ingredient—still marvelous but just not right.

"I believe I can manage to control myself," he said dryly.

"All right, then. You may accompany me back to the palace." She stopped and stared at the massive home. "It is a palace, isn't it?"

"One of the grandest in England," he stated. "Makes my home look like a country cottage."

"Oh, I hardly believe that," she said. "You are an earl, after all. I imagine earls live in very nice houses."

"It is nice. Quite lovely, in fact. My uncle was a very astute businessman. He saw the agricultural depression coming years ago. It was very unfashionable of him, you see, to have business investments, to actually work for a living. My only regret is that I didn't spend more time with him learning how to manage it all. I'm afraid I had to hire business managers to do all that for me. I am learning, however, and I imagine at some point I'll take it all over."

"You sound absolutely despondent." He noted she seemed rather thrilled by the idea of his misery.

"It will simply take me away from things I'd rather be doing."

"Such as balls and hunts?"

"My dear," he said, "you are looking at England's foremost bibliophile."

He was uncertain whether he was pleased or annoyed by her expression of complete disbelief. Most people who did not know him well could not picture him wading through piles of books to find the exact copy of a fifteenth-century tome, but it was, by far, his favorite thing to do.

"You're not joking, are you?" she asked, as if he'd said he collected human bones.

"One of the reasons I am here, other than to entertain you, is to assist His Grace in restoring his library. It was indeed tragic what happened here."

"Oh?"

"The old duke sold every book. It was perhaps one of the greatest collections in England. They had original manuscripts from Archimedes. My God, just thinking of it."

"I didn't even know you could *read*," she said, clearly jesting him.

Edward forced a smile, but truthfully, he was more than a little insulted by her amazement, something she immediately noted.

"I see I have struck a nerve. I had no idea you were so serious. You were much more fun to needle in Newport, Lord Hollings. Not nearly as sensitive. I do believe you've become entirely too stodgy since returning to England. Is it the air, do you think, that has stolen your sense of humor?"

"It is the responsibility."

Maggie looked properly chastised, for which he was glad. This happy banter of theirs was somehow not nearly as satisfying as it once was. Perhaps because it was all so meaningless and could lead to nothing. Why flirt with someone he could never have, after all? She was engaged to marry another man, which made her more unattainable than had she been married. She really was none of his business. Whether she found books as fascinating as he did was of no consequence whatsoever. In fact, he didn't know what had possessed him to ask her on this walk with him.

"Do you love him?" he blurted. Well, hell, he hadn't even realized he was going to ask such a nonsensical thing until it came out of his mouth.

He watched in dreaded fascination as her cheeks bloomed with color.

"Whom do you mean?" she asked, being purposefully obtuse.

"Your fiancé," he ground out, thrusting his hands behind his back to prevent him from shaking her.

"Love Arthur? Of course I do."

His heart plunged more than he would have admitted, even upon threat of death. "Then that explains why you are marrying him."

She swallowed; he watched the slim column of her throat move. She was still staring at the palace, and now it was clear to him that she was simply finding the home so fascinating because she did not want to look at him. She moved her hands up in front of her and grasped them together before pushing them down to her sides, where she fisted them in her skirts.

"I don't think I could ever marry someone I didn't love," she said finally and with odd emotion.

"No. I don't suppose you would," Edward said, wishing this Arthur fellow was here before him so he could pummel him.

Maggie shrugged, and with her dark curling hair and fair complexion, she looked decidedly French. "We found we suit each other quite well. He adores Egyptology. Mummies and all that. It's quite . . . fascinating."

Edward chuckled. "You do not find it fascinating at all, be honest."

Maggie looked up at him with all innocence. "I find it as fascinating as listening to you talk about books," she said, which only made him laugh aloud.

"For your sake, I hope you do. There are enough miserable married people in this world without adding to them."

"I agree wholeheartedly. And I know you do as well."

Her fervent agreement and her reminder that she knew he was opposed to the state of matrimony bothered him. He recalled when they met in Newport her saying she was opposed to marriage, but he hadn't really believed her. He didn't like being proved correct this time. It was incredibly annoying to realize Maggie would never agree to get married unless she were madly in love and that thought only depressed him further.

"If you are engaged, then I have a proposition for you."

"This sounds positively intriguing."

He explained his sister's request. "She very much wants a season and I cannot come up with a good excuse not to give her one. The only one I had, the lack of a chaperone, could easily be remedied by you and your mother, if she was willing." He nearly choked on the next. "And you could have a season as well. American girls are all the rage in England about now."

"Rich American girls," she reminded him. "Why on earth would you deny your sister a season?"

He let out a big-brother beleaguered sigh. "She breaks hearts the way Matilda's children break fine vases. Often and without conscious thought. I think, despite her grand age of nineteen, my dear sister is far too immature to be on the marriage market, though I daresay I would never tell her that."

Maggie laughed. "Then she is like every other girl searching for a husband. You do remember the duchess, do you not? She believed herself to be in love with a scoundrel. Girls do the most foolish things for what they believe is love."

"And what foolish thing have you done?" he asked.

"I've never been in love, so I wouldn't know," she said, smiling brilliantly at him before she realized what she said. "Except for Arthur, of course. And I haven't done a single foolish thing." She smiled again, and for just an instant, he was fooled by that smile.

"There's no shame in doing foolish things for love," he said, and watched with fascinatiom as she struggled mightily to maintain her smile.

"Spoken by a man who has never been in love," she said, giving up any pretense of a smile. "As for a season, I am sorry, but I do not believe my mother and I will be staying here that long. We have plans to visit my aunt in Savannah when we return home. My mother hasn't seen her in more than two years, you see. We were supposed to be there now, but for the duke's request that we come here for the birth. It's quite impossible."

Edward found himself making a valiant effort to not show his disappointment, when he hadn't truly been aware that he'd at some time in the past day decided he wanted them to stay for the season. "I'm sure I can dig up some spinster aunt from somewhere to do the deed," he said.

"I thought England was full of spinster aunts."

"Quite so. Then again, perhaps my step-aunt will be able to act as chaperone. Janice may be feeling better."

"What is wrong with her?"

"No one can say, though God knows nearly every doctor in England has examined her. She's a little slip of a thing. Nothing to her."

"It must be difficult for Lady Matilda."

"It is. For all of us, really. Of all her children, Janice is the sweetest little thing. She never complains, not even when it is clear she is suffering. A little trooper, that one."

As they got closer to the home, those who were still on the veranda stood up as if anticipating their return. Maggie trudged along, relieved that her first time alone with the earl had gone so smoothly. She'd flirted lightly, managed to talk to him in a manner that almost seemed normal, almost like that lifetime far away that was Newport. She hadn't given in to the urge to touch him, to tell him that she'd missed him.

Maggie could see Amelia on the veranda, waiting with visible anticipation for them to appear. Behind her sat Maggie's mother and Elizabeth, both smiling at the girl who stood clutching the rail in barely contained eagerness. As they walked up the shallow marble steps, Amelia ran to greet them.

"Oh, Edward, the most wonderful news. Mrs. Pierce has agreed to chaperone me this season."

Chapter 8

Maggie was not a woman who got angry, and if she did, she always managed to hide it well. But she could not hide the flood of irritation she felt upon hearing Amelia's happy news. What was her mother thinking? How could she accept such an invitation when they had no money, no clothes, and no way of obtaining them?

"Mother," Maggie said in such a sharp tone, Amelia stopped her happy chatter and looked from daughter to mother with dismay. Maggie forced herself to remain calm, when inside she was burning. "Perhaps we should discuss this."

"There's nothing to discuss. It's perfect. We can order your trousseau. And I've always wanted to experience a season in London. Why, since you were a little girl it's always been something I've dreamed about. We could visit Mr. Worth, perhaps. Or maybe Her Grace has some recommendations."

It was almost as if Maggie could feel her blood begin to boil. "Mother, may I have a word with you?"

"I'm sorry," Amelia said softly. "Did I do something wrong?"

Maggie felt immediately contrite, and gave the girl a reassuring smile. "Not at all. It's only that my mother and I had other plans after Christmas and staying for a season was not something we'd thought of doing. I would like to discuss this with my mother before we make any final decisions." What on earth was her mother thinking? It was almost as if she truly believed they had to purchase a trousseau, as if they had the money to do so, as if her father was not in prison, leaving them destitute.

"All right. Of course," Amelia said, but Maggie could see the dreams of a wonderful season dying in her pretty blues eyes. She nearly gave in, then and there, but her reasons against a London season were so many she could not.

"Oh, dear, I'm afraid my daughter is quite angry with me," Harriet said with a laugh. "I'd best go have it out with her."

Maggie could not even pretend a smile. As she was leaving, she heard Lord Hollings gently chastise his sister. "You should not have said a word until you spoke with me."

"I know," Amelia said, in a voice that told Maggie she was clearly on the verge of tears, which made her feel even more like a shrew. A correct shrew, but one nonetheless.

When they'd reached their private apartment, Maggie waited for her mother to sit like a chastised child.

"I don't know what you are so upset about, my dear. This is the opportunity of a lifetime for us."

Maggie ignored her. "Do you have any idea what

it costs to finance a season, Mother? How am I going to buy the necessary gowns? I will not be able to. So you will chaperone a girl while I sit at home—a home we shall not be able to afford, I might add. Did you not think of that?"

"Oh."

"Mother, how could you have agreed to something without giving it any thought?"

Her mother worried her hands in her lap. "You have some lovely gowns," she said, then stopped as if finally recalling how desperate their situation was, and she slowly deflated, shrinking before her daughter's eyes. "*Had* some lovely gowns." Then, to Maggie's horror, her mother started to cry copious tears. Her mother, who couldn't bear to see anyone sad, buried her face in her hands and sobbed in an almost childlike way.

Maggie knelt beside her, grasping her hands. "Mama, please don't cry. I'm sorry. It's just we have to be more practical now. We hardly have the funds to return home and go on to Savannah. You know I spent hours trying to budget this trip." She'd sold her best gowns, her piano, all her jewels to fund this trip. They literally had nothing left to their names.

"I don't know what I was thinking. I wasn't thinking, I suppose. I just wanted to be normal, to go to balls, to . . . pretend," she ended on a whisper.

Lord, Maggie wanted that, too. But she was obviously far more practical than her mother.

"I'll tell Amelia I cannot. It wouldn't do for me to go to balls and dinners and concerts and leave you home. How will you find a husband if you do not come with us?"

Maggie felt a tingling of fear that her mother was

losing her mind. "Mama, you know that is impossible now," she said softly.

Something fierce and rather terrifying crossed her mother's features. "It is not only not impossible, it is imperative that you find a husband. I have given it much thought and it is the only answer."

"After what I told you . . ."

"You told me nothing that will prevent you from finding a husband." She said the words as if she truly believed them, as if she had no recollection whatsoever of their conversation.

Maggie shook her head in disbelief. She did not know this woman, for she did not resemble her mother at all.

"I don't see how I can pretend to look for a husband when I am supposed to already be engaged," Maggie pointed out reasonably.

Her mother stared at her blankly for a moment. "We can say he's broken it off," she said calmly, as if they had not argued this point not a day before and agreed it was vital that Maggie maintain the lie she was still engaged. "You will receive a heartbreaking letter from Mr. Wright. You will cry. Not too long, of course. That would grow tiresome and we really do not want anyone to think you were too attached to Arthur. We want them to believe you are ready to move on. Then we could—"

"Mama . . ."

"Do not argue with me!" she shouted, throwing her hands to each side of her head, almost as if she were holding it together.

And Maggie stopped, because she had a terrible feeling that had she said even a single syllable more, her mother would have shattered right in front of her.

"A season sounds like a wonderful idea, Mama," Maggie said, smiling. "We'll figure it all out."

Her mother lowered her hands and after a few long moments, gave her daughter a tenuous smile that nearly broke Maggie's heart.

"Yes. A season in London will be lovely," she said. "Quite lovely."

Edward watched his younger sister playing like a child with her cousins, even though many women her age were already married and with children of their own. They were playing "statue," the goal of which was to remain completely still for as long as possible when someone shouted "statue." Matilda had suggested the game, knowing that for long minutes the children would be quiet and still. That was the goal, at any rate. But children being children, they found it much more fun to giggle and collapse on the floor in mirth when one of them got themselves into an impossible-to-hold position.

Amelia was in high spirits, for not minutes ago, Mrs. Pierce had announced that she and her daughter would be happy to participate in the season. Edward suspected Miss Pierce was not pleased, though for the life of him he didn't know why. Maggie had seemed to him to be one of those women who adored balls and dinners and concerts and all that participating in a seasoned entailed. Perhaps now that she was safely engaged, such amusements had dulled.

"Miss Pierce," Amelia called, having spied her walking furtively by the room. "Oh, do come play

statues with us. And you, too, Edward. You must."
With a mischievous smile, Amelia came over to her
brother and dragged him into the fray of children.

"I really should be helping out His Grace. I've not
done anything about his library since I've been here
and have wasted far too much time entertaining you."

Amelia pouted. "You are absolutely ancient," she
said dramatically. "Is he not, Miss Pierce?"

"Why, I'd guess no more than thirty-five," she said,
a wicked gleam in her eye.

Amelia let out an unladylike laugh. "She thinks
you *are* ancient, Edward. He's actually only twenty-
eight. Older than His Grace, of course, but still not
old. Not *ancient*, anyway."

"It must have been the gray hairs," Maggie said,
gazing at his temples.

And even though he knew she was joking, he
found himself touching the side of his head as if he
would be able to feel gray hairs sprouting there.

"Only one or two," Mary said, happily joining in
on the teasing. "And I don't think he'll be truly bald
until he's a bit older."

Maggie laughed aloud, and he realized it was the
first time he'd heard her laugh so since he'd seen
her, a sound full of joy, holding no reserve. "Shh,"
she said, putting a finger to her lips. "Gentlemen do
not like to be reminded they are losing their hair. It
makes them decidedly grumpy."

"I am not losing my hair," Edward said, even though
he knew arguing would only fuel their teasing.

"Bald men can be quite handsome," Amelia said,
as if defending her poor hairless brother.

"Mary didn't say he was bald," Maggie said, studying
his thick, wavy blond hair. "Bald*ing*, perhaps."

"I am not balding," he said forcefully, but he was starting to think that perhaps he was.

"No, you are not," Maggie said, coming to his rescue. "And it's a good thing, too. Someone with such an oddly shaped head would not bald well."

Amelia had to sit she was laughing so hard. "Please stop torturing him," she said, waving a hand in front of her face as if cooling it.

"A good idea," Edward said dryly.

"I think it is good to sometimes make overly handsome men think that perhaps they are not," Maggie said pertly.

"Are you calling me an overly handsome man?" Edward said, ridiculously pleased though trying hard not to show it.

"Uncle Edward, you may not be as handsome as His Grace, but you're not as ugly as Jonathon Peters," Mary said, mentioning a poor unfortunate boy who lived nearby their estate whose head was strangely overlarge for his body.

"Thank goodness for that. How did this discussion start?"

"I asked if you could play statues with us, and you declined," Amelia supplied.

"And you," he said, tapping his sister on her nose, "said I was ancient."

"Well, will you play?"

"Do you really want me to?" he asked, and couldn't help looking to Miss Pierce to gauge her reaction.

"I cannot," Maggie said. "I have about a dozen letters to write."

"That I believe," Edward said. "Miss Pierce is a very prolific letter writer." He was gratified to see her flush, that at least she perhaps recalled the pages and pages she'd written to him when he was on his tour in America with Rand. "As it is, I cannot take time to play, either. I have His Grace's library to rebuild. Perhaps, Miss Pierce, you can write your letters in the library and keep me company."

He could see her struggling to come up with some sort of excuse why she could not. "Of course. Let me get my things."

Maggie went to her rooms in search of her address book, cursing herself for being unable to come up with a quick and believable excuse why she could not write her letters in the library. Lord Hollings would be far too great a distraction—and a temptation, if she were honest. It was rather awful to be in love with him and realize she could not have him.

When she reached her room, she peeked into the sitting room she shared with her mother. She was sitting in a chair facing the empty fireplace, a book held limply in her hands.

"Mama, there you are. Why are you sitting here all alone?"

Harriet lifted her head as if startled. "Oh, my, I dozed off," she said, sounding slightly muddled. "I'm so tired lately."

Maggie gave her mother a worried look, then kissed the top of her head. "I'm going to be writing letters in the library," she said. "There's a lovely old desk in there. Very majestic. I shall pretend I am a duchess." Her mother smiled, then furrowed her brow a bit.

"What are we going to do?" she asked, sounding

so pathetic, Maggie's heart wrenched. She wasn't certain which was worse, her mother when she was unhinged or pitiable. Neither was tenable.

"Don't worry, Mama, I shall rescue us," Maggie said grandly. "I shall be the toast of the season. A feisty, daring American that none of these stodgy old Englishmen can resist."

"I feel as though I'm as bad as Elizabeth's mother for asking you to do this. Worse, perhaps. But I have thought and thought and, other than both of us going into servitude, I cannot think of another escape."

"Please don't, Mama," Maggie said. "It is time for me to marry. I know that. I have, I think, the same romantic soul as you. I hoped to marry for love, but if that is not the case, I shall marry a man who can take care of all of us. I do hope I find someone to love like you did."

Harriet let out a bitter laugh. "Yes, you can see where that got me."

Maggie smiled, glad to hear her mother sounding a bit more herself. These past few months had been one trial after another. It was almost as if she were slowly watching her mother fall apart, little pieces left behind with every bad thing that happened. She feared if her mother ever discovered how she bargained away her virginity with Charles Barnes, it would completely destroy her.

"I'll let you rest, Mama. I'll see you at dinner. I hear the Lady Matilda's children are putting on a little play tonight. They are so charming, are they not?"

"If you say so," Harriet muttered.

"It's a wonder you kept the boys and me," she said, smiling. "I'm going to be writing to them both. I shall send them a hello from you."

Maggie gathered her writing materials with far more enthusiasm than she should have, telling herself it was perfectly acceptable to look forward to spending time with an old friend. An old friend she had kissed. Last summer in Newport seemed so long ago. Likely her memory had distorted every wonderful thing that had happened because life had become so difficult since. Elizabeth had been miserable, dreading her upcoming marriage to the duke, but Maggie had had the most thrilling summer of her life because that was the summer she'd fallen in love with Lord Hollings. What a wonderful, terrible time that had been, for she'd never thought she'd allow such a disastrous thing to happen. At least, it had been disastrous for her. Lord Hollings had gone home, without saying good-bye, without a note, with nothing but memories that were made all the more painful knowing that all that time, she'd meant nothing more to him than a pleasant distraction. She tried not to dwell on everything about that summer, particularly that kiss. It had only been once and thankfully she had pretended it meant nothing. "I am afraid if you continue on in this amorous way, you will be in danger of falling in love with me," she'd said, pretending that kiss had been part of their game to keep any possible suitors away. "I do not wish to be a party to breaking your heart when you leave for England. I must ask, then, for the sake of us both, for you to never kiss me again." And he hadn't.

Not even once.

Oh, why was she thinking about such a thing when she was willingly closeting herself in a room with the man?

Maggie, who had lied to her mother about a grand

desk in the library (she was finding that mendacity was becoming more and more easy), was shocked when she walked into the cavernous room. Squares of light streamed through the dust, giving the room a haziness that was out of place in such a well-run home. Crates were piled on the floor and upon sturdy tables, and books were stacked, seemingly without thought, nearly everywhere. In fact, at first look, Maggie not only couldn't see a desk; she couldn't see a clear spot upon which to work. Other than the dust, crates, and books, the room appeared to be empty until she heard a thump coming from one corner.

"Lord Hollings?"

He stood, appearing behind a stack of crates, and smiled. "I just found a complete Book of Hours. My God, it's the Rothchilds."

"Is that good?"

"It is arguably one of the most beautifully illustrated fifteenth-century books ever created. Though some could make an argument against that. I daresay I wouldn't."

Maggie couldn't help but smile at his enthusiasm. In all their dances together and walks, never had Lord Hollings shown this side of himself. It made him all the more attractive to her, that he should have such a serious passion. "What exactly is a Book of Hours?"

"A prayer book. Come, look at this." Edward moved around the crate and hastily pushed a stack of books aside, wiped down the table with a pristine handkerchief, and laid it carefully upon the surface. Using yet another handkerchief, he opened the book, revealing an intricate illustration of the crucifixion with equally ornate letters alongside and beneath the picture.

"What does it say?"

"Who knows? It's the art that is important. At least for these types of books. It's Latin, though, and I'm afraid Latin was not my strongest subject."

"Is it very old?" Maggie asked, becoming interested despite herself. The thought of someone hundreds of years ago gazing at this very same illustration when it had been newly made was fascinating. She went to touch the page, but Lord Hollings stopped her, deflecting her hand gently away from the page.

"The oils from your skin could be quite damaging," he said. The shock of his touch nearly overwhelmed her senses, and she looked up, locking gazes with him for perhaps two breaths, before dragging her gaze back to the page. God, she'd forgotten how very blue his eyes were, how his mere touch made her instantly heat. "That's why I put these on." He took out a pair of pristine white gloves; then she looked dumbly down at her clean fingers expecting to see the oil.

"Oh, I'm sorry," she said.

"No need," he said cheerfully, then gingerly closed the book. "Not everyone is as careful as I am. But it is rather old, fifteenth century, and His Grace thought it gone forever. I don't want to be the caretaker who led it to ruin."

She moved away from him, wishing she hadn't come, for it was clear her feelings hadn't changed and neither had his. He was cheerfully going on and on about books, when she was finding it difficult to stand next to him without touching him. "Where did all these books come from? Were they in storage somewhere?" she asked, not really caring.

Lord Hollings frowned. "They were sold. His Grace's father and brother, the late dukes, sold nearly everything from this house that had any value at all. Including nearly every book from this library. I've volunteered to track them down. At least the finest of them. It's been extremely interesting."

"If you say so," Maggie said, streaming one finger through the thick dust on the table.

"I don't want to bore you," he said, sounding endearingly hesitant, and Maggie immediately felt contrite.

"You could talk about rocks and not be boring," Maggie said, and was rewarded with a rather glorious smile. "My goodness, I didn't know your ego needed such incessant stroking."

He promptly frowned, but in a way that she knew he was joking. "I live for the tiny crumbs you throw me."

There, they were firmly back on the easy-banter ground where Maggie felt safest, where nothing was serious, including their flirtations. "How did you get so interested in books?"

"My father was a bookworm, constantly reading. Much to my mother's chagrin. She could have an entire conversation with him and he wouldn't have the vaguest idea what she was saying if he was reading. I still remember the first book he gave me, *All But Lost* by G. A. Henty."

"I've never heard of it."

"It was a great adventure. My father said I should be very careful with it, for books were magical things." He shrugged. "I've been completely obsessed ever since."

"Are all these crates filled with books? It will take a lifetime to sort out," Maggie said, again taking in the complete chaos around her.

"It likely will take a rather long time," he said, sounding quite happy.

"Don't you have work to do at your estate?"

"Not trying to get rid of me, are you?" he said, removing more books and crates from the table. "Your desk, mademoiselle," he said, sweeping a hand to indicate the now-empty, but still dusty space.

"Of course I'm not trying to get rid of you. Your sister and step-aunt are quite lovely and I enjoy their company immensely."

"Their company alone? You have wounded me yet again."

Maggie shot him a look of disbelief. "You are lovely as well," she said. "But I am growing fond of your sister and aunt. They are both quite charming."

Lord Hollings felt a bit sheepish. "I'm afraid they are leaving in a few weeks and I shall remain until right before Christmas. I have promised His Grace to work on this library and I never renege on a promise."

"Very gallant."

"Not really. I feel as if I've died and gone to heaven. My own library is depressingly complete. The fun of books is in finding them."

"I thought it was in reading them," she said, using her hand as a dust rag only to find his handkerchief thrust in front of her.

"Oh, I don't want to ruin your handkerchief," she said, eying the already-dusty, but finely monogrammed material.

"As you can see, the damage has been done."

She studied the monogram for a moment. "EHH," she read. "What does the other *H* stand for?"

"Horatio," he admitted.

"Don't feel too bad. My middle name is Zilfa."

"It doesn't suit you," he said.

Maggie shrugged as she dusted, feeling far more like a Zilfa these days. The cloth was completely covered with dust. "What shall I do with this?" she asked, and laughed when he simply stuffed it into his pocket. "Your valet will want to murder you."

"He can join the line of people who do. Including the man who sold me half these books. I got them for half what they're worth," he said happily. "But for twice as much as they were sold for by the old duke."

"I suppose I should start writing to my brothers," Maggie said.

"And your fiancé."

"Of course." Maggie forced a smile, because she somehow knew he was saying that simply to be contrary. It was almost as if he already knew her engagement was a farce. She was not looking forward to the scene her mother envisioned, of her receiving a letter from Arthur breaking off the engagement. Should she cry? Act morose for days on end? She wasn't certain whether she could pull off such a charade, especially beneath the watchful eye of Lord Hollings. He'd always had a way of seeing through her, and she'd felt him studying her more than once since her arrival, though that was likely her imagination. Maggie was quite certain that her gift of hiding her true feelings was diminishing.

She set out her writing supplies, placing her pen and ink carefully in front of her, then her borrowed stationery from Elizabeth. The expensive paper had the Ducal crest on it, and it tickled Maggie to be writing upon such rich stuff. She could hear Lord Hollings moving books, muttering beneath his breath. She thought he'd forgotten all about her, for she was finished with one letter when he said, "Do tell how it is you fell in love with Arthur, when you used me all last summer as a pawn to avoid being with the man."

Maggie pressed her lips together and stared at the blot of ink that just appeared on her paper, marring her otherwise perfect penmanship.

"You were not a pawn. You were a diversion," she said.

"A diversion."

"Yes. I did not know Arthur that well. If you remember, I was trying to avoid all the Wright brothers equally. And then after you left, Arthur came calling," she said, telling precisely what had happened as she continued to write. "He was very pleased you left."

"So your scheme worked."

Maggie looked up. "What scheme are you referring to?"

"The scheme to make yourself more attractive to the Wright brothers," he said rather darkly.

It dawned on Maggie that her quick engagement to Arthur bothered Lord Hollings, perhaps had even made him jealous, and she smiled to herself. She had no illusions that he cared for her, but rather that his ego was feeling a bit bruised. "That was not at all my intention," she said with complete honesty. "As well you know. However, the end result was marvelous. Arthur, it turns out, had been hanging back for weeks last summer, nearly green with envy. In *that* our scheme worked. He thought you were courting me and my cachet increased dramatically. And then when you left, he came to call."

"And you fell in love."

"Yes, I did," Maggie said, but in her heart she meant that she'd fallen in love not with Arthur, but with him.

"Hmmmm."

For the next several minutes, they each silently worked, and Maggie thought he'd dropped the subject.

"I stopped by, you know."

"Oh?"

"Before I left New York. I stopped by."

Maggie vividly remembered that awful afternoon, when she'd gone out with her cousins only to find out that while she'd been gone Lord Hollings had stopped by their New York brownstone. Maggie had agonized for weeks about that missed visit, wondering if she'd been home, what would have happened. Would he merely have said good-bye, or would he have asked her to come to England with him? She'd hoped, ridiculously so, that he had fallen in love with her the way she had with him. But he'd left New York without seeing her, without leaving a note, without a word. If she hadn't been invited to visit Elizabeth, she never would have seen Lord Hollings again, because obviously that was the way he wanted it. She'd come to the rather harsh conclusion that Lord Hollings was a flirt and was completely unaware of the affect he had on women, particularly her. It likely wasn't even a conscious thing, but simply part of his charm.

She looked up and smiled, a curious smile. "Stopped by where?" Oh, she so enjoyed torturing him.

"Stopped by your home," he ground out. "I wanted to say good-bye."

"You didn't leave a note," she said, her tone not quite disbelieving, but certainly full of skepticism.

That seemed to fluster him a bit, which Maggie enjoyed immensely. He would never know how devastated she'd been, how completely heartbroken when he'd gone without saying good-bye.

"Didn't your mother tell you?"

Maggie shrugged helplessly. "I don't think so." As if she'd forget.

"It's no matter," he said slowly, but it was clear that it did, indeed, matter.

He began working again, this time a bit more loudly than before. Books were unceremoniously dumped on the floor, and Maggie wasn't certain whether it was because he was angry with her or with the fact he couldn't find something he was looking for.

"Why didn't you leave a note?" she asked.

He stopped working suddenly, and with great care put the book he was holding in front of him and stared at it as if the book would give him his answer.

"I'm sorry, I didn't know that was a difficult question. It seems to me it was important that I knew you stopped by, and yet when you did *apparently* stop by, you didn't leave a note. Just wondering."

"Apparently? Are you saying you think I'm lying?" He turned to her, his blond hair disheveled, hands low on his hips, looking so completely handsome it was all Maggie could do not to openly stare at him.

"Not at all," she said, all innocence.

"I didn't leave a note—"

"Yes, I know."

"I didn't leave a note," he said more forcefully, "because I didn't know what I should write."

She looked at him and slowly raised one eyebrow, silently challenging him to come up with a better answer.

"Letter writing is *your* forte," he said with an irritated nod toward her half-finished letter.

"I'm so sorry," Maggie said, though she was not sorry at all. "I can imagine how difficult it would be to come up with the proper words. 'Sorry I missed you. I'm leaving for England tonight.' Yes," she said thoughtfully. "I can certainly understand your dilemma."

He let out a sound of irritation, a cross between a growl and the word "bah" before returning to his books. A long silence grew interrupted only by the soft sound of books being placed on shelves and the scratching of her pen.

"I suppose Mr. Wright is a prolific writer."

Maggie smiled down to her paper. He was so wonderfully annoyed. "I wouldn't know," she said rather mournfully. "You see, we've never been apart for more than a day. I do expect a letter from him any time now. Actually, *letters*. He promised to write every day and I'm sure that he will."

"Smitten, is he?"

"Apparently." She smiled up at him, fully happy with her teasing, and he jerked back, as if revolted by her joy.

"I suppose he would be," he said softly.

And Maggie, just to be ornery, pretended not to hear. "Excuse me?"

"I said, I suppose he is smitten," he said loudly. "The fool obviously proposed."

Maggie's smile instantly disappeared. "And what makes you think Arthur is a fool?"

"He's getting married, isn't he?"

"Is it marriage in particular you object to, or me?"

The muscle in his jaw contracted. "Of course I meant no insult to you," he said rather formally.

"Of course."

Edward clenched his jaw again. This was not at all what he had planned when he'd invited her to spend time in the library. He'd just wanted to be close to her, alone with her. He'd, perhaps, thought he might get her to kiss him as he was dying to do. Even though, with her being engaged, that would be so, so wrong. It was pure agony being with her and seeing her eyes alight with happiness at the mere mention of her fiancé. What kind of idiot brings up a woman's fiancé when he's in love with her himself? It was almost as if he wanted to punish himself for being imprudent enough to fall in love with her.

He hadn't meant to insult her. Or perhaps he had. He was suffering and she was, well, disgustingly happy. It wasn't fair.

And then, while he went back to blindly placing books on shelves, it hit him like a blow. He had become one of them. One of those ridiculous lovesick idiots that he'd made fun of since he was in short pants. He was literally feeling ill at the thought of her marrying another man. It wasn't the altar and flowers that passed through his fevered brain, but nightmarish images of her beneath a faceless man thrusting into her, her face in thrall, her body arched in ecstasy. He wanted to shake her. No. He wanted to love her. But most of all, he wanted her to love him.

Oh, Lord, how in hell had he allowed himself to go this far over the edge? Keeping her letters had been pathetic enough, but at least he could rationalize it in his ever-rational mind. But this . . . *feeling*. This sick, wonderful, horrible, weak feeling was absolutely untenable. He dared look at her and she was lovely. She was smiling down at her paper the way she would no doubt look down into her Arthur's eyes when he was making love to her. She paused in her letter writing and gazed up at the ceiling, and his eyes moved from her perfect mouth to her neck, soft, slim, and enticing, and he nearly groaned aloud.

Goddamn her. Goddamn Arthur Wright. But most of all, goddamn him for being foolish enough for falling in love.

Chapter 9

Elizabeth laughed aloud at the face Maggie was making as she squeezed into another of her old gowns.

"My goodness, Elizabeth, I had no idea you were quite so . . ."

"Diminutive?" she suggested.

"Scrawny," Maggie said, looking down at the two quivering mounds of flesh that were nearly bursting from her neckline.

Elizabeth waved away her complaint. "Take it out a tad and it will be a perfect fit," she said. "Other than the bosom, it's quite lovely." Maggie was more than lovely, Elizabeth thought, looking at her friend fondly. Maggie might have gone through a sad time, but she was the same girl she remembered, the bubbly, happy, ever-optimistic person she'd known nearly her entire life. Despite what must have been a horrific time, she was still Maggie, still lovely with her huge brown eyes and dark curling hair, still Maggie with her carefree smile.

Maggie looked in the mirror, her eyes widening

comically at her reflection. Elizabeth had to admit that Maggie looked like one of those Wild West dance hall girls she'd seen in some rather naughty publications her cousins had once shown her. "I can't breathe," Maggie said with an exaggerated wheeze.

Elizabeth ignored her friend's discomfort and eyed her critically. "Sophia, can you fix these gowns?"

Sophia was Elizabeth's seamstress, a young girl from the village who'd been worked to near starvation by her mistress. It had come to Elizabeth's attention that Sophia was designing and sewing all the local gentry's gowns and Madame DeMarin was getting all the credit. Elizabeth, who hadn't thought about anyone other than herself for the first nineteen years of her life, was finding it rather satisfying to help others. She'd already accumulated an impressive list of the downtrodden who were now gainfully employed by the new Duke and Duchess of Bellingham. One local resident actually had some of his wooden carvings being displayed in the Museum of Metropolitan Art in New York. Sophia, now in the coveted position of personal seamstress to a duchess, was only her latest project.

Sophia eyed Maggie critically before saying, "Yes, Your Grace. It will simply be a matter of letting them out a bit." Sophia, much to Elizabeth's vast relief, did not fawn over her like so many others she had encountered. She was painfully blunt and wonderfully honest. "Perhaps some added lace around the bustline." She was examining poor Maggie's quivering mounds as she said the last.

"See?" Elizabeth said.

Maggie looked down at the rich deep blue gown. Even in the days when she'd owned ball gowns, she'd never had anything of this quality on her back. Seed pearls adorned the sleeves, hem, and neckline, held in place by gold thread. "It is beautiful," she said, letting a bit of yearning in her voice.

"I wore it once and I shall never wear it again," Elizabeth said, smiling down at her ever-growing stomach. "Rand says he never wants me thin again and I am more than happy to comply."

Maggie gave her friend a withering glance. "The only fat thing about you is your belly."

Elizabeth pinched her cheeks. "I am positively plump," she said, "and that is the way I'm going to stay."

"It is true that a baby changes a woman's body forever," Sophia said matter-of-factly.

"Does it feel very strange?" Maggie said, finally asking the question she'd been dying to ever since seeing the clear evidence that her friend would, indeed, have a baby.

"Only when she moves," Elizabeth said solemnly, then laughed aloud. "Rand insists it's a boy, but I think he secretly is wishing for a girl. It's almost as if there's a melon in there rolling about. A melon with feet to kick me. And I'm extremely awkward, waddling about everywhere."

"I don't know how I shall do it," Maggie said. "I cannot sleep if I'm not on my stomach. And that looks to be quite impossible." She eyed her friend's stomach with a bit of awe tinged with horror.

Elizabeth laughed at her expression. "I'm not a monster."

Maggie shot her a guilty smile. "Sorry. It's just so very strange seeing you like this. It's so . . . so . . ."

"Out of character?"

"Well, yes."

Elizabeth clapped like a child about to be given a treat. "That is exactly what I'm trying to do: the opposite of everything I did before I met Rand. My children will play in the mud until they're thirty. And they shall climb trees and sing at the top of their lungs while slouching terribly. And eat whatever they want. Well, perhaps not that, I really do want healthy little children."

"How many do you plan to have?"

"Twelve. But three or four would do as well," Elizabeth said.

Maggie made a face, thinking that she wouldn't want to have relations with a man more than once or twice. "I think I'll have one," she said firmly.

"How many does Arthur want?"

For just a moment, Maggie didn't know what her friend was talking about; then she recalled her lie and turned away to look at her reflection. "We haven't discussed children yet," she said, and even though that was true, it still felt like a lie.

"Men want a brood. Proves their manliness," Sophia mumbled through the pins in her mouth.

"Are you married, Sophia?" Maggie asked.

Sophia looked up at her with an almost hostile look on her face, as if the question was somehow insulting to her. "No."

Maggie shot a look at Elizabeth, who shook her head slightly in a warning not to say anything more.

After Maggie had tried on more than a dozen gowns, she collapsed into a large chair, completely exhausted. Sophia had gathered up the huge mound of silk, wool, velvet, and lace and promised all the gowns would be ready in time for any Christmas festivities and certainly by the time the season was in full swing in April.

"I think you are conspiring with Amelia to get me to stay," she accused. "You know very well that my lack of appropriate gowns was the only remaining obstacle to my staying here for the season."

"I adore Amelia, and there was a real danger she would have to miss her season if she could not find a chaperone. The person I must truly apologize to is Arthur. I'm certain he expects you home earlier than June."

Maggie thought she would scream if Elizabeth mentioned Arthur one more time. As soon as it was possible for the post to have arrived from the States, she was going end this charade that she was an engaged women. Between Elizabeth and Lord Hollings mentioning him at every other turn, she was going to scream out the truth. She hated this mendacity, especially when it meant lying to her best friend. Lying to Lord Hollings was perhaps less awful, because it gave her some satisfaction to know that her engagement was a source of irritation to him.

Maggie let out a noncommittal "*Mmmmm*" without meeting Elizabeth's eyes. Compounding her guilt was the knowledge that Elizabeth had shared everything with her, including her ill-fated plan to elope with Henry, the man she'd thought she'd loved.

"I hope you'll forgive me for saying this," Elizabeth said cautiously. "But . . . oh, never mind." Elizabeth shook her hand in front of her as if erasing her thoughts.

"What do you want to say?" Maggie asked, even though she dreaded what the question was going to be.

"It's just that—and you are not allowed to get angry with me if I am completely wrong. You have to promise."

Maggie gave her friend a look of exasperation. "I promise I will not get angry. At least I will not let you know that I'm angry. How's that?"

"Perfectly acceptable." Elizabeth braced herself, and Maggie got an uncomfortable feeling that somehow she had suspected the truth about Arthur and was not about to confront Maggie about it. "It's about Arthur."

Maggie felt her stomach knot uncomfortably.

"I get the feeling, and please correct me if I'm wrong, that you don't love him." She said the last quickly, then winced.

Maggie took pity on her friend and smiled. "It is not a mad, crazy love. More of a mature deep liking." That was exactly how she'd felt about Arthur, that living with him would not have been awful, but certainly not wondrous, either.

"Oh," Elizabeth said, clearly disappointed. "Is it because of your . . . situation?"

"It is that. And the matter that no one else has seemed even remotely interested in me," Maggie said, laughing. "The only other man who paid any attention to me was Lord Hollings, and he was only *pretending* to be interested to keep all the other mamas away!"

"I'm so sorry," Elizabeth said, and to Maggie's surprise her eyes glittered with tears.

"For goodness' sake, Elizabeth, it is not a great tragedy," Maggie said, even as she remembered that what had truly happened to her was, indeed, fairly tragic. She almost gave in to hysterical laughter at that moment, the result of which made her appear to Elizabeth ecstatically unconcerned about her situation.

"It's just that to find a great love is so completely wonderful." Maggie, who could count on one hand the times she'd rolled her eyes in disbelief, rolled her eyes. "It's true," Elizabeth said earnestly. "There is nothing better in the world than to love someone with all your heart and know, *know*," she said, putting both hands over her heart, "that they love you as much or even more."

"Oh, Elizabeth," Maggie said, amused and touched by her friend. "You truly are the luckiest girl."

Elizabeth beamed a smile, and Maggie prayed she wouldn't bring up the topic of Arthur again, at least until she produced the fake letter from her fake fiancé.

Two weeks later, Maggie and her mother received their first post from America. It was a letter from Aunt Catherine, which she'd apparently written a week before they'd even departed so it was considered rather miraculous that a post arrived so soon after their own arrival. The Pierce women had the same thought at the same time: they could use the aunt's letter as a ruse and claim it was from Arthur, breaking off his engagement to Maggie.

So when the letter was presented to Maggie, she picked it up, held it against her breast rather melodramatically, and raced to her private suite on the pretext of reading a love letter in private. Harriet followed discreetly behind, acting like the perfect, curious mama who is so thrilled she has found a husband for her only daughter.

When her mother entered their sitting room, Maggie nearly succumbed to a bout of hysterical laughter and she handed over the letter to her mother.

"This couldn't be more perfect," Harriet said, clapping her hands together. Her cheeks were flushed, her eyes glittering with excitement. "Now you shall have to cry. Or at least appear as if you have been crying." Her mother tapped the unopened letter thoughtfully against her palm. "Onions ought to do the trick. The only question is how to get them here without anyone knowing." Maggie watched in fascination as her mother considered the problem a bit more, then shook her head. It was almost like watching a farcical play; this could not be her real life, could it? "These servants are militant. The other day I asked one of them to light the fire in the grid and you might have thought I'd asked him to invent fire. Apparently only the maids are supposed to *light* fires. I shall never be able to retrieve an onion myself and I cannot think of a reason why I should ask for one."

"You might say you're afraid of vampires," Maggie said dryly.

"That's garlic, my dear." Harriet squinted her eyes together as if doing so would give her an idea. "Can you cry?"

"You've trained me not to."

Harriet pulled a face. "I don't need your fresh mouth at the moment, Margaret. I need your tears. Certainly enough awful things have happened in the past six months that you can produce a few. Think about poor Papa in jail. He's cold and alone. Or worse, there's a positively awful man with him in his cell. He's uneducated and . . . he smells and is particularly ugly. Papa is missing us terribly and especially the opera." Her mother's voice got suspiciously tight. "He's all alone and here we are, living in a palace without a care in the world, planning the most wonderful season and he's . . . he's . . ." With that, her mother buried her face in her hands and began crying copious tears.

"Mama, I'm supposed to cry, not you," Maggie said, coming over to embrace her mother, who continued to sob. She knew she should not laugh, so used all her willpower not to.

"I suppose it will seem particularly real if it looks as if I've been crying, too," Harriet said in a rather waterlogged tone. "But you are not doing your part."

"I am trying," Maggie said, allowing herself to laugh. "See?" She put a great effort toward becoming somber and pointed to her eyes, which were completely void of tears.

Harriet didn't think Maggie was very amusing, and her comment only served to produce even more tears from her mother. A dry-eyed Maggie continued holding her mother, trying to absorb her bodyracking sobs. Suddenly, Harriet thrust her away, the expression on her face almost hateful.

"Why ever did you do that?" Maggie asked warily.

"*You* should be crying, not I," her mother said angrily. "*You* are the one who got us into this mess. You are the one who gave your virginity to a man without the benefit of a wedding. *You* are the cause of your father embezzling money, the reason he's rotting away in prison. Do you think he would have felt such pressure for money if not for your lofty ambitions? *You* had to go to Newport. *You* had to attend all the same balls as Elizabeth, which meant more and more ball gowns and jewelry, things we couldn't even begin to afford but which you happily accepted without a single thought to their cost."

Maggie shook her head in shock, all levity of the moment completely wiped away by her mother's horrible words, and her eyes flooded with tears, spilling over to course down her cheeks. "But that's not true. I never asked for any of that. I was grateful, but how could I have possibly known what Papa was doing in order to fund all of those things?"

Harriet let out a sound of disgust. "You threw away the only man who was ever willing to marry you. Do you truly think you are such a catch? Do you really think you'll find any man to marry you? Perhaps if you trick him. Is that what you were trying to do with Arthur? Is it?"

"My God, Mama, no. Stop. Stop," Maggie shouted, putting her hands over her ears and squeezing her eyes against the horrible things her mother was saying to her.

"None of this would have happened if not for you."

She heard those words through the roaring in her ears, and was tempted to tell her mother just how low she'd sunk in her vain effort to try to help her father. Had it been guilt that had driven her to such a depraved act with that man? Was there some truth in what her mother said? No. She'd never asked for anything, had simply enjoyed what her parents had given her never once questioning whether they could afford such luxuries. If she was guilty of anything, it was only ignorance. Her mother's hateful words rang again and again in her ears, drowning her, killing the small amount of joy she still held in her heart.

"You can't believe that," Maggie said, sobbing now as she looked at her mother.

And then her mother smiled and pulled her into an embrace. She resisted, but her mother held tight. "Of course I don't." She put her hands on each side of Maggie's face and used her thumbs to wipe her tears away. "Look at all those wonderful tears."

"Wh-what?"

"You look like you've been crying for a week," her mother said rather happily.

It dawned on Maggie slowly that her mother had been saying those horrid things simply to make her cry. "You are quite possibly the worst mother on earth," Maggie said darkly, wiping tears off her face.

"It was quite apparent you were not going to cry until I was perfectly awful." Her mother gave her another tight hug. "You do know that nothing I said was true. Don't you?"

"I suppose."

"I am not convinced. Truly, I'm shocked that I was able to spout such venom."

"No more than I," Maggie said, still reeling from her mother's words and not completely convinced she hadn't meant a great deal of it.

"Oh, darling, forgive me. Please? It worked. You look positively dreadful. What do you say we head back to the common sitting room and make our announcement before your face recovers? I do wish you could manage a few more tears in front of everyone."

"A lady does not show emotion in public," Maggie

ground out, trying, and failing, to completely forgive her mother.

"Yes, but it would add a ring of authenticity, don't
you think?"

Maggie followed behind her mother thinking that
she was stepping a bit too lightly for a woman who'd
just heard the terrible news that her daughter had
been jilted. One more lie and then all the lies would
be over. She wouldn't think about the poor man she
would someday dupe into marrying her. She didn't
want to think about her wedding night, the fear she
knew she'd feel that her unsuspecting husband
would somehow discover her secret. Virginity, unless
lost to one's fiancé in a moment of passion, was expected . . . and demanded. She'd read that some
members of the royalty had to prove their virginity
before marrying. She had no idea how one went
about such proof. That was a nightmare she could
do without, thank you very much. For now, she
wouldn't think about the fact she was a soiled dove.
She wouldn't think about how she was duping her
best friend, the man she loved, and her future husband, whoever that might be.

She would only think about strangling her overly
joyful mother.

Edward watched Maggie enter the room and immediately knew something was wrong. Clearly, she'd
been crying, and he curbed the urge to go to her. A
quick look to her mother showed that she'd been
crying as well. He wasn't the only one who noticed.

"What has happened?" Her Grace said, rising
awkwardly from her place by the fire.

"The most terrible news," Mrs. Pierce said loudly. "Terrible. Horrible news."

"Oh, dear, has someone died?" Elizabeth said, grasping the older woman's hands.

"Worse," Mrs. Pierce said, and Edward could have sworn Maggie was trying not to smile. How odd.

"Mr. Wright has broken it off," Mrs. Pierce announced, then promptly collapsed into a nearby chair. For some reason, Mrs. Pierce had taken the news far more badly than Miss Pierce—at least that was how it appeared at the moment. Then again, it was obvious Miss Pierce had been crying; the evidence of those tears was quite apparent. Her skin was blotchy, her eyes red-rimmed and slightly swollen, and he could actually see some tell-tale tearstains on her bodice. She'd been crying and by the looks of it, quite a lot.

"No, he *couldn't* have," Elizabeth said, immediately going to her friend. "In a letter? That scoundrel."

"That's awful," Amelia said, standing up as if she were ready for fisticuffs with the gentleman. "How dare he? I'll tell you, it's a lucky thing he lives across the ocean. Right, Edward?"

Edward, who'd been studying Maggie's face, and wondering why she appeared more irritated than heartbroken, realized abruptly that his sister was talking to him. "Right what?"

"It's a good thing Mr. Wright lives across the ocean."

"I hardly think it is your brother's concern," Mrs. Pierce said, and for some reason, Edward found that statement rather distressing, for it meant he had no claim on the Pierces, no right to protect Maggie's honor. He was merely an acquaintance, someone certainly not expected to call someone out.

"But surely someone must take him to task," Amelia insisted.

"Mr. Pierce will surely handle things," Harriet said calmly.

"Mama."

"What, dear?" Oddly, both mother's and daughter's tones held a note of warning, as if they each feared the other would say something she oughtn't. There was some undercurrent between the two women that Edward could not begin to understand.

"I don't want Papa involved," Maggie said. "I don't want to think about this at all. I'm sorry. I don't mean to be so emotional in front of you all."

If anything, it was the lack of emotion that was so curious, Edward thought. Then again, he knew Maggie tried very hard to not let anyone know her true feelings, and when she beamed them all a rather convincing smile, he knew that he was right. The poor girl was completely heartbroken and trying valiantly not to show it.

"I do believe this is all providence," Mrs. Pierce said, strangely chipper of a sudden. "Had we been in New York, this would have been far more humiliating. But we are here, and here for months to come."

"Oh, Miss Pierce," Amelia gushed. "Now you can have a true season. I shall make it my duty to find you a fine English husband. You can be assured no English gentleman would ever jilt his fiancée so."

Maggie looked pained, as if the idea of going about looking for a husband was the last thing on her mind. "Amelia, Miss Pierce surely is not thinking about obtaining a second fiancé when she is still recovering from losing her first," Edward said. Of course, he didn't mean a word of it, for it was nearly impossible to stop the surge of joy at the realization that Maggie was now free. He had only to wait until she'd recovered a bit before making it clear to her that he intended to court her. A week ought to do it.

"I say when the horse throws you, get right back on it," Amelia said with a nod.

"Thank you, Amelia, but your brother is right. The last thing I need now is another suitor. I really cannot even think about such things right now."

Perhaps two weeks, Edward thought begrudgingly. Surely in two weeks she would be over this Arthur person.

"Of course not," Elizabeth said, drawing Maggie down to sit next to her. "Oh, dear, we planned a supper tonight with some local gentry. Twenty guests in all. Please don't worry if you cannot dine with us."

"I'm perfectly fine and I wouldn't miss the play the children are putting on for the world. It will be a good distraction. I need that right now, I think."

Three weeks and no more. The girl couldn't possibly pine for the man for longer than that.

Chapter 10

Apparently, Miss Pierce had recovered far more quickly than the three weeks he'd thought it would take if her ability to flirt with every man in a room was any indication, Edward thought sourly not four hours later. Lord What's-his-name had been hovering over her all night, as well as Sir William, a very nice person from what he knew, but who was old enough to be her father. She was sparkling and witty and decidedly *un*melancholy. For some maddening reason, Her Grace had placed Maggie beside her and between two men in what Edward thought darkly was a ridiculously transparent attempt to get her mind off her fiancé.

He was seated between two young and exceedingly annoying women, another ridiculously transparent attempt by Her Grace to marry him off. One of the women had just said something to him, using a voice so soft he was forced to lean over to hear her, forcing an intimacy he did not want to participate in.

"Did you enjoy America?" she asked, and Edward

actually thought he detected a slight tremor in her voice. God, he wasn't that frightening, was he?

"Very much so. But I found it entirely too sunny."

The girl looked at him blankly, then gave him a shy smile. "You are teasing." Then she looked down at her plate as if she'd said something unpardonable.

"Yes," he said, slightly ashamed to tease a girl who clearly was not used to being teased.

"I don't think I would like it there. I find Americans rather loud," she said, and in that instant, Maggie let out a laugh that was filled with abandon. He jerked his head to see if he could determine what was so god-awful funny at her end of the table, and found two men staring at her as if she were some sort of goddess. He frowned, and the twit next to him took his frown as agreement that, indeed, Americans were much too loud.

"Her Grace is rather nice." *For an American,* came the silent part of that sentence. "But . . ."

Edward turned toward the girl, reassessing his earlier opinion. She was not a shy, awkward thing, she was a crafty, miserable thing.

"But her friend is rather unsophisticated."

"Your brother seems to find her fascinating," Edward said darkly.

"I know," she said feelingly. "I'm certain she is a very nice person, but my brother is heir to a *barony.* And she is . . ."

"She is what?" Edward asked, and something in his tone must have warned her to be a bit more discreet.

"Well, she is not *English.*"

Just like that, he was transported back to Newport. He'd been dancing with Maggie and announced that not only was he not interested in marriage, but he certainly was not interested in marrying an American girl. "I have no intention of marrying for at least another ten years, and certainly not an American," he'd said, full of arrogant confidence. "My not wanting to marry an American girl is completely snobbishness on my part, I confess. Given the choice, I'd rather marry a girl from my own country."

Maggie had understood, but wondered aloud what would happen if he met a girl and fell madly in love. He'd scoffed. "I have known some of the most beautiful women on this planet and have not succumbed to that irrational state. I feel sorry for the men that do. And what of you? How can you predict the future?"

Maggie had tilted her head; he could still picture her looking up at him as if deep in thought. "But I've already met everyone there is to meet and I have not fallen in love, so I can safely say that I will remain unmarried. And happily so."

And not two months later, she'd gotten engaged. Fickle woman. Of course, in a shorter time than that, he'd fallen in love, madly so, with Maggie. So who was the bigger fool?

"Not that being English makes someone perfect," the girl continued.

"Are you one of the perfect ones?" Edward asked, deciding to flirt with the girl after all. It certainly wouldn't do to sit there seething every time he heard someone on at the opposite end of the table laughing.

The girl blushed and took a breath that could only be described as triumphant, as if she could already picture the two of them marching down the aisle.

"Are you at Bellewood long, Lord Hollings?" a woman across from him asked. He knew instantly he was staring into the hopeful eyes of a Desperate Mama. He'd seen enough of them over the years to recognize them immediately. This one was definitely an older version of the girl sitting next to him. He didn't remember her name, even though they'd been introduced.

"He's here until Christmas," chimed the girl to his left. He did know her name, a Miss Sterling who was a daughter of Viscount Sterling.

Until inheriting his uncle's title, he'd not been a member of the ton, had not attended balls and the London season. He was only recently an earl and forced, because he was his sister's guardian, to ensure that she found a suitable husband. It had become vital, overnight, that Amelia not only marry, but marry well. She was the sister of an earl, not simply the sister of an officer in the British Light Guards. If not for Amelia, he would have been perfectly content to search for books, attend a few gentlemen clubs, be happily single until . . .

He'd always pictured a plump, rosy-cheeked English wife. Someone comfortable and comforting. Not in a million years would he ever have admitted to such a thing to his friends, for that was not at all the type of women he'd spent so much time with in his youth. Any of his friends would have described Edward's perfect woman as someone overtly sexual, beautiful, lithe, and elegant. But what he really, truly wanted, the woman he imagined gathering up his children and putting them to bed, was . . .

Maggie.

Maggie, with her brown eyes, her lush mouth, her wonderful curves. He'd only kissed her once, barely touched her, really, yet he could imagine what it would be like with her. God had cursed him with a wonderful imagination, and lately it had been driving him insane with its vivid details. Just then, the woman of his vivid imagination laughed again and laid a hand on the older gentleman's arm in a gesture that could only be seen as flirtation. Unless one was dead. And from the look on Lord William's face, he was very much alive. And very much interested.

Maggie hadn't had so much fun in months. Feeling the weight of a lie lifted from her shoulders, she was finally allowing herself to have a little fun. She was surrounded by extremely jolly people, so it was a bit difficult to remain morose given that she hadn't felt so happy in months. In a tiny corner of her mind, it was frightening, this feeling, as if at any moment her laughter could turn into hysterical tears, as if she were hanging on to this small bit of joy by the very tips of her fingers.

Elizabeth had done well selecting her guests, for they all seemed like pleasant people who were genuinely curious about New York and living in America. The dining table easily fit the company, which had been nicely divided into ten men and ten women. Forgoing the traditional seating according to rank, Elizabeth appeared to have seated her guests according to their interests and state of marriage. Maggie was slightly put out that Lord Hollings had been seated farther down the table between two lovely girls, both blond, both hanging on his every word as if he were the king himself.

Maggie sat near the head of the table where Elizabeth presided next to a baronet and across from a Sir John Somebody who had apparently been recently knighted, whatever that meant. Surely it didn't mean he was going to don a coat of armor after dinner. Maggie wasn't at all certain what being knighted entailed, but she'd acted impressed when informed of this development. Sir John was a young man, handsome enough, with a straight fringe of bangs that lent him a strangely medieval air, which she supposed went with his new title.

"You seemed to have recovered nicely," Elizabeth said, beaming a smile at her friend.

"I have, haven't I? You know me, Elizabeth, I have never been one to dwell on the past."

Elizabeth raised one eyebrow. "But you found out only hours ago that your fiancé was calling it off."

"Yes. That is true," Maggie said, forcing a frown that didn't come near to reaching her merry eyes. "And I forgot to thank you for your discretion this afternoon," she said, lowering her voice. "My mother doesn't want anyone to know of our situation."

"So I gathered when she announced that your father would handle Mr. Wright," Elizabeth whispered.

Maggie smiled, but her mother's mercurial moods and apparent love of deception were wearing on her. It was becoming more and more difficult to know which lie was still out there, who knew which lie, and who knew the truth. At least she no longer had to perpetuate her engagement to Arthur. As far as she knew, Elizabeth was the only one who knew her father was in prison, her mother was the only one who knew she'd lost her virginity, and she was the only one who knew Arthur hadn't taken it.

If it wasn't all so horrid, Maggie might laugh. In fact, she felt like laughing and so found herself staring at her wonderfully tender roast beef with intensity in an effort not to dissolve into hysterics.

"Is there something wrong with your beef?" Sir William inquired.

Maggie gave the gentleman next to her a startled look. "Oh, no. I was merely thinking about something amusing and was trying to stop myself from bubbling up with laughter. I'm afraid you all would have had me committed to Bedlam."

Sir William Matthews, a baronet and the duke's neighbor, had been charming all evening, regaling her with tales of trying to raise five sons on his own. The sons were all grown up now, all married but one, which surprised Maggie because he didn't seem all that old to her. She'd thought when they'd met he was in his forties, perhaps even younger than her father. But he had sons in their thirties, so he certainly must have been closer to fifty.

"Would you care to share? I do appreciate a good chuckle."

"I'm afraid you would not find this particularly amusing. Sir William, I wonder how it's possible that you have a grandchild. Did you perhaps marry when you were ten?"

He gave her a smile somewhere between disbelief and appreciation, which was really quite charming. "Are you trying to ascertain my age, Miss Pierce?"

Maggie flushed slightly. "It's only that my father

appears older than you, but I've determined that you must be older than he."

Sir William, putting on a wounded look, said, "Now you have crushed me. Shall I produce a cane and prove my age? Here I was, thinking I was impressing a young lady, thinking my skills of flirtation weren't as rusty as I'd thought, and the girl compares me to her father."

"Favorably," Maggie said, laughing.

"I think I shall turn the tables, Miss Pierce, and, at the risk of making me feel even more ancient, ask you how old you are."

"I've just turned twenty-one this past September," she said. "Ready to be put on the shelf."

Sir William muttered something under his breath.

"Sir?"

"You are younger than my youngest child and hardly ready for any shelf." He was acting disappointed, as if he'd actually been contemplating courting Maggie. For now, that wasn't entirely too horrifying, for the chances were he was simply flirting with her.

"Nearly all my friends are married, many with children," she said, with a nod to Elizabeth, who was completely embracing the latest fad in England to appear in public *enceinte*. And then, because she knew Sir William had been flirting with her all night, she stated with a straight face, "Are you trying to play matchmaker with your son?"

Sir William, who had just taken a sip of wine, nearly choked. Maggie kept her look of innocence as long as possible before smiling.

"You have put me firmly in my rocking chair," he said.

"Don't be silly," she said lightly. "I have no interest in your son. I should tell you that I was recently jilted by an extremely immature young man, who refused to marry me because his parents were not completely in accord with the idea. He did not stand up to his mama and so our engagement was ended. Frankly, the idea of ever being courted again by someone who has to answer to his mama or papa is distasteful in the extreme."

"You are a remarkable young woman," Sir William said, then turned back toward his own meal, as if he was embarrassed to have been so forthcoming.

"I don't feel so very young, sir. And by the way, you very effectively changed the subject from you to me and never assuaged my curiosity."

"So you admit it."

"Yes, I admit I am curious about your age. I would have guessed forty," she said, looking over his still-full head of hair, which was only slightly salted with a bit a gray at his temples.

Sir William smiled. "You are a very dangerous young woman, I think," he said.

Maggie laughed aloud. "No one has ever called me dangerous. I can't even frighten mice away." At his look of disbelief, she said, "It's true. We had mice roaming around our house when I was a child and they seemed to find my room particularly welcoming. Most likely it was because I hid all the traps Nanny put about the room and they somehow knew it was a safe haven."

"I am afraid of mice," said the knighted young man across from her with enough charming self-deprecation to force another grin from Maggie. She was surrounded by charming men this evening.

Without thinking, she looked down the table toward Lord Hollings and found him scowling fiercely. Well, she thought, most of the men were charming. Lord Hollings, whom she had found so delightfully refreshing when he'd visited Newport last summer, had been decidedly less so since her arrival in England. She wondered idly if he'd requested that she not be seated next to him now that she was an eligible woman.

"I find all rodents rather frightening, actually," the young man admitted.

"Surely not rabbits, sir," Maggie said, teasing him. He shuddered dramatically.

"I can't stand snakes," Sir William said, inserting himself back into the conversation.

"You know," Maggie said thoughtfully, "there isn't a creature on earth that I'm frightened by now that I think of it. My brothers used to call me to dispense of the spiders in their room. I already told you about the mice. Bats, perhaps. I wouldn't want one flying into my hair, I suppose. But I've never really been around enough bats to know if I'm frightened by them or not. They can't kill you, can they? They could make a nightmare of my coiffure, I suppose. No, not even bats frighten me."

"So you are one of those fearless American girls, riding astride bareback fighting Indians," Sir William said. "Like Annie Oakley."

"I saw Annie Oakley," Amelia gushed from across the table. She was seated next to the knight, and Maggie wondered if Elizabeth had been trying to pair them up. "She was magnificent. Can you ride like her?"

Maggie laughed, shaking her head. "I'm sorry if I

gave the impression that I am a younger version of Annie Oakley. I can ride, but not astride. I think my mother would faint."

Amelia warmed to the discussion. "There's an American Wild West show touring in London. I saw a flyer . . ."

"I heard it's not nearly as good as the original. With Wild Bill and all that. Not the sort of show that would bring out the queen, like the original one did," the knight said.

"I don't care," Amelia said, her eyes sparkling. "Real cowboys in England. Can you imagine?"

"It's been my experience that cowboys are rather rough sorts. Uneducated roustabouts who prey on pretty English girls," teased Elizabeth.

"Oh, but you should have seen the flyer. It had this cowboy, or was he supposed to be an outlaw? I don't know but he was dressed all in black and looked very mysterious."

"And handsome?" Maggie asked, smiling at Amelia's obvious crush on the unknown cowboy. "I hear the artists take certain license when depicting their stars. No doubt he's fifty years old and with a paunch."

Next to her, Maggie thought she detected Sir William sit a bit straighter as if sucking in a paunch.

"I would so love to see the show. I was so young when the Wild West show came, I hardly remember any of it. Can we go, Edward?"

Lord Hollings looked around the table for some help, and seeing none, he said, "We shall see, right, then?"

Amelia instantly put on a mulish expression. "I suppose I will have to plague you daily until you agree," she said, sounding rather happy at the prospect of hounding her brother.

"Perhaps you should relent now, Lord Hollings," Elizabeth said, laughing.

The final course was delivered, ending the conversation, leaving Maggie making idle chitchat with Sir William and Sir John. She didn't mind in the least that Elizabeth had placed her near two eligible men, and she wondered if her friend would be surprised that she was enjoying Sir William's company far more than the younger man. The fact that she could enjoy anyone's company was a complete shock to her. She'd thought, well, she'd believed she was so damaged by what she'd done that she could never behave normally again. And yet here she was, enjoying a dinner, flirting and chatting with men as if she were the same girl she'd been six months ago.

"Elizabeth," she said, drawing her friend's attention. "I want to thank you again for having me. You cannot know how much I needed this."

Elizabeth smiled warmly at her. "As much as I did, no doubt." Elizabeth turned to Sir William, who was pretending not to listen. "Maggie and I have been friends forever and I found I could not survive any longer without her with me."

"She does seem rather special, actually," Sir William said, clearing his throat.

Maggie inexplicably felt a bit panicky hearing his words of praise, and she hoped he hadn't misunderstood her bit of flirtation. Elizabeth used to warn her, though Maggie never once believed her, that men could become enamored very quickly with her. And tonight she felt as if she'd drunk too much champagne even though she'd not touched a single drop. She knew she was flirting, knew that perhaps she was making Sir William think she was interested in him, but did not care. Besides, Sir William was a very nice man who seemed inordinately gentle and completely harmless.

Moments later, the duke rose, and everyone else followed suit. The men went off to have cigars and port and the women gathered in the main parlor, a breathtakingly lovely room with gilt trim and intricate moldings that gave the space a kind of fairy-tale beauty.

Maggie found herself sitting by Amelia. "Are you enjoying your stay so far?" the younger girl asked, then blushed. "Except, of course, for this afternoon. I'm sorry."

"Don't be. I do believe there was a part of me that believed we would never marry."

"Star-crossed lovers," Amelia murmured, and Maggie found herself stifling a laugh.

"It wasn't as romantic as all that," she said. "In fact, it wasn't romantic at all. Arthur was a nice man, good-looking enough, I suppose. But I'd known him for years. We went to the same birthday parties as children. He was more like a brother to me, really. So perhaps it's just as well."

"I can't wait to fall in love," Amelia gushed.

"From the way you were describing that cowboy, I'd say you already have," Maggie teased, then felt bad when Amelia flushed. "I once had a crush on my mother's portrait artist. I was very young, much younger than you, just thirteen. I thought he was magnificent and he knew I thought him so. When I look back, he really was quite cruel, but then, perhaps he didn't know how to handle a little girl's crush."

"What happened?"

"I proposed," she said.

Amelia let out a laugh. "You didn't."

"I did. I was quite ardent, quite passionate, as you can imagine a thirteen-year-old being."

"What did he do?"

"He laughed. I suppose it was rather amusing, but I'll never forget that feeling of being made to feel foolish for having fallen in love."

Amelia scowled. "The cad," she said fiercely.

"And so you see, I have not had very much success with men. It's been one rejection after another since then," she said airily. She couldn't help but think of Lord Hollings as being perhaps the most painful of those rejections.

"My brother has had little success, either. I keep threatening him that I will not marry until he does, but I fear it is an idle threat and he knows it. He has absolutely no interest in marriage."

"Yes, I know," Maggie said. "Did you know that the very first time I met your brother he announced to me he had no intention of marrying and had a particular aversion to American girls?"

Amelia opened her mouth in horror. "He didn't."

"He did."

"No wonder he's still a bachelor," Amelia said, rolling her eyes. "I do worry about him."

Something in her tone sparked Maggie's curiosity. "Why is that?"

Amelia let out a sigh. "He is so very responsible in every other way. When our parents died, he immediately bought a commission in the Light Guards, hired a governess for me, made certain I was educated at the best schools even though I know it was difficult financially for him to do so. At that time he was only a mister with no thought of titles or wealth. He was the son of a youngest son," she said, shrugging. "He came to visit me whenever he could. When the other officers took their leave, they went off with their friends, but Edward always came home. Always."

"How did your parents die?"

Amelia looked down to her lap. "I was twelve, Edward twenty-one and still in university. When he came home on holiday, he was ill. But he was young and strong and got better. My parents had spent that winter fighting one sickness after another. They weren't frail by any means, but a bit worn down. And then we all got Edward's sickness. I was abed for more than a week and my parents . . . well, they both died. It was quite the most awful time for us." Amelia blinked quickly, obviously fighting tears. "I'll never forget Edward. I was only twelve and so very sad. Unbearably so. But Edward was, well, he was never the same after that. He's become a bit of a tyrant, to tell you the truth."

"How do you mean?"

"For two years after that, he would not let me leave the house for fear that I would contract some horrid disease. He ordered my governess to contact the physician if I so much as sneezed. If he himself gets ill, he refuses to see anyone until he is completely better. He has no close friends but for the duke and that is only because His Grace will not allow him to abandon him." Amelia looked about the room, then into her lap. "I probably shouldn't have told you all that."

"Don't worry. I have absolutely no one to gossip

with here," Maggie said lightly, trying to put her at ease.

"Neither do I," Amelia said, pouting. "I've become quite isolated. I've been begging for a season for two years now. I'm nineteen! I can hardly believe that he's agreed to let me go. Hopefully, he'll attend some of the events himself and find a wife."

"What about those two?" Maggie said, leaning forward and whispering while she gave a furtive look to the two women who'd been flirting all evening with Lord Hollings.

Amelia wrinkled her nose. "All those two talk about is gowns, floral arrangements, and my brother."

"Oh?"

"I do believe they both think they are vying for his hand, though nothing is further from the truth."

Maggie studied the two women, a pretty girl with bright blond hair and another with an unfortunate nose.

"They've only met him one other time, and I'd wager my brother doesn't remember either one of them."

"Has your brother ever fallen in love?" Maggie found herself holding her breath, as if it were possible that not only had Lord Hollings loved her but had actually told his little sister of his feelings.

Amelia shook her head. "I thought once, but if he did nothing came of it. I'm probably wrong. I blamed his bad mood on a lost love. I am a bit of a romantic."

Maggie swallowed her disappointment. "So I guessed. The cowboy."

Amelia smiled, no longer embarrassed by her infatuation. "Have you *seen* that poster? I have never before seen such a magnificent man in my life. He's so . . . so . . ." She let out a sigh. "American."

Maggie laughed. "I had no idea that was such a good thing."

"It's fascinating. English men are so proper, so completely bound by society and its rules. I want a man who will be his own man."

"And ride a horse?"

"Yes," Amelia said with a firm nod.

"I lived in America my entire life and never met a cowboy. I do believe there are more cowboys in England than in America," Maggie teased.

"Who knows?" Amelia said pertly. "Perhaps I'll meet one here." Then she scowled. "Lord knows my brother would never let me go to America and find one for myself. I might catch the sniffles."

Just then the men filed in, looking flushed from their port and smelling of expensive cigars. The two young women vying for Lord Hollings began whispering furiously to each other, probably fighting over who would get him down the aisle first. Nose apparently lost the argument, for she looked to be near tears when Pretty One smoothed out her dress and moved toward where Lord Hollings was talking with His Grace.

"I truly dislike her," Amelia said, glaring at the girl. "I'd bet my best dress that she said something horrid to Miss Sterling."

Maggie was about to go to the poor girl when her mother swooped down on her and tugged her to the side. The poor girl was obviously suffering a blistering attack for her lack of attracting Lord Hollings. She kept shaking her head, looking as if she wished she were any place in the world but this particular drawing room. Maggie knew that feeling well and again felt a tug of compassion for her.

"Maggie, I wonder if I could have a word with you," Elizabeth said, drawing her aside. "Amelia, could you please rescue your brother?"

"My pleasure," Amelia said, looking much like a soldier going into battle.

"Is everything all right?" Maggie asked, seeing a pained look on Elizabeth's face.

"I'm not feeling very well. I really shouldn't be in public at this stage anyway. I'm as big as a house. I think I shall lie down and I was wondering if you and your mother could handle the hostessing duties."

"Of course," Maggie said. Elizabeth let out a sigh. "What is it?"

"I haven't told Rand yet. He's going to overreact and call for the doctor. I'm sure it's nothing. The baby's not due until Christmas and it's only mid-November."

Maggie sensed that Elizabeth was far more concerned than she was letting on. "Tell me what's happening."

"I just feel strange. It's difficult to explain, but it's almost as if someone is tightening a corset inside me."

Maggie and Elizabeth moved to a more private corner of the room and Maggie waved her mother over. "Tell my mother."

Elizabeth repeated what she'd told Maggie, and Harriet smiled. "Completely normal. Believe me, Your Grace, you will know when labor is starting. It's quite painful and very obvious." She leaned in and whispered, "And can be quite messy."

Elizabeth's eyes widened. "Messy?"

"I was confined, thank goodness, but my water broke in my bed, quite ruining the mattress. I stood up and Mr. Pierce thought I'd had an accident. I was soaked."

"Soaked? With what?"

"My dear, hasn't anyone told you what to expect?"

To Maggie's dismay, her friend's eyes filled with tears. "There's no one here but servants. And Rand certainly doesn't know what to expect. The doctor, well, he's talked a bit about what will happen when we first learned I was *enceinte*, but I was so overwhelmed I confess I hardly was paying attention."

"The baby is happily floating in water right now. When the time comes for the birth, the water breaks in some women. In others, it happens later. But either way, you will know when the baby is coming because it is quite painful."

Elizabeth swallowed. "How painful? I know it hurts, everyone knows that. I've seen colts born. Oh, God, is it like that?"

Harriet chuckled softly. "Not quite, dear. And while it is painful, it's not so bad. After all, every one in this room was born and most everyone has more than one sibling."

Suddenly, Elizabeth grasped her stomach. "Oh, there it is again."

"Is it pleasant or painful?"

"Well, I wouldn't describe it as pleasant. But, no, it doesn't hurt."

"Then you've nothing to worry about."

"Go lie down," Maggie said. "Mother and I will take care of hosting duties."

"Of course we will. That is what we are here for, to make this time easier for you. And, Your Grace, if you have any other questions, please don't hesitate to ask."

Elizabeth grasped Harriet's hand. "Thank you."

Maggie watched as Elizabeth went to the duke and whispered into his ear. The way he looked at her, God, if a man ever looked at her that way, she would know what pure love was.

Edward saw her coming from the corner of his eye and resigned himself to the fact that he was about to engage in yet another tedious conversation with his dinner partner. Pittswell. *Yes*, he thought with a small bit of triumph, *her name is Miss Pittswell.* Or was that the other one, the one with the large nose? He rather liked her better, come to think of it, and he looked past the blonde to see if the other girl was following. Instead, he saw her. With *him.* Again.

Sir William was a dratted good sort. Solid, dependable, rich enough, if the cut of his clothes said anything. He lived in this district, close to Bellewood, and raised horses, which explained why his friend Rand had taken such a liking to the man. It turned out that some of Sir William's horses had been sired by the very horseflesh once gracing the ducal stables. He'd never seen Rand get so excited about something as when he showed him a stallion and mare that were descendants of his grandfather's breeding.

Unfortunately, the handsome Sir William was not one to bore you with the details of his horse rearing if he had any indication that his partner was not interested. He was a well-rounded, well-traveled man who'd spent years abroad with his sons, exploring nearly every continent. He was damned fascinating. Legends more interesting than he himself was. He fairly cringed when he thought about how he'd explained about his books to Maggie, how he'd gone on and on, sounding much like a stodgy old professor about how one could tell a real treasure from a worthless bit of pulp. Maggie had been too polite to tell him just how exceedingly boring he was, but now thinking back, he was lucky she hadn't drifted off to sleep.

Sir William *was* old. That was one thing in Edward's favor, if indeed he was vying for her hand. Edward was younger, richer, had a better title, and was probably slightly more charming when he wasn't boring people to tears by talking about books. He knew, with a slightly sick feeling, that his title meant nothing to Maggie. She appeared completely uninterested in it, in *him*, if he was honest.

"Lord Hollings, are you looking forward to tonight's performance?" Miss Pittswell asked, as if it was the last thing on earth he would look forward to. He hoped it was Miss Pittswell, so he thought he'd just take the plunge and call her that.

"As a matter of fact, Miss Pittswell, I am. I enjoy the children and they've been working very hard."

Miss Pittswell (he must have been right, for she hadn't corrected him) pursed her lips a bit, as if recognizing her strategic error. "Indeed. I do remember putting on little shows when I was small. I'm quite certain they were horrid."

"I'm sure they were," he said rather distractedly, and only realized what he said when she let out a small gasp.

Edward laughed aloud. "I do apologize. I did not mean that as it came out."

Miss Pittswell laughed as well, but it came out as

such a false sound that Edward found himself trying not to laugh again. It was so absurd, all this social dancing, this *please like me, please dance with me, please marry me* rot. He'd only been an earl for a little more than two years and already he was weary of it all. The thought of escorting his sister to a multitude of balls and soirees, to the operas, to plays, to Hyde Park, it was almost more than he could bear. No wonder some men married the first pretty thing that interested them; they simply wanted it all to end so they could pursue the women they really wanted. Edward was about to make some excuse to leave the room, that he needed a smoke, that he needed some air, that he needed to be anywhere but in the same room with eligible women, when his sister came to his rescue. It was such an obvious rescue that Edward couldn't help but beam a smile at her.

"Edward, I wonder if you could help with some of the scenery," Amelia said. "Some of it's quite heavy and I fear the children and I could hurt ourselves."

How wonderfully inventive. "Of course," he said, then bowing to Miss Pittswell, "If you'll excuse me."

"Can I be of any help?" she asked.

His sister, thank God, didn't miss a beat. "My goodness, Miss Pittswell, that is very brave of you. I fear we'll be getting very dusty, and the spiders." She gave a shudder. "I wouldn't want you to ruin your beautiful gown. Is it Worth?"

Miss Pittswell preened, as Edward was sure his sister planned, and agreed that the last thing she wanted was to get her gown dirty.

"That was lovely," Edward said when they were alone.

"Thank you. But you should really give credit to

Her Grace, for she directed me to save you. Or perhaps she wanted to make certain Miss Pierce was alone with Sir William," she added thoughtfully and without a hint of guile. "In any case, we really don't need you unless you want to help."

Edward scowled. "I'll help. There's nothing else to do."

"My, you sound exceedingly grumpy. Is Miss Pittswell all that bad?"

"It's all the Miss Pittswells of the world. They all run together into a single marriage-minded girl who wants only to sink her claws into my title."

Amelia laughed aloud. "Poor, poor Edward. What you need to find is a girl who has absolutely no interest in your title. Miss Pierce would have been perfect. But I fear she's already been taken." Amelia gave her brother a sly look, which he immediately recognized for what it was: a transparent attempt to see if he was at all interested in her.

"I have no interest in any woman here," he said, using all his willpower to not look toward Maggie, who at that very moment let out a delighted laugh. Sir William was a rather entertaining fellow, apparently.

Amelia pouted, then almost immediately brightened. "Don't worry. After the holidays you'll have plenty of time to find the right girl."

"I cannot wait," he said so dryly that Amelia snorted her disbelief.

The children put on a rather entertaining rendition of *Hansel and Gretel*, with the addition of a few more woodland creatures and an extra hostage or two to make certain all the children had a part. Maggie sat next to Sir William, who seemed to genuinely enjoy the production. Amelia played an outlandishly wicked witch, complete with a very large and very crooked false nose. In between her scenes, Amelia ran to the piano and accompanied the action on the "stage" quite wonderfully.

After the show everyone congratulated the children on a job well done, then bid the children good night, led by the harried Lady Matilda. Maggie did not envy her the job of settling that brood down for bed.

"Well, that was rather good, now, wasn't it?" Sir William said, after the children were out of the room. They stood off to the side, a bit apart from the other adults. "Quite impressive."

"Far better than my own performances when I was a child. Of course, it was only my brothers and me trying to do all the parts. We weren't terribly successful."

"I'm sure you were charming."

"Actually," Maggie said jauntily, "up until about a year ago I was a little hoyden, completely unmanageable. Ask my poor mama."

"Miss Pierce," Sir William said, sounding terrifyingly serious.

"Yes?"

"Your mother is younger than I am by quite some years. I am more than old enough to be your father."

"That is all quite true," Maggie said cautiously.

Sir William moved even farther from the others until they were completely on the other side of the large room. "When my wife died, I had no interest in marrying again. I already had children, was quite content, and frankly no other woman since my wife's death . . ." He cleared his throat. "I've been by myself for a long time. And quite happy. Really."

"I'm sure you have been," Maggie said, pretending she didn't know where this awkward conversation was going.

"I know I am much older than you."

Maggie pretended surprise only to make him laugh and to make this moment slightly less excruciating for both of them.

"I was wondering if you could ride out with me, Miss Pierce."

Maggie placed a dramatic hand over her heart. "Oh, thank God, I thought you were proposing, Sir William. Yes, indeed, I think I can handle a riding out with a fine gentleman like you."

Sir William laughed. "I'm a bit out of practice, talking to women, as you can see."

"You have done wonderfully all night," Maggie said, putting him at ease. What else could she have done, after all? Sir William was a nice gentleman and she could find no objection to taking a drive with him. Going for a drive with a man didn't mean she was hoping for a proposal.

Then a thought, completely unbidden, struck her like a small bolt. What if she *did* marry Sir William? He was old, and likely wouldn't be too demanding in the bedroom. She decided that if she had to endure such humiliation, at least having it infrequently would be more acceptable. He was wonderful company. He seemed kind and intelligent and she felt completely at ease around him, unthreatened. Calm. Safe.

Sir William stirred none of the feelings she felt

when she was around Lord Hollings, who made her heart beat too, too fast, who made her wish and wish and wish for things that could never be.

Besides, Lord Hollings hadn't asked her to go for a ride. Sir William had.

"When shall we go, sir?"

He smiled at her and she chose to ignore the fact his teeth were rather yellow and slightly crooked. No one was perfect. She pushed her mind firmly away from the thought of Lord Hollings's straight, white teeth. Perhaps next time she was near enough to him she'd really study his teeth and find them less than perfect.

"If it is a fine day tomorrow, how about then? I'd love to show you my team. Finer horseflesh you'll not see in all of Britain," Sir William boasted. Maggie didn't realize why he'd suddenly started talking rather loudly until she noticed His Grace stop dead in his tracks.

"If they are a fine pair," the duke said drolly, "then it is because they are descendents of Bellewood stock."

"Ah, Your Grace. I didn't see you there," Sir William said with a wink to Maggie.

"Sir William is helping me to get my stable back in order," Bellingham explained. "And I do believe it tickles him that a duke is so beholding to him."

"I am not that shallow a man," Sir William said, completely insincerely. "I am more than happy to bring your stables up to my standards."

Bellingham threw his head back and laughed and Sir William joined in. The older man, though far beneath the duke in rank, clapped the younger man on the back companionably.

"I take it Sir William is showing off his horses to you, Miss Pierce," Bellingham said.

"Yes, Your Grace. After all this discussion I hope to be suitably impressed."

"Don't get your hopes up too high," he said dryly.

Sir William leaned over to her and said in a staged whisper, "He will not forgive me for beating Black Knight at Aintree last spring."

Bellingham laughed again. "I already have my sights on next year. If you will excuse me, I'm going to check on my wife," he said with a small bow. "Enjoy your ride, Miss Pierce."

Sir William nodded and Maggie gave a bit of a curtsy, slightly embarrassed by her lack of social graces. Did one curtsy to a duke only at his arrival or also at his departure? She wondered how Elizabeth got everything straight in her head, but she seemed to have taken to this world of British nobility quite quickly.

"I never know when or whether to curtsy. Or how deeply or to whom," Maggie confessed.

"I make it a practice to curtsy to everyone," Sir William said, making Maggie laugh by modeling his curtsy. "As a mere baronet, I am the low man on the totem pole, so I must defer to everyone."

"What, precisely, is a baronet? I've heard of barons, but I confess I haven't heard of baronet. I thought," she said with a smile, "that perhaps it was a female baron."

Sir William laughed, which is what she intended.

"You two seem to be having quite the time," Lord Hollings said.

"Sir William was beginning to explain the intricacies of the British nobility. Apparently, he's a mere baronet, which is much better than being a 'mister' but beneath a duke."

"Or an earl," Sir William pointed out, with a nod toward Lord Hollings.

"I find all this Sir this and Lord that and His Grace rather confusing. And I never know what to call the women. Or daughters. Or sisters. Your sister is a Lady, is she not?"

"Yes, but only since I got the earldom."

"Lord Hollings's wife will be a countess," Sir Williams said.

"Fancy," Maggie said, pretending to be enthralled.

"Except he's never going to marry, so there will be no countess." Amelia had come up to them, apparently drawn by their *joie de vivre,* beaming a smile at her older brother.

"Not marry? Why ever not?" Sir Williams asked.

"He claims he cannot find a suitable bride. England is positively filled with girls who would give anything to be his bride. And he doesn't even need an heiress," Amelia said, clearly goading her brother.

Maggie watched as Lord Hollings attempted a smile, but it was so far off the mark of what she knew he was capable of, she burst out laughing. "Oh, surely you can do better than that," she said.

"Better than what?"

"Better than that smile you're plastering on your face. Hardly your best and I think most certainly insincere."

"He doesn't like to discuss marriage," Amelia said.

"Do not continue to speak for me nor about me as if I were not standing in front of you," Lord Hollings said overly pleasantly through gritted teeth. He turned to Sir William. "I apologize for my sister. She is extremely young."

"Only compared to you," Amelia said, in pure little sister fashion.

"Your sister was only telling the truth, sir. I don't think you should get upset with her for that." Maggie decided that goading Lord Hollings was, indeed, amusing.

Lord Hollings turned to her and for an instant the heat she saw in his eyes was almost frightening. It was so quickly masked that she thought perhaps she'd been mistaken. Then he forced a smile. "I adore talking about marriage," he said. "Whom do you think I should marry, Miss Pierce? Is she in this room, perhaps? Please be so good and point her out. Put a blindfold on and turn around and find my bride for me. My sister seems to think it is that easy."

"I told you he doesn't like to talk about it," Amelia said.

"I enjoyed married life, myself," Sir William said in an obvious attempt to deflect whatever was going on, for though the words spoken were innocuous, it was clear there was an undercurrent of meaning being passed around.

"Shall we talk about something more pleasant?" Maggie asked with forced joviality. "Perhaps the plague?"

Everyone laughed, and Lord Hollings had the good grace to look a bit sheepish. She silently prayed the subject would change, for it was becoming a bit painful to hear even though she knew she was responsible for bringing the subject to the forefront. She wondered if Lord Hollings even remembered their discussion of marriage, if he'd agonized over it as she had. Probably not. If she brought it up, he'd likely look at her as if she were daft. But she remembered nearly every word, every expression, every heartbreaking syllable he'd uttered.

It had been at Elizabeth's wedding and they'd been having such a lovely time. After not seeing Lord Hollings for weeks, she'd been so ridiculously happy to see him, though she'd tried her best not to show it. He'd held her and angrily told her he didn't love her, wouldn't marry her, cutting her with those words he'd spoken so vehemently. "I shan't get married," he said. "Not for years and years. Even if I did get married, I wouldn't marry you," he'd said. "Because I . . . I . . ." He'd lowered his head, unable to finish.

"Because you?"

"Because I couldn't bear it," he'd said.

She didn't know what he'd meant then, and she didn't know now. All she did know was that Lord Hollings had left soon after, leaving her heartbroken and confused and determined to never be hurt again. Particularly not by him. It was no use pining for a man who had a strange aversion to marriage, one that he, apparently, had no intention of reversing.

While she'd been basking in her own miserable memories, Sir William had been talking to her and she lifted her head, startled, when he said, "What do you think, Miss Pierce?"

"Oh. Yes." She prayed she wasn't saying yes to something horrid, like eating raw oysters or playing chess.

"You're sure you don't mind?" That was Lord Hollings, eyebrows raised, as if he were startled by her answer. Oh, dear, she'd have to confess her wandering mind.

"I'm sorry," she said with an embarrassing laugh. "What have I just agreed to? I'm afraid I was lost in thought and haven't a clue what you're talking about. I hope it's not too horrid."

"Certainly not," Sir William said, but Maggie got the sense that he was not entirely pleased. "We've just invited Lord Hollings to accompany us on our ride."

Chapter 11

"Of course I must go. You certainly cannot go out with two single men on your own," Harriet said as she pushed the final hat pin into her rather ragged-looking peacock-feathered hat. Each time Maggie noticed something like that about her mother—a frayed collar, a faded skirt—it reminded her just how desperate their situation was. At times it seemed as if her mother's mind was becoming as frayed as her clothing and that Maggie only had to fix her clothes to fix everything else that had gone wrong with their world.

"I know it would be unseemly. It's only I wish Elizabeth could come. Not that I don't enjoy your company, Mama," she said, giving her mother a peck on the cheek.

"If it had been only Sir William, I would have allowed it. After all, he is an older gentleman who certainly would not take advantage of a young girl."

"Mama, it was Sir William who asked me to ride with him. I think he is considering courting me."

Her mother eyed her skeptically. "He is older than

your father. And if that is the case, why did he invite Lord Hollings? A man his age cannot compete with a young, handsome earl."

"Lord Hollings invited himself. And don't fool yourself into thinking it was his interest in me, it is not. He wants to see Sir William's horses."

Harriet let out a heavy sigh. "Sir William does seem taken with you. I suppose you could do worse."

"Much worse," Maggie said with false cheerfulness. She did like Sir William, but the thought of him kissing her made her want to giggle. She simply could not imagine wanting him to kiss her, never mind everything else that marriage required. At the thought of that, she closed her mind and pushed that image away. She should only think about how happy her mother would be not to worry so much.

"Do you like him?"

"I suppose. I've only just met him, Mother. Surely you don't expect me to make a decision about marrying a complete stranger so quickly."

"Of course not," Harriet said, but there was a bit of pique in her tone, as if she did, indeed, think Maggie should make such a decision.

"He hasn't asked," Maggie said in a teasing tone.

Harriet's face suddenly looked strained, almost as if she were trying desperately not to cry. "What if he doesn't? What if no one does?"

"Papa won't be in prison forever."

"By then we'll be destitute. It will be nearly impossible for your father to find employment," her mother said bitterly.

Maggie hugged herself, hating that she could no longer have a conversation with her mother without bringing up how dreadful their situation was. "Sam has a good job now and Aunt Catherine—"

"Samuel can hardly care of himself. He's living in a one-room flat, scraping by because no one with any connections will hire him. And my sister cannot support us all."

Maggie hated how suddenly their entire family's future rested on her shoulders. "I've told you I would find a position, if worse comes to worst. Really, Mother, people do work for a living."

Her mother reared her hand back as if to slap her. Maggie couldn't have been more shocked. Harriet, her face red, her breathing audible, dropped her hand. "If you had told me what had happened before we left New York you would have been safely married to Arthur. I would have insisted on it. To think he got away with such a thing with no repercussions sickens me. And to think you kept such a thing a secret and allowed him to . . . to . . ." Her mother's words came out as gasps.

"Mama, please calm down," Maggie said, wanted to scream and scream that it wasn't Arthur who had taken her virginity. Her mother took a deep, shaking breath.

"Oh, my. I told myself I wouldn't think about it. It does make me angry. Not with you, darling," she said, giving her daughter a tremulous smile. Maggie wanted to believe her, but how could she when she'd come so close to striking her? Such a thing would have been unheard of just a few months ago.

"Let's try to enjoy this day, Mama. And promise me you will not push me. You've always told me that men sense a desperate girl and it is a most unattractive trait."

"That is true. But desperate mamas can be forgiven,"

she said lightly, tapping Maggie on the nose as if she hadn't just been on the verge of slapping her.

Maggie felt sick inside, but forced a smile. "Let's go. The men await."

Edward stood beside Sir William feeling a bit foolish, which was not something he often felt. He realized, soon after he'd gotten the begrudgingly offered invitation to join Sir William on his ride with Maggie, that he should have gracefully declined. It was, after all, what Sir William had expected him to do. No doubt if the older man had thought for a moment he would say yes, the invitation would never have been offered. But the thought of Maggie riding alone with Sir William drove him a bit mad.

Now he felt out of sorts and out of control. Edward was a man who liked being in control, which made life extremely difficult for him because thus far he'd had very little control over what happened to him and those around him. He couldn't stop himself from getting ill, he couldn't stop his parents from dying, and now it seemed he couldn't stop the woman he loved from going on a drive with another man. He supposed that was why he'd enjoyed the military life so much. Everything was regimented, there were clear rules to follow, clear consequences.

The two men, a generation apart, stood together in a small sitting room that was part of Bellingham's private quarters. Sir William wore the uniform of a country gentleman: a tweed coat, brown, over a darker brown jacket, which at the moment rested in the crook of his arm. For some reason, he hadn't wanted to hand it over to the footman. His boots were expensive but had the necessary wear and tear to prove they were well worn and not simply for show. He was shorter than Edward by several inches and pounds heavier, which made Edward slightly pleased. Edward hated sizing the man up but simply couldn't help himself. He knew he was a rather vain fellow and for the life of him couldn't understand why Maggie was showing Sir William such interest.

"I do hope I'm not intruding," Edward said, hoping nothing of the sort.

"Oh, no. Miss Pierce is probably glad to have someone her age along," Sir William said in that self-deprecating way of his. Edward put himself on guard. It had been his experience that humble men had traplike resolve and were especially attractive to women.

"She actually didn't seem all that pleased," Edward said truthfully.

"Do you think so?" Sir William brightened noticeably, which made Edward even more uncomfortable. What if he was right? What if Maggie did have her sights on Sir William and the feeling was mutual? What if he had to stand by and watch her fall in love with another man?

"Do you know Miss Pierce well?" Sir William asked.

No, but I managed to fall in love with her anyway. "No. We met in the States when His Grace was there. She is the duchess's best friend and as I was traveling with His Grace, we did see each other quite a bit." That sounded nicely neutral.

"She was engaged?"

"Not when we met."

"Hmmm."

Edward didn't like the sound of that "hmmm." It was full of meaning, but Edward couldn't decipher exactly what it meant, so he gave Sir William a questioning look.

"I suppose I was thinking myself lucky you found Miss Pierce so completely undesirable," Sir William said with a little chuckle, a man who could not believe his good fortune.

"I don't find her completely undesirable," Edward said carefully. "I'm simply not in the market for a wife."

"Neither am I," he said, as if surprised to find himself contemplating such a thing. As if he were actually thinking of marrying Maggie. Edward's gut twisted.

"I loved my wife and I never thought I'd think about marrying again."

"You've just met her," Edward pointed out, wondering what it was about American women that made British men fall so fast and so hard for them. Rand had fallen for his duchess within days of meeting her, even though she was hardly interested in him. And he himself nearly made an idiot of himself over Maggie, the very same Maggie who had Sir William smitten with her in a single evening.

"I know, I know. There's just something about her. For one thing she's beautiful. And her eyes are . . ." Sir William stopped, his cheeks growing ruddy. "They are quite striking. Not just brown, but . . ."

"They have flecks," Edward said, growing testy with the man's gushing.

"Flecks?"

"Green and gold."

"Oh. You certainly are observant," Sir William

said. The older man gave Edward a thoughtful look, which made Edward feel even more testy.

At the sound of female voices, both men turned, Sir William with a genuine smile and Edward with something far less than a smile.

"Ladies, how delightful you look," Sir William said, walking toward the women.

They did look delightful, at least Maggie did. She wore a green wool dress that hugged her body, making every delicious curve on her seem even more delicious. It was modest, with a neckline that curved at the base of her throat, but for some reason it had Edward thinking of sheets and beds and impossibly soft skin. He clenched his jaw and had to look away for fear he'd become aroused.

Sir William gave Mrs. Pierce a small bow, then grasped Maggie's outstretched gloved hands, bringing them up for a gallant kiss. Mrs. Pierce tittered next to her daughter and it was all Edward could do not to roll his eyes to the ceiling. He was beginning to feel like a fifth wheel.

"How delightful that you're still coming along," Maggie said, with just the slightest emphasis on *still.* He doubted anyone else in the room detected that small nuance, but to him it screamed that he was an unwanted addition to their little party.

"Ladies," Sir William said, holding out the crook of his arm, which Maggie promptly took, her mother beaming a smile at Edward as if he were in on this little courtship.

Edward might be miserable, but he still had enough presence of mind to admire Sir William's landau and his bays. The horses were beautifully matched bays, strong and calm, being held by

Bellingham's uniformed livery. It was a brisk, but clear day, so the top was down.

"Will you ladies be warm enough?" he asked, feeling the cool air through his light coat.

"The sun is wonderful," Maggie said, lifting her face to its warmth. Edward felt a rush of lust and longing so fierce he stopped breathing altogether.

"She is delightful, is she not?" Sir William said next to him.

Edward started, then nearly collapsed in relief when he saw Sir William gazing fondly at his landau and realized that was the "she" he was referring to. "And your pair is nicely turned out," Edward said. "Beautiful animals, sir."

"Thank you, though I daresay Bellingham likes to take the credit for them," he said, handing Mrs. Pierce up into the landau. She sat facing the horses and Maggie sat across from her. Edward swung himself up and took the spot next to Maggie, ignoring her small gasp, just to be ornery, his back to the two bays.

"Sir, I would never forgive myself if I allowed an earl to sit backward."

Edward looked up, slightly bemused, but saw steel determination in his eyes, which made it nearly impossible for Edward to remain seated next to Maggie.

"Such formalities are unimportant to me," Edward said truthfully, even though he knew it was a lost cause.

"I'm afraid they are rather important to me. I'm a bit old-fashioned, it would seem." He stood there, waiting for Edward to move, and so he really had no choice in the matter. Once he was seated he didn't miss the look of self-satisfaction on Sir William's face, nor the smug one on Maggie's.

It seemed to Edward for the next hour Maggie delighted in torturing him. It was likely his over-lusted imagination, but each time she looked at Sir William she smiled that brilliant lovely smile of hers and each time she looked at him she scowled. Her mother chatted with him, making it nearly impossible to hear everything the two lovebirds said to each other. Clearly, he no longer had an ally with the mother. For some reason, he had been taken off the list of eligible bachelors, relegated to a man who'd had his chance and failed and so was discarded out of hand. Mrs. Pierce was polite, she tediously described a house they were building in New York, then went on to talk about her husband's famously well-honed investments. Every once in a while, Maggie would give her mother a warning look, no doubt afraid that her mother's bragging would appear unseemly. Which it did.

But Edward indulged the older woman simply because doing so allowed him to sit across from her daughter and once in a while stare unabashedly as she flirted with another man. It was exquisite torture.

At the moment, Sir William was regaling her with stories of his travels in Europe. Edward had to admit he was an entertaining fellow, the sort he would naturally have been drawn to if not for the fact that his thigh at that very moment was grazing Maggie's. He was congratulating himself on not dragging the man to his feet and throwing him from the landau when Sir William, laughing at something Maggie said, actually reached out and briefly laid his hand upon her knee. Maggie was enjoying herself so much, she hardly noticed, but Edward found himself jerking forward, hand outstretched, ready to yank the offending hand off her knee. By the time he'd done so, the hand was gone and Edward was left looking rather foolish in midlunge and was staring into the startled expressions of Maggie and Sir William.

"I think a bee stung my back," he said, improvising quickly.

"A bee? This time of year?" Harriet asked, looking around as if she might actually see the nonexistent bee.

"Something bit me," Edward insisted. "But all is well now." He smiled at Maggie, who narrowed her eyes suspiciously at him. "You were telling us about Mount Vesuvius, I believe," Edward prompted.

"Yes, when I was on the continent as a much younger man, the volcano erupted. Quite a sight." Sir William continued on with his story about lava and Neapolitans who'd gone about their business ignoring the steam spewing from the famous volcano. Edward stared at the passing scenery, laughing when the others did, making responses when asked a question. But for the most part, he was ignored, perhaps even merely tolerated.

When the group returned, all smiling faces, cheeks rosy from the brisk air and sunshine, Edward bid them all good day and headed to the duke's library. Or rather, escaped to the library to brood and be alone.

For the next several days, he threw himself into his work, pausing only to say good-bye to his aunt and her brood when they returned to his estate. Apparently his aunt had found an exciting prospect for a governess, a young woman who'd been the oldest of a large family and who was used to the chaos of children. In one week Advent would begin, and the children, excited that meant Christmas was growing closer, wanted to be home.

Maggie, who had been using the library to write her letters, stopped appearing. Edward didn't see her, didn't want to see her. He was doing the gentlemanly thing and bowing out. He'd lost, and it appeared Sir William was going to win. He'd be better off without someone like Maggie in his life anyway. Just look what she did to him, turned him into a blathering idiot, a besotted fool, the very kind of man he used to ridicule. It was likely only lust anyway. He hadn't sought out his regular female companionship in months, so it was clear to him he just needed a good bedroom romp.

On the third day of his self-imposed exile, he stood in the center of the library and looked about. Every crate had been emptied, every book briefly examined. The room was beginning to look more like a library than a warehouse. Now would come the meticulous cataloging, comparing old lists of books from the former dukes, determining whether he should pursue those books, their worth. It seemed like an endless task, he thought rather happily. Thanks to his meticulous uncle, his estates ran exceedingly smoothly, so he didn't feel at all guilty for ignoring his own holdings. Well, perhaps a small twinge. For some reason, it was taking far longer to organize his friend's library than he'd thought, considering the amount of time he'd been devoting to the task.

It was warm in the room, the duke's new central heating kicking on with a vengeance. It was either fiercely hot or downright chilly in any given room of the mansion, but he didn't say a word. The duke and duchess seemed inordinately pleased with the heat and would beam smiles at each other every time they heard the pipes clanging loudly indicating the furnace was on. Their obvious happiness with every aspect of their lives was becoming annoying.

Loosening his collar and tossing his cravat aside, he was heading toward the nearest window when he heard a female laugh and stopped dead. The sound came again and Edward realized it was his sister, not Maggie. Then his sister let out a squeal so loud his heart nearly jumped from his chest. He turned about, rushing from the room to see what horrible thing had just occurred, when the sound came again.

He found her clutching a piece of paper, her face alight with joy, jumping about as if unable to contain the happiness that little piece of paper had wrought.

"Good God, Amelia, I thought you were being murdered."

"I shall die of pure happiness," she said dramatically, waving the paper, which he now saw was an invitation, about in the air.

"I take it that is a well-coveted invitation," he said, quickly losing interest.

"Only to the Lady Rotherham's Christmas Ball!" Another earsplitting screech followed.

"Do we know Lady Rotherham?" Edward asked, craning his neck to see the invitation.

Amelia looked at her brother as if he were crazy. "Of course we don't. We've never met. We never go anywhere, so how on earth would we know Lady Rotherham?"

Edward gave his sister a strained smile. "Then I fail to see why you are so excited."

Suddenly her demeanor changed. "I'm not. Not really. It's just that I've never been to a Christmas ball and I daresay it sounds wonderful. I do love the Christmas season. It seems as if we haven't truly celebrated Christmas in years and years."

Edward felt a sharp twinge of guilt. Since his parents' deaths he'd avoided such family festivities, thinking that Amelia felt the same as he. Now he realized his sister had missed out on nearly every Christmas tradition he'd grown up with. He hadn't even put up a tree for her.

"The ball is in London," Amelia said, a tiny bit of distress in her voice, as if he would reject the invitation because of that. Was he such an ogre? "There will be all sorts of interesting people there. It's not that important," she said, so seriously that Edward knew immediately that she would kill to attend the ball. "But I suppose I would like to go. I could wear my new gown."

Edward held out his hand, clearly expecting her to place the invitation into it. He had every intention of escorting her to the ball, but it wouldn't hurt to make her squirm a bit. She stared at his extended hand, pretending not to know what he was requesting.

"If you don't mind, I'd like to see the invitation."

Amelia made a small face, then dutifully handed it over, crossing her arms impatiently. It was a simple invitation, requesting the honor of their presence. He handed it back slowly, a gesture full of suspicion.

"What?"

"You tell me." His sister put on a familiar mulish expression. "Tell me or I will not accept."

"Oh, you are truly the most horrid brother a girl could have," Amelia said, but it was clear she did not mean it. "I heard through Miss Sterling that Carson Kitteridge is going to be an honored guest. That's all." She gave a shrug as if it didn't warrant any further conversation.

"Carson Kitteridge?"

"The American cowboy."

Edward gave his sister a blank stare as his mind recalled the conversation at a recent dinner party in which his sister was gushing about some poster she'd seen. "And that's what has you screeching to high heaven? You are very lucky you didn't break any of the duchess's fine crystal."

Amelia scowled at him. "He's far more exciting than anyone around here. At least he's *lived*."

"Carson Kitteridge, hmmm? It sounds like a made-up name. A stage name. His name is probably Elmer."

"Or worse, Edward."

It was Edward's turn to give his sister a face. No one watching the pair would have thought Edward was an earl and Amelia a lady.

"Well. Can we go? Miss Pierce will most certainly want to attend. Do you think you could get an invitation for her? Or perhaps I should ask the duchess. Or perhaps Sir William received an invitation and plans to ask her." She smiled at him and he smiled right on back.

"Perhaps. And yes, you can go." She jumped into

his arms, letting out yet another happy squeal. "I'll see what I can do about Miss Pierce. I'm certain once Lady Rotherham realizes she is a guest of the duchess an invitation will be forthcoming. When is it, anyway?"

"December seventh." She calculated quickly in her head. "Two weeks!"

"I cannot wait," he said dryly. Edward turned to go, but his sister stopped him. He was surprised to find her expression sincerely somber.

"I think Sir William is going to propose. So does Miss Pierce." She studied his carefully passive face. "I thought you might want to know."

"I am happy for them both," he said, keeping his voice carefully neutral, a Herculean task given what his gut had just done.

"Are you?"

Edward let out a beleaguered sigh. "I really cannot say why you would think I even care."

"All right, Edward." Amelia brightened immediately. "I'm going to hunt down the duchess and talk to her about the ball with Miss Pierce. Too bad she's stuck in bed, she'll miss all the fun this season. It shall be the event of the winter. Everyone says so."

With that, she ran away, happily clutching her invitation.

Maggie thought her face just might crack for all the smiling—sincere and false—that she'd had plastered on her face all week. When she was with her mother, it was a sort of hysterical smile, one that begged her mother to please, please return to the mother she'd known most of her life, the sweet, distracted, gentle woman. When she was with Sir William, the smile was sincere. She truly enjoyed his company. She did. Just as long as he didn't look at her in that certain way that fairly made her skin crawl. It was very distracting to realize that the man she'd targeted to be her husband, the one who seemed to want to be her husband, was the one she least wanted to kiss.

And when she smiled in front of Lord Hollings, on those rare, wonderful, horrible times she saw him, her smile was utterly false. She'd tried avoiding him, which wasn't all that difficult since he spent most of his time in the library, but when she saw him it was as if something sucked the wind from her lungs, made her heart stop for just an instant. Made her wish he'd look at her with something more than the indifference she saw in his eyes. She was not paying attention to Sir William to make Lord Hollings jealous, but it would have been a bit grati- fying if he were. She'd thought that first day when he'd forced himself upon their carriage ride that's what he'd been doing. But he'd been quiet, almost sullen on that ride, and since then nearly completely absent from all the house's activities. Sir William had become rather a fixture in the grand mansion, coming to dinner, inviting her for strolls, sitting with the family in the evening to listen to Amelia and her play the piano. She realized Lord Hollings had never heard her play.

Just now was the most genuine of smiles as she looked at her dearest friend, bed-bound, surrounded by more pillows and blankets than an entire family should need. Her husband was rather frantic that his wife be as comfortable as possible, especially since the young Dr. Walton had suggested that, given her size and since it was her first pregnancy, the duchess might be—*might be*, he'd stressed—carrying twins. Elizabeth had said the doctor had been half joking about it only because her belly was so large, but the duke had taken it as near fact.

That was the day the duke tried to assert his absolute authority over his wife and demand that she remain abed until the baby or babies were born. It rather deflated the duke's bluster, and served only to increase his concern, when Elizabeth readily agreed.

And so it was upon Elizabeth that Maggie shone her most wonderful smile.

"Twins. You always had to be better than anyone else," Maggie said in mock anger.

"One is frightening enough. I cannot imagine two. I've never even held a baby, can you believe it? Rand is impossible. I wish Dr. Walton had never mentioned such a possibility. Before he was nervous. Now he is an absolute wreck. He has vowed to never touch me again."

Maggie sat down on the huge bed next to her friend. With the doctor ordering bed rest, Elizabeth was put in a separate room from her husband. It was a pretty room and Elizabeth's bed was set so that she could gaze out the window and look out to the garden below. Dr. Walton felt that as she could go into labor at any moment, she should be put into the birthing room, the general idea being that the birth and the mess associated with it should not be part of the marriage bed. The doctor's words were still bouncing off the walls when the duke called the servants to ready the special room. If the doctor had told him Elizabeth should eat toad tongues three times a day until the birth, no doubt he'd be force-feeding her toad tongues.

"So," Elizabeth said, her hands resting on her large abdomen. "What is all this I hear about Sir William?"

Maggie knew her friend was curious, but she wished she hadn't brought the subject up quite so quickly. She'd hoped to enjoy her visit a bit longer before addressing her most pressing problem. "I have no idea what you've been hearing," Maggie said evasively. "Do you feel as if you've got two babies in there?"

"No, I don't. I've heard that Sir William is showing interest. Perhaps more than interest."

"I'm curious who would be gossiping about me. Most unbecoming. Perhaps you're carrying three. I have heard of such a thing."

Elizabeth continued their strangely disjointed conversation. "I have one large baby. And my husband has been relegated to telling me all the goings-on of the household since I am stuck here. It is my understanding that Sir William is besotted."

"With whom?"

"Maggie!"

"Don't 'Maggie' me."

"What are you thinking? I know you do not love him."

Anger surged, unexpectedly. "You don't know anything of the sort."

Elizabeth's eyes widened. "Do you?"

Maggie looked down, feeling her cheeks flush. "No. I don't." Then she gave her friend a fierce look. "Did you love the duke when you met him?"

"You know I didn't. But the situation was entirely

different," she said, waving a dismissive hand. "My mother forced me to marry him. You can choose who you want. I'm not saying that Sir William isn't a fine man, but . . ."

"But?"

"He *is* very old, Maggie."

Maggie let out a sigh. "I know." She fiddled with the blanket, wondering how much she should tell her friend. "My situation is actually far more dire than yours was. I have to marry to save my family. My mother. Oh, Elizabeth, I'm so worried about my mother. I fear she is coming unhinged. Everything that has happened has affected her far more than I would have imagined. The only thing that seems to calm her is the idea that I will marry."

"I had no idea," Elizabeth said.

"She is obsessed with the idea. And because Sir William has shown such interest, she has sunk her teeth into him—"

"Like a rabid dog."

"—and I fear she won't let go until he proposes. Which I believe he will."

"And you'll say yes?"

Maggie looked helplessly at her friend. "I don't know what else to do. He's not an *awful* man. Quite the contrary. I actually quite like him. It's just that . . ."

"He doesn't make your head spin."

"My head?"

"When he kisses you. He doesn't make your head spin."

Only one man's kiss has ever done that. "He hasn't kissed me yet. Goodness, Elizabeth."

"Rand kissed me, rather soundly as I recall, at

the Astor's Summer Ball," Elizabeth confessed. "He was angry because I'd been meeting with Henry beneath the beech tree and I do believe that kiss was meant to punish me. I've never told him this, but I quite enjoyed it. He made my head spin. So I slapped him."

Maggie let out gasp. "You didn't."

"No, I didn't," she said on a sigh, then giggled. "I wanted to, though. I've never in my life come so close to doing physical harm to another person."

"Sir William has been the consummate gentleman. If it wasn't for the way he looks at me, I'd think he simply enjoyed my company."

Elizabeth wrinkled her nose. "How does he look at you?"

"You know, like a man looks when he *wants* to kiss you. And don't look like that. He's really quite handsome."

"For an old man."

Maggie narrowed her eyes and pressed her lips together so she wouldn't smile; she wanted Elizabeth to think she was at least a little angry. "He's not so old and you know it. Fifty-one is not old."

"True enough," Elizabeth said without conviction. "Do you want him to kiss you?"

"No," Maggie groaned. "But I do like him. Maybe when he does it won't be so bad."

"Maybe," Elizabeth said doubtfully. Then she gave her friend the biggest of smiles. "We'll be neighbors! Oh, Maggie, if you marry Sir William we can be like sisters again. Our children will grow up together, we'll grow old and sit in rocking chairs with our horrid shawls wrapped around us. Two American crones ruling English society." She let out a rather cronelike cackle.

Maggie couldn't help but get caught up in the idea that if she did marry Sir William she could be near her friend forever. Everyone would be happy, her mother, her friend. Everyone but her. There were worse things than marrying someone you didn't love. Far worse.

"If he asks, I'm going to say yes," she said, almost feeling something like happiness envelope her.

Elizabeth suddenly looked worried. "I would never ask you to do something you didn't want to do simply because I miss you so."

Maggie grabbed her hand. "I know that. It will be the best thing for everyone if he does propose. But I'm not going to get my hopes up too high. You know what happened the last time," she joked.

But Elizabeth did not smile. "Does he know about your father, about your situation?"

"No, but I am going to tell him." She just wasn't certain exactly what or how much she was going to tell him, for she was a girl who had a lot to hide.

Chapter 12

Maggie tugged on her gown, worrying over the tight fit of the bodice. The poor seamstress could only let out so much material, it seemed, to Elizabeth's old gowns. While Elizabeth and Maggie were the same height, Maggie had far more curves than Elizabeth, whose mother had fairly starved the poor girl to achieve her tiny waist. Maggie let her corset do most of the work, something that was decidedly uncomfortable but absolutely worth the pain.

Everything about this evening was decidedly uncomfortable. She and her mother were staying in Lord Hollings's London town house at the insistence of Amelia. For practical reasons, she knew it made sense to accept the invitation; they could not have afforded a hotel in London. But the place was his. He'd sat in nearly every chair in the sitting room. His hands had touched the gleaming mahogany banister, he had been in this very room, no doubt looked into the very mirror she was looking into.

Maggie let out a sigh. Lord Hollings would be at the ball tonight and no doubt he'd ask her to dance, but she would be escorted by Sir William. In the past week, Sir William had become inordinately contemplative. She would find him staring at her and she knew he was thinking about what sort of wife she would make. No doubt, he'd get "that look" in his eyes when he saw her in this formfitting gown.

Still, she thought, gazing into the full-length mirror, the gown was pretty and she wouldn't change it. It was a deep burgundy, cut lower than she was used to, and revealing far more of her than she was entirely comfortable with. It was a wonderfully rich color in keeping with the holiday season. She bit her lip in indecision, whirling when she heard a gasp behind her.

"You look stunning," Amelia gushed.

"It's one of Elizabeth's old gowns," Maggie admitted. "I hardly fit into it."

"It makes you look so . . . so . . ."

"Womanly?" Maggie suggested with a slightly sick look. "I'm not used to this." She fluttered her hands to her exposed cleavage. "I don't remember Elizabeth wearing this, but I certainly don't recall her revealing quite so much flesh."

"You do have more flesh," Amelia said, trying to suppress a smile. "I wish I had more flesh. Look at me. I look like I'm twelve."

Maggie laughed. Amelia did not look anything like a twelve-year-old. The gown was a deep navy and her hair, like her brother's, was a sun-kissed blond. Tonight it was upswept, lending Amelia, who usually did look quite young, an air of sophistication. "You look beautiful. You and your brother have nearly exactly the same color hair and eyes."

"The girls are always going on and on about my

brother's eyes, 'Oooo, they're so bluuue. Oooo, he's so handsome.' Honestly, he hates it all."

Maggie laughed. "How awful to be cursed so."

"He does hate this. I'd take pity on him if I was a grander person. As it is, I refuse to stay home simply because I know he loathes balls."

"I've never noticed that. Honestly, he never seemed uncomfortable at any of the balls we all attended in Newport. He seemed quite relaxed as a matter of fact."

Amelia looked shocked. "But surely all the American mamas were ready to sink their talons into him. No offense."

"None taken," Maggie said, laughing. "Actually, we came up with the perfect solution. He pretended to court me and I pretended to be interested in him so the mamas stayed away from him and a certain group of brothers stayed away from me."

Amelia looked positively stunned. "That," she said, "explains a great deal."

"Do you think I should wear my hair down like this? Or all up?" Maggie said, quickly changing the subject.

At the moment, Maggie's voluminous dark curls were pulled back, leaving a trail of spirals down her back. It was a lovely affect and even she knew it, but she didn't want to talk about Lord Hollings or Newport any longer.

"It looks pretty as it is," Amelia said, squinting at her. "But I think you need a simple tiara. Nothing too gaudy, don't worry. I have just the thing from my come-out ball." As she rushed from the room she said, "That was nearly a year ago, so you can see why I am so excited about this night."

Maggie knew why Amelia was so excited and it had little to do with her lack of social outings. It had everything to do with a silly poster from what looked to be a rather seedy-looking Wild West show. It seemed the English were far more fascinated with the American cowboy than were Americans. They arrived at Hanover Square yesterday morning and Maggie accompanied Amelia on a last-minute shopping expedition. Quite suspiciously they'd ended up near the entrance of the show. Maggie hadn't even noticed it until she heard Amelia say, "Oh, my."

Maggie looked up and saw a large poster depicting an impossibly handsome and rugged cowboy. His teeth were straight and white, his hair rather long and wavy, and he sported the fullest mustache Maggie had ever seen. He certainly was a sight. Oh my, indeed. Amelia sighed just gazing up at this example of American male.

"Isn't he the most handsome man you've ever seen?"

The artist had even put a twinkle in his gray-blue eyes, a twinkle that no doubt had all the English ladies swooning at the sight of him and begging their husbands, fathers, and brothers to take them to the Real Wild West Show. The brightly colored poster announced the Real Wild West Show would be departing the isle "Forever" in January.

"He is handsome," Maggie said as she scrutinized the large poster. "He actually looks a bit like your brother. Put that hair and a mustache on Lord Hollings and he'd be the image of Kit Carson."

"Carson Kitteridge."

Maggie had laughed. "I know. I'm kidding. Kit Carson is a real American frontiersman."

"Mr. Kitteridge is real." Maggie didn't have the heart to set Amelia straight.

"Here it is," Amelia said, interrupting Maggie's thoughts. She was holding a lovely, delicate-looking tiara, and Maggie smiled. "It's just the thing, isn't it? Sit down and I'll put it in." After a few moments of scalp-scraping and hair tugging, Amelia proclaimed her finished. She stood behind her as they both gazed into the mirror. Maggie had to admit she'd never looked prettier. She wasn't used to looking so beautiful, and she credited Elizabeth's gorgeous gown for her transformation.

"My goodness, Maggie, there isn't a man in London who isn't going to fall instantly in love with you."

"My God, who is she?"

Edward stood with an old friend, Lord Havershaw, his body so tense he ached with it. "She's an American girl staying with Bellingham for a few months. Miss Pierce." Nothing in his voice betrayed the gamut of emotions he felt watching her, watching men want her.

"Weren't you staying with Bellingham? What do you know of her?"

Edward tried not to let his irritation show, but it was a difficult task. Lord Havershaw wasn't the only man gazing at Maggie with avarice. Hardly a man in the place could take his eyes off her, and if he did it was to look at his own sister. He didn't know which was more grating. Both women seemed completely oblivious of the sensation they were making, but as a pair they were, Edward had to admit, delectable. Amelia, with her blond hair piled atop her head, looked entirely too old for Edward's liking. He wondered where the scraggly little girl that he'd known all his life had disappeared to. The sooner he had her married off to some nice sort, the better because he was quite certain he would not be able to keep his fists unclenched if one more ne'er-do-well ogled his little sister. And next to her stood Maggie, those dark curls frothing around her head, her striking eyes seeming to take in everything at once. Except, of course, for the fact that every man from sixteen to eighty was drooling for her.

"I know only that she is an American. She's pleasant enough, I suppose."

"Not interested, Holly?"

"She's practically engaged," Edward said, cursing the pain in his gut that erupted at those words.

"But nothing formal?"

Edward forced himself to say no, she wasn't officially off the marriage mart.

"That never stopped you before," Havershaw said, laughing.

"Miss Pierce is not the sort of woman to trifle with. She's marriage-minded and I am not." Edward had no idea why he was lying to this man. He was within moments of stalking across the ballroom floor and dragging her from this room and hiding her away forever so that no other man could look at her, never mind touch her. Of dragging her to the nearest church and demanding an instant marriage. All this taking the high road and bowing out to the better man was not going at all as he'd planned. He was ready to scrap the entire plan and begin courting her in earnest himself. And he would have if he'd gotten even the slightest indication from Maggie that she would be receptive to the idea.

"Well, I wasn't suggesting you bed the girl. I was simply wondering why you didn't pursue her for yourself." Havershaw sounded defensive, which meant Edward must have sounded testy, which meant he was allowing too much of what he felt to show.

"As I said, I have no interest in getting married."

Havershaw laughed and slapped Edward on the back. "I have to tell you that up until that girl walked in, I didn't have marriage on my mind, either." It sounded so much like what Sir William had said, so much like what he himself felt, Edward nearly winced. "Would you mind making introductions?"

Edward minded very much, but he said nothing. He had a feeling Havershaw would not be the last man that evening to express interest in an introduction. "She's not an heiress, if that's what you're thinking."

"Actually, I hadn't even given the matter any thought," he said, as if amazed by his indifference. "Though you know I would adore an heiress. Things are a bit tight. But I'd live poor if I could wake up to her every morning."

Edward smiled tightly and resisted the nearly overwhelming desire to punch the man in the face. "Come on," he said. "I'll introduce you."

Maggie was completely oblivious to the stir she was creating. In fact, if someone had said something, she would have told them they were insane, that it was Amelia the men were staring at. She was aware only of one man and that was, to her great disgust, Lord

Hollings. He was standing with another gentleman across the dance floor apparently talking about something interesting. What it was, she couldn't imagine. Perhaps books.

Maggie had been to any number of American balls, but this one seemed to hold an extra bit of excitement, a thrum of anticipation. Perhaps it was simply the Christmas trappings that lent the evening such an air of expectancy. The ballroom was decorated throughout with boughs of greenery. In one corner stood the largest, most elaborately decorated Christmas tree Maggie had ever seen. It towered over the guests and was festooned with lighted candles, little presents wrapped in golden paper and bright red ribbon, and sprigs of holly. It was all beautiful and Christmassy, but no decorations could keep her mind off Lord Hollings. Maggie pretended to be admiring the decorations when in fact she was snatching glimpses of Lord Hollings. She'd look around and let her eyes rest, torturously, on him for just a few seductive seconds, before forcing herself to look away.

And when he looked up at her and scowled she pretended it didn't matter. "Your brother looks displeased," she said to Amelia, who'd been spending every ounce of energy looking around the room for her cowboy.

"My brother always looks displeased," she said absently.

"And he's coming this way with another gentleman. Do you know him?"

Amelia squinted her eyes at the man making his way around the ballroom with her brother. "I believe it's Lord Havershaw. Single. Boring. Poor."

Oh, dear, boring *and* poor. Lord Havershaw had been dismissed before he'd even arrived.

"He was at my coming-out ball. I suppose he's nice enough." Amelia shrugged and continued her search around the room, her frustration growing. Clearly any man not wearing spurs and a cowboy hat was far too boring for Lady Amelia.

"Is your dance card full?" Maggie whispered.

"No, but he's not coming here for me. He's coming here for you," Amelia said. "He hasn't taken his eyes off you all evening."

"Miss Pierce."

God, even his voice could make her insides swirl. Maggie turned to find herself looking into his eyes, those blue eyes that so many girls apparently swooned over. "Yes, Lord Hollings?"

"May I introduce to you Lord Havershaw? Lord Havershaw, Miss Pierce."

Maggie gave a small curtsy then extended her hand, which Lord Havershaw took and held briefly. He was a good-looking enough fellow, rather nondescript, the kind of man you'd meet in the evening and need to be reintroduced to the next day. He had brown hair, parted in the middle, brown eyes, and a mustache, trimmed thin over his upper lip. That mustache was the only distinguishing thing about him. Maggie decided she like clean-shaven men, even if it wasn't the style of the day.

"How are you enjoying London so far, Miss Pierce?" he said, in a strange rushing way, as if he'd run a mile to ask her that question. Maggie darted a look to Lord Hollings and saw him looking at his friend with slight bemusement.

"I haven't seen enough of London to really form

an opinion, but what I've seen so far is very lovely.
I've been staying at Bellewood and I've only been in
London this one day, you see."

"You'll need someone to take you sightseeing,
then," he said, pouncing on the opening like a
hungry cat.

"I'm afraid I'm bringing Miss Pierce and my sister
back to Bellewood tomorrow," Lord Hollings said.

Both women turned to Lord Hollings in surprise.
It was the first time they'd heard such a thing.
Maggie would have been perfectly happy to go back
to Bellewood, but Amelia actually stomped her foot
in dismay.

"Tomorrow! Why, we've only just arrived in London.
Surely we can stay longer than that," Amelia pleaded.
"I wanted to see the Wild West Show. I promised Miss
Pierce we'd go."

She'd done no such thing, but Maggie didn't say
a word because she knew how much Amelia wanted
to see the silly show.

"Sorry to cause such an uproar," Lord Havershaw
said with a nervous smile. "No need, no need. I'll
just content myself with a dance. Miss Pierce. If you
would do me the honor?"

Maggie looked down at her dance card, nearly full
thanks to Sir William's introductions but for a hand-
ful of dances—a quadrille, a galop, and a waltz. "I do
so adore dancing the galop," she said of the lively
dance.

Lord Havershaw looked instantly worried and
began emitting an odd humming sound. It took a
few moments before Maggie realized that the sound
was coming from the gentleman in front of her.

"I think perhaps a quadrille?" he asked hopefully.

"Lord Havershaw has two left feet, you see, Miss Pierce," Lord Hollings said. "Pencil me in for the galop and a waltz. One near the end of the evening."

Maggie flashed him a look of irritation. He hadn't asked to dance, as the other gentleman had, but simply demanded it.

"A quadrille it is, Lord Havershaw," Maggie said, smiling sweetly at the gentleman, who'd begun humming even louder. How very odd.

"And my dances, Miss Pierce?" Lord Hollings smiled at her expectantly, as if completely unaware that she was slightly miffed with him.

"The galop is next," Maggie said, with some dismay.

"Excellent," Lord Hollings said, holding up his arm for her to take.

He immediately began leading her toward the dance floor, forcing her to call back to poor Lord Havershaw that she'd been happy to meet him and looked forward to their dance.

"That was quite rude, you know," she said as they took up their positions and waited for the orchestra to begin.

"I thought if you stayed standing near him for much longer the man would explode."

Despite herself, Maggie giggled. "It was him humming, wasn't it?"

"A nervous habit. One that was extremely annoying, not to mention sometimes dangerous, when we were in school together."

The music started and they stepped simultaneously to the lively tune.

"Dangerous?"

"We were schoolmates at a place called Thereford's. It was very strict and the punishment for even the slightest infraction was quite severe. Poor Havershaw would begin that god-awful humming every time one of the schoolmasters walked by. We must have been nine or ten."

"How terrible," Maggie said, though she was trying not to laugh.

"No matter how many times we tried to get him to stop, he simply could not. The more nervous he was, the louder the humming. One time a few of the boys, myself included, snuck into the kitchen after dark. They hardly fed us, you see, which was quite shocking considering how much our parents were forced to pay for the privilege of sending us there. One of the boys knocked down a pot and it made a terrifying noise. We all hid beneath this large wooden table in the center of the room."

"You poor things."

"Yes, well, Havershaw was with us."

"Oh, no."

"And he was quite, quite nervous."

Maggie began to giggle.

"One of the boys, it might even have been me," he said disingenuously, "suggested giving him a pop to knock him out."

"You didn't," she said, beginning to get a bit breathless, for the galop was quite a vigorous dance.

"No. Though later we wished we had. His humming led the headmaster directly to our hiding place. We went two days with nothing more than gray porridge and water. And we got whippings, too."

Lord Hollings was smiling, as if the memory was a fond one.

"It sounds like an absolutely horrid school."

"It was. But I'll tell you what, Maggie mine, in all

my years I've never had closer friends. We still call each other friend today."

Maggie nearly stumbled when he called her "Maggie mine." Clearly, he was so comfortable, he was unaware that he'd called her anything but Miss Pierce. He had never done so before, and to have it slip out so casually was odd, indeed.

"Did you ever go away to school?" he asked, and it wasn't simply to make conversation. It was clear he was interested in her answer. That's when Maggie felt it, the way she'd felt it all those months ago in Newport, that tug, that pull, that strange sensation of falling toward him even though she knew she wasn't. He was doing it to her again, making her feel comfortable in his arms the way she'd never thought she would again. She could simply melt into his arms and stay there forever, and she would have if she'd truly thought he would be there to catch her.

"My father would have none of it," Maggie said, smiling at the memory of her dear father. He'd been so adamantly opposed to her going away. "He could not bring himself to send me away to school even though I begged him to. At the time I was quite angry with him, but now I realize it was only because he has such a soft spot in his heart for me." Suddenly, her throat closed and she found she couldn't speak. She stared at his cravat, willing herself not to cry.

The music had stopped, they'd stopped dancing, and she hadn't even been aware of it. "Maggie." She felt a gentle finger beneath her chin as he lifted her face. "Are you all right?"

She smiled shakily at him. "It's only that I miss my father."

"You'll be home before you know it," he said, and that nearly was her undoing, because she was quite certain she wasn't going home, not for a very long time. He dropped his hand suddenly, making her acutely aware of where they were.

"Excuse me. Miss Pierce? Lord Hollings? I believe this next dance belongs to me."

Maggie turned to find Sir William staring daggers at Lord Hollings.

"So it is, sir," Maggie said brightly. "I do so love the polka."

"It is our waltz," Sir William said curtly.

Flustered, Maggie curtsied to Lording Hollings, thanking him for the dance.

"My pleasure, Miss Pierce," his said, then walked away.

Maggie immediately went into Sir William's arms, smiling brightly, pretending with all her skill that she didn't want to run after Lord Hollings.

"That was such a tender moment I interrupted," Sir William said, sounding quite unlike himself.

"Lord Hollings stepped on my toe. It was quite excruciating and he was awfully sorry. It was rather a surprise, really, because Lord Hollings is usually such an accomplished dancer," she said.

Sir William tightened the grip on her hands. It didn't hurt but she could tell he was angry. "I am not one of your stupid young men who can be so easily misled, Miss Pierce."

Maggie instantly lost her false smile and stared over Sir William's shoulder mutely, trying not to cry. It was a rule for young men and young women to look pleasant when they danced with a partner no matter how unpleasant one felt. But Maggie truly could not bring herself to smile, not when she was thinking of her father, not when she could still feel Lord Hollings's touch.

Sir William led her from the dance floor, giving up the pretense of a happy couple, a hand firm on her upper arm, almost like a father would lead a naughty child.

"You must tell me what is going on between you and Lord Hollings. I thought from the beginning that there was some sort of undercurrent between you two. More fool I, I thought it was because you disliked each other, but I now have the feeling that it is quite the opposite."

Maggie clenched her jaw, giving him a mulish expression. "I have never behaved in a way that would make you think such a thing," she said, knowing she was being purposefully vague.

"Perhaps it is the way Lord Hollings behaves around you. I am sorry if I am mistaken about your own feelings." He didn't sound at all sorry, he sounded angry.

"If you must know, Sir William, Lord Hollings mentioned my father, which is an extremely painful subject to me. I planned to tell you in a more private setting, but as I can see you are angry, I will have to tell you now and hope it does not taint your view of me." She took a bracing breath. "My father is in prison and will be for five years. He embezzled thousands from his friends. Lord Hollings does not know this, very few people here do. My mother is ashamed, of course, and wants it to remain a secret, or at least not something we mention in casual conversation. I do not like pretending to be happy when I am not, and when Lord Hollings mentioned my father I fear

I was unable at that moment to pretend to be happy. In order to explain my tears, I told Lord Hollings simply that I missed my father, and Lord Hollings, trying to cheer me up, told me I would see him soon, which could not be further from the truth. My father is deeply humiliated by this experience and has not yet allowed us to visit. I was quite over- whelmed and Lord Hollings, being apparently more sensitive to my emotions than others," she said pointedly, "was only trying to comfort me like a gen- tleman. He asked only if something was wrong." It was mostly the truth. She'd only left out the part where she was completely and utterly in love with Lord Hollings.

If Maggie thought she would shame Sir William with her overly dramatic description, she was wrong.

"He touched you."

Maggie lifted her chin. "We were dancing."

"He touched your face. He looked at you as if . . ."

"As if what?"

"As if he wanted to kiss you."

Those words hurt far more than Sir William could know. "You are mistaken," she said, looking straight into his eyes.

Sir William let out a sigh. "I am sorry for your father," he said, his voice softening. "If you are wor- ried that it has somehow lessened you in my eyes, you are wrong." He looked around the vast ballroom and let out a soft chuckle. "I am very fond of you, Miss Pierce. You must know that."

Maggie tensed, dreading that he would ask her to marry him at this moment. *Not now*, she pleaded silently. *Please not now.*

"I suppose I must get used to men staring at you.

It will not be easy. You are very beautiful." Those words were the closest he'd come to a declaration. *I suppose I must get used to men staring at you.* It was as if he'd marked her as his.

"Thank you."

"You are still angry with me."

Maggie couldn't help but smile. "Only a little. It is very difficult for me to remain angry with anyone. It really is a curse."

"A wonderful curse," Sir William said, obviously relieved that she was no longer speaking to him in a monotone.

Just then, the ballroom changed, conversations grew silent and then the dancers, noting the change, stopped dancing, and finally, the orchestra members lowered their instruments. Maggie let out a giggle, quickly stifling it. For standing at the entrance to the ballroom was the most ridiculous-looking man she'd ever seen.

Carson Kitteridge had arrived.

Chapter 13

"Oh, my goodness, he's even more beautiful in person," gushed Lady Amelia as she clutched her brother's arm, not seeing the look of complete disbelief in his eyes.

Carson Kitteridge stood at the entrance of the ballroom dressed in white from head to toe, except for the large silver embellishments on his hat, fringed shirt, pants, and spurred boots. He swept the hat off his head revealing long, wavy hair that was tied loosely in back with a white and silver string. At his throat, he wore a strange little tie and a large silver medallion that seemed to hold the tie in place. He looked more dazzling than the star at the top of the Christmas tree. As his eyes swept the crowd, each woman sighed in turn as his gaze touched upon them.

"Oh, good God," Lord Hollings muttered.

"Isn't he the grandest man you've ever seen?" Amelia asked.

"He certainly is . . . different," Edward said. He knew only what he'd read in the *Times*, that Carson Kitteridge was supposedly a hero of the great Indian wars, rode with General Custer, and was generally considered an American hero. He owned a large ranch in Texas, was a member of the famous Texas Rangers, and was in England as a sort of ambassador for the great American wilderness. In between, of course, putting on two shows a day, which Edward had heard had little resemblance to the famous Buffalo Bill Cody Wild West Show that had all of England so enthralled six years ago. That show, which Edward had actually attended, was quite spectacular, featuring real Indians and real cowboys. Queen Victoria had even attended during the Golden Jubilee. This show, however, was considered far more pedestrian and less exciting than the original. Still, Carson Kitteridge was managing to engage London's female population.

He was a large man, standing above most of the men in the room, something, Edward noted, he seemed to enjoy. He wore a pointed beard and a large mustache that curled upward, no doubt helped by wax. Edward had to admit he was a fine specimen, though for the life of him he couldn't understand why any woman would find him more attractive than, say, him.

He looked about the room and found her, Maggie, and was immensely relieved when he saw her hiding a smile behind her hand. As if knowing he stared, she looked at him and her smile broadened as she rolled her eyes—just slightly—to let him know just how absurd she thought the man was. God, he loved her.

Carson Kitteridge, looking like a king walking among his adoring subjects, entered the room flashing a smile that fairly made the gaslights and

Christmas decorations seem dim. The orchestra resumed playing and ladies with their gentlemen began dancing while pretending not to look for the famous Carson Kitteridge.

Edward chanced another look at Maggie and found her still standing next to Sir William, watching as the American cowboy started to mingle. Holding her in his arms tonight had been sheer torture. And he still had a waltz to live through before the grand Christmas feast. He simply could not keep his eyes off her and wondered why he should even continue to try. As he watched, she said something into Sir William's ear, something only the older man could hear, and the man smiled. She'd made him smile. Damn him to hell, but even that made him insane with jealousy. Loud laughter filled the room. Apparently Mr. Kitteridge had said something impossibly witty. Maggie looked across at him and crossed her eyes.

At that moment Edward vowed the evening would not end before he kissed her.

"You must introduce me."

Edward gave his sister a sick smile, which Amelia chose to ignore. "Must I? I fear all that glitter on him will blind me if I get too close."

"If you don't, he'll end up dancing with someone else during the last waltz. Look," Amelia said, holding up her dance card. "I've saved the last waltz for him."

"Isn't that a bit presumptuous?"

"I am going to ask him to dance."

"You are doing nothing of the sort," Edward said firmly.

"Then introduce me, please," she said, feeling a bit of panic grow in her chest. If she didn't get a chance to dance with him she'd just die; she could feel herself beginning to expire at that very moment. "You are an earl, Edward. You never use your rank for anything. You might think you were still a mister the way you act. Please do this for me."

"You want me to *make* him dance with you?" he asked.

Amelia let out a puff of air. Edward didn't understand. How could he? He'd never been in love. Not that she loved Carson Kitteridge. Even she knew how ridiculous it would be to claim she loved a man she'd never met. But still . . . there was something about him that drew her, made her feel like she'd never felt before. He was the first man she'd ever seen that she could even consider kissing. "Please just introduce us."

Her brother looked down at her as if seeing a foreign creature standing before him. Indeed, that was what she felt like, foreign, completely unlike herself. She'd never made a fool of herself for a man; she'd never wanted to. But Carson Kitteridge was standing in the very same room as she and he was even more handsome than she could have imagined. The artist had not done him justice at all. He was far grander and taller and impossibly more handsome than the poster of him.

"Very well," Edward said, holding out his arm for her to take.

Amelia clapped her hands together, unable to contain her happiness, then put on a look of sedate interest that didn't quite mesh with the excitement in her eyes. They stood for a few moments on the fringes of the crowd that surrounded Mr. Kitteridge, before Amelia lost all patience and elbowed her brother.

"Mr. Kitteridge," Edward said during a brief break in the conversation. The cowboy turned her way and Amelia, who'd never even felt light-headed her entire life, felt like she might swoon. The physical impact of him looking at her was like nothing she'd ever experienced. It felt as if her entire insides had just melted, just like that, and puddled to her slippers.

"Sir?" His voice was a deep baritone, smooth and rich.

"I would like to present to you my sister, Lady Amelia. She is an admirer of yours apparently."

"Mr. Kitteridge," Amelia said. "It is a pleasure to make your acquaintance."

Just like that, Mr. Kitteridge abandoned the throng surrounding him, took Amelia's hand in his, and lifted it to his mouth, stopping just short of kissing her gloved hand. "Lady Amelia," he said, looking into her eyes with his striking gray ones, "the pleasure, surely, is all mine."

He had the most delicious accent Amelia had ever heard, drawing out his vowels so that it seemed as if each syllable deserved special attention.

"Have you seen the show?" He was still holding her hand and Amelia wondered if he was ever going to let go. She hoped not.

"No, I haven't, but plan to before we leave London." She looked to her brother, who was looking at their hands. "Isn't that right, Edward? Oh, I'm so sorry, this is my brother, Lord Hollings. He's an earl."

"An earl. Well, that's mighty fancy."

"Oh, no. Not really. Edward is a regular sort, aren't you, Edward? In fact, he's just become an earl. Before that he was just—"

"Amelia," Edward said, giving her a look that told her she'd gone quite insane, and indeed she felt a bit insane. It was as if Mr. Kitteridge's hand burned through her glove and melted the parts of her that weren't already liquid.

"I'm not certain we'll have the time," Edward said, surely just to make her crazy.

"Of course we have the time," she said to Mr. Kitteridge. "I've only been looking forward to it forever. Some people say it's even better than Bill Cody's show." No one had said that, and Amelia didn't know why she'd just lied, but there it was. At the mention of Bill Cody, Mr. Kitteridge's smile faltered slightly and Amelia wished she hadn't said a thing.

"Our show is very different than Mr. Cody's and I think far more entertainin'. We have two shows tomorrow. I would be honored, Lord Hollings, if you and your sister could come as my guest."

Then he winked at Amelia, as if he knew he'd just trapped her brother into going and was sharing their little victory. Amelia's brother could do nothing but nod and thank Mr. Kitteridge for his kind offer. If they hadn't been standing in a ballroom, Amelia would have jumped up and down with joy. Imagine not only going to the show but being Mr. Kitteridge's special guests.

"I wonder, Lady Amelia, if there is the smallest chance that you have an empty spot on that there dance card."

Amelia didn't even pretend to look. "Why, I do have one dance remaining, Mr. Kitteridge. A waltz."

Mr. Kitteridge's smile broadened. "If you would do me the honor," he said, bowing grandly.

"I shall pencil you in now," Amelia said brightly, carefully shielding from him that, other than her brother, his was the only name on her card.

"Oh, my, I do think our Lady Amelia is in love," Maggie said to Sir William.

"With whom?"

"Carson Kitteridge, the American cowboy she's been talking about so endlessly. I do hope she doesn't let herself get too involved."

"I don't see how she can. We're going back to Bellingham in a few days and that show isn't going to be in town much longer. Can't see what any female sees in him. Look at that hair," he said, laughing.

"Some women like a man who's different from everything they've ever known. Perhaps that's why I like Englishmen," she said, allowing herself to flirt a bit. Flirting with Sir William had lost a bit of its charm ever since he began taking it all so seriously. He would get this look in his eyes, much like a dog when its master mentions offhand that it's time to go for a walk but then sits down in a comfortable chair. She almost wished he'd get angry with her again; it had been rather refreshing.

"All Englishmen or someone in particular?" he said, smiling down at her.

"Just one," she said, squeezing his arm. It was the least she could do, after all. She was glad he'd forgotten about Lord Hollings and apparently believed her when she'd said he was merely comforting her. "But I do have to warn you that I have another dance with Lord Hollings and if you plan to turn into a jealous toad, I want you to leave the room," she said, teasing him.

"Perhaps I'd better. You may not be interested in him, my girl, but I can tell you he is vastly interested in you."

"Lord Hollings is interested in all women," Maggie said, ignoring that her heart picked up a beat at his words. She looked across the ballroom to where Lord Hollings seemed to be happily holding court with three young ladies. Despite Lord Hollings's protests that he did not like the attention women gave him, he certainly appeared to be having a wonderful time chatting with three of them at once. She tried not to stare across the bobbing heads of the dancers, but it seemed it was impossible for her.

"When is your next dance with Lord Hollings?" Sir William asked with forced nonchalance.

Maggie knew, but she pretended to scan her dance card anyway. "The last waltz," she said. "Oh, I should have saved that for you. I'm sorry."

Sir William smiled. "No worries, my dear. I got my waltz in, didn't I, and there's no need to get tongues wagging by dancing two waltzes with you, eh? Ah, here comes Lord Woodbury," Sir William said, nodding to his friend whom he'd introduced to Maggie earlier in the evening. Her dance card was nearly filled with men in their fifties and older because it seemed as if Sir William wanted to introduce her to every man he'd ever been acquainted with. Other than Lord Hollings, no one was near to her age. Maggie told herself she didn't mind, in fact wouldn't mind when they were married. She didn't realize how very little she had in common with the older generation until she spent an evening with them. They either treated her like a little girl or looked at her in a way that made her feel exceedingly uncomfortable. For some reason, Sir William didn't get angry with his friends for leering at her, only at Sir Hollings for touching her face.

After her dance with the gentleman, she went in search of Amelia. She was supposed to help her mother chaperone the girl, and so far this evening she had not done a very good job of it. When she found her, Maggie's heart plummeted, for she was looking up at Carson Kitteridge like a girl fully in the throes of her first crush. The man was standing far too close, with one hand braced against the wall as he hovered over her. Amelia wasn't a small girl, but she looked tiny looking up at Carson Kitteridge, who seemed to loom over her like a hungry wolf. With determination in her step, she marched over to where they were standing, fairly fuming that her mother wasn't doing a better job with her chaperoning duties. In fact, Maggie couldn't recall seeing her mother all evening. *Wonderful. Something else to worry about.*

She deftly pulled a long strand of hair from her hair clip as she approached the pair, and said, "Lady Amelia, there you are. I need your help with my hair."

Amelia, looking rather dazed, practically had to shake her head to clear her vision. Then she actually frowned at her friend. "They have maids in the retiring rooms for that," she said, then turned back to Mr. Kitteridge. "Besides, my dance with Mr. Kitteridge is nearly here. I'd hate to miss it, you know."

Carson Kitteridge looked from one girl to the other, apparently vastly amused.

"Could you introduce your friend, Lady Amelia?" he asked with his Texas drawl. Though Maggie had never traveled to Texas, she was quite certain she'd never heard a drawl so pronounced before, and she narrowed her eyes at him. "Do I detect an American accent?" he asked.

Clearly, the man was a genius. "You do, Mr. Kitteridge. I'm Margaret Pierce from New York." She was quite certain he wouldn't have any knowledge of her father's embezzlement. He did not seem to be the sort of man who read the *New York Times* regularly.

"Miss Pierce is here as a guest of the Duchess of Bellingham," Amelia said, and Maggie had the suspicion that she was trying to impress the cowboy.

"That the one who up and married that duke?"

"The very one," Maggie said, forcing a smile and quickly reassessing the cowboy. If he knew about Elizabeth, that meant he read newspapers; she prayed he didn't know about her father.

"You here to fetch yourself a duke, Miss Pierce?" he asked, and his smile was so charming Maggie, who was already suspicious of the man, couldn't help but smile. God help Amelia if she was falling for him.

"No. I'm afraid I'm not much of a catch for a title."

Mr. Kitteridge let out a low chuckle and there was a bit of the devil in his eyes. "Now, I wouldn't go sayin' that, Miss Pierce."

Maggie gave him a look as if he'd quite lost his mind. He was clearly flirting with her even though he'd spent most of the evening talking with Amelia. The younger girl didn't miss the obvious bit of flirtation, either. In fact, Maggie was quite certain that if Amelia had claws, she would have sprung them at that very moment. Mr. Kitteridge gave her a self-effacing smile, a sort of facial shrug that told her he simply couldn't help himself, he flirted with all women.

"Miss Pierce is practically engaged," Amelia said.

"Is that right? Who's the lucky fellow?" he asked, scanning the room as if he might pick him out. Then he stopped dead. "That there fellow," he said, nodding across the dance floor.

"No," Amelia said, giggling. "That's my brother. It's the gentleman in the corner. The one standing next to that bald elderly man."

Mr. Kitteridge looked down at Maggie and she looked stubbornly up at him.

"You don't say?" he drawled, his eyes flickering up again to Lord Hollings before resting on her. "Well, good for you, Miss Pierce."

"Nothing is official," she said through partially clenched teeth.

Then, in one deft move, Amelia grabbed the piece of hair she'd tugged free and quickly secured it into place. "There. Now you are free to dance the night away. I think I see your next partner coming this way."

Maggie turned to see a man who must have been nearly seventy coming her way. Suppressing a groan, she smiled at the approaching man whom she remembered as being extremely knowledgeable about raising prized hunting dogs.

"Don't you have a dance partner?" she asked Amelia, feeling testy.

"No one has asked," she said, bringing out her laced dance card as proof.

"Aren't I just the luckiest fellow in England?" Kitteridge said, and he smiled that smile that likely caused a hundred girls to faint dead away just at the glory of it.

Maggie narrowed her eyes, giving the man a silent warning before turning to her next dance partner.

It was nearing midnight when the small orchestra began playing the Emperor's Waltz, one of Maggie's least favorite Strauss compositions. It wasn't because the piece wasn't lovely, but because it began strong and lively, then turned so soulful she rarely was dried-eyed by the end. And she was dancing with Lord Hollings.

Her emotions were already frayed from Sir William and her inability to find her mother. It was possible she was playing cards with some of the other older ladies. Perhaps going to a ball without her husband was too painful for her. Maggie wished she had been smart enough to disappear somewhere, for she didn't think she'd be able to get through the Emperor's Waltz in Lord Hollings's arms without completely breaking down.

"Miss Pierce," he said, coming up behind her.

She nodded, praying he couldn't hear her heart, which was pounding so painfully, and she held up her arms, carefully placing one in his firm hand, the other on his shoulder.

He held her lightly as they began to move among the other dancers. "As I recall, this is not your favorite Strauss," he said, completely surprising her.

"I cannot believe you remember that."

He smiled. "It seems I am cursed to remember

every detail about you." He tightened his hold just then, and she let him. Something was different about him. He kept his eyes on hers, his gaze holding a strange, dark intensity that made a flood of heat nearly consume her. *Oh, dear God.*

They danced without speaking, without smiling, and a casual observer might think they were a couple who was bored, with life, with each other. But someone who was watching intensely might have seen Maggie's parted lips, the way her breath was catching oddly in her chest, the way his arms pulled her subtly closer and closer until they were nearly fully embracing.

When the music stopped, Lord Hollings pulled her out of the ballroom and to the empty veranda. He didn't say a word. Neither did she.

Even when he pressed her against the cold stone of the mansion, even when he brought his mouth against hers, even when he pressed his aroused body to hers, even then, they were silent. She pulled him against her, reveling in the feel of his mouth, his tongue, his hands that seemed to touch her everywhere, her breasts, her neck, between her legs. And she, oh God, she touched him on his face, his neck, his chest, and fleetingly, because she simply could not help herself, his arousal.

He pulled away, breathing harshly, staring at her as if she'd bewitched him. Swallowing heavily, he finally spoke.

"He can't have you."

And then he pressed a finger against her lips, to stop her from speaking, and then put that same finger against his mouth. He left her there, just as another couple walked onto the veranda, giving her a silent warning to remain still and silent.

Maggie remained on the veranda until the other couple, driven back inside by the cold, left. She hadn't realized just how frigid the air was until they were gone; then she began shaking violently, tears streaming down her face.

Chapter 14

Maggie wiped her tears and took a bracing, shaking, breath. She'd been outside perhaps two minutes; the kiss had lasted no more than thirty seconds. Yet she felt completely ravished.

Her lips were slightly swollen, her breasts felt strangely heavy, her entire body almost painfully aroused. Never in her life had she felt this way, out of control, ready to jump out of her skin.

And she had to go back into the ballroom and face Sir William and pretend nothing had happened. She had to sit and eat supper, chat with her neighbors, smile, all the while she would still feel Lord Hollings's hands on her. Would be wishing she was still with him, touching him, tasting him.

Oh, goodness, what was happening to her? She felt as if she were about to come apart, fly into a million pieces and blow away into oblivion.

"There you are. They've just called everyone for dinner. You look flushed, my dear." Sir William seemed genuinely happy to see her, which made her feel even more guilty. She almost wished he suspected something; it would only serve her right.

"I went outside for some fresh air. It's frigid out there. I don't know why, but I never picture London as being as cold as New York. My cheeks are like ice."

He put the back of his hand against her cheek and it took every bit of self-control not to back away. Somehow it seemed duplicitous to allow two men to touch her tenderly in a single evening.

"You are like ice," he said. "Some sherry will warm you up."

Maggie rarely had spirits, but right at that moment, she thought she just might down an entire decanter of sherry.

"Sir William, have you seen my mother? She seems to have disappeared."

"Can't say that I have. She's likely off somewhere playing whist."

"That's what I thought. If you don't mind, I need to go to the water closet."

He nodded. "I'll wait by the entrance of the dining hall."

Maggie wished he would simply go inside and sit at their table, but didn't argue. It really was the proper thing to do, but at the moment she just wanted to get away from him and perhaps from her own guilt.

Maggie emerged from the water closet when she saw Lord Hollings coming quickly toward her. "I've found your mother," he said, and something about the way he said it made her instantly worried. The passionate interlude they'd shared might never have happened the moment he said those words.

He immediately turned down a long hallway and she followed him, her anxiety escalating.

"Is she all right?"

"You could say that," he said, sounding as if he was trying to suppress a laugh. "She's plowed."

Maggie stopped dead. "Do you mean drunk?"

He shrugged his shoulders. "It would appear so."

"But she doesn't drink," Maggie said, bewildered. "Where is she?"

Lord Hollings continued to lead her down the deserted hallway to a closed door. "I couldn't help myself. I wanted to check out their library," he said, opening the door. "And that is where I found her."

"Good Lord," Maggie whispered. Her mother lay slouched in a large chair, her legs splayed as far as her gown would allow, her hair completely askew, her mouth wide open and emitting a noise quite unlike anything Maggie had ever heard. She rushed to her side, and, even though the evidence was staring her in the face, she was still shocked when she smelled the alcohol on her mother's breath.

"She's drunk!" Maggie whispered harshly.

"So it would seem. Now we have to figure out a way of getting her out of here without anyone being the wiser."

Maggie pressed her fingers against her temples. This was all too, too much. "It's impossible."

"Nothing is impossible," Lord Hollings said, going over to the large windows and examining them. "I could carry her through here." He sounded doubtful, for there was at least four feet between the bottom of the window and the floor.

"I've never even seen her take a glass of wine," Maggie said, still in disbelief. No matter how much she wanted to reject the idea that her mother was passed out at her first London ball, she knew she could not. She recalled images of her mother over the past weeks, cheeks flushed, napping in the middle of the day, her strange outbursts, her easy tears. Maggie had attributed all that to the undo stress her mother was under. But apparently that stress had led her mother to the bottle.

"Honestly, I don't know if I can take much more," Maggie said softly.

Edward assumed she was talking about her fiancé's abandonment, and now this. "We'll get her out with none the wiser," he said with false bravado. The truth was, Edward wasn't at all certain he'd be able to sneak an unconscious woman in full ball dress out to their carriage with none being the wiser. "Let me get the carriage round and see if we can discreetly get her out. Then I'll find Amelia and tell her we must go."

"She'll be so disappointed."

"By the look of things with that cowboy, it is probably just as well. I fully expect her to go on bended knee any moment and ask him to marry her."

Maggie giggled, which is exactly what he was aiming for. Edward walked over to her, hating to see her so sad. "Don't worry," he said, kissing her lightly. "Everything will be all right."

She looked at him as if he were delusional, and it was his turn to chuckle.

"I'll meet you back here in ten minutes," he said, taking out his watch. "I'll bring Amelia here. I know she can be trusted to be discreet." Just then Maggie's mother let out a loud snort, shifted a bit, then resumed her snoring. Maggie gave him a sick smile.

He resisted the urge to pull her into his arms; she looked so damned fragile at the moment, so unlike her confident self.

"Lord Hollings," she called after him. "Sir William is waiting for me to join him for dinner. Could you—"

"I'll tell him your mother is not feeling well and we must bring her home immediately."

"Thank you."

The last thing he wanted to do was talk to Sir William, but at that moment he likely would have done anything to ease Maggie's worries. He found Sir William pacing at the entrance to the vast dining hall. Inside, the sound of muffled voices and clinking silverware told him dinner had begun.

"Sir William, I'm afraid Miss Pierce will not be joining you. Her mother has taken ill and must go home. She sends her regrets, of course."

Sir William eyed him almost hostilely. "So you are taking her to home."

"Of course."

"I see no reason why Miss Pierce cannot stay. I'll take her home myself."

"I'm afraid Miss Pierce wants to stay with her mother," Edward said, trying not to lose patience with the man. Of all people, he understood Maggie's charm. He almost felt sorry for the old man, for there was absolutely no way he was going to allow Maggie to marry him. He fully intended to marry her himself.

Sir William clenched his jaw, clearly not happy with the events. "Where is she, then? I'd like to bid her good night."

Edward smiled. "I really couldn't say."

"You what?"

"I have to find my sister, sir. If you'll excuse me."

"What do you mean, you cannot say?"

Edward turned, all pretense of pleasantness wiped from his face. "Good evening, sir," he said in clipped tones, and stalked off to find his sister.

Amelia was sitting next to Carson Kitteridge, laughing, her eyes sparkling, and Edward felt just a twinge of remorse that he would have to drag her away. He'd never seen his sister having so much fun. Whispering in her ear, he relayed what had happened and was gratified when she immediately stood.

"I'm so sorry, Mr. Kitteridge, but my friend's mother has taken ill and I must go."

"I sure would like to call on you," he said, looking from Amelia to Edward.

Edward, knowing when he was defeated, agreed and Amelia rewarded him with a quick hug.

"Good night, Mr. Kitteridge. And thank you for being such a wonderful companion this evening. It really was the most wonderful of nights."

"The pleasure was all mine, Lady Amelia," he said, looking sorrowful.

Brother and sister walked from the dining hall, stopping only to thank Lady Rotherham for a beautiful evening. "I'm sorry you had to leave," he said.

"I am, too. Now, what happened? Is she truly plowed?"

Edward chuckled to hear such slang from his little sister's mouth. "Extremely so. I don't have to tell you that is it extremely important that this go no further than us."

"Of course not," Amelia said, slightly offended.

"I must say I have to credit you for not making a fuss at leaving early."

Amelia smiled. "I'm not happy about it, but Mr. Kitteridge had already promised to call on me. Is he not the most gallant man you've ever met? Did you know he's a Texas Ranger? He's captured criminals, murderers even. He's a true American hero. And imagine, he's coming to call on me!"

"Yes, I'm quite certain the sun dims in his presence."

Amelia batted her brother's arm. "I do believe you are jealous of his wonderfulness."

"Absolutely green."

"How is Miss Pierce? She must be absolutely mortified."

"She is quite upset. And worried we'll not get her mother out before anyone notices."

Amelia was silent for a few moments before stopping her brother. "I caught her drinking," she whispered. "I was looking for Miss Pierce and found her drinking straight from one of the duke's decanters. I think it was brandy," she said, wrinkling her nose. "She didn't see me, and I didn't tell a soul."

"Maggie told me her mother didn't drink."

Amelia grinned. "Oh, *Maggie* told you, did she?"

"Miss Pierce told me."

"I do believe you said 'Maggie.'"

"A slip of the tongue. This is all quite upsetting."

They'd reached the library, so Amelia stopped her teasing. "Oh, goodness," she said when she spotted Mrs. Pierce.

"Amelia, I'm so sorry about this. I know how much you were enjoying the ball."

Amelia waved away her apology. "Don't worry.

He's coming to see me tomorrow," she said, hugging herself happily. "I do believe I'm in love."

Edward looked at his sister in wild disbelief. "You do not love Carson Kitteridge. You are deeply infatuated. You hardly know the man."

Amelia scowled at her brother. "You are such a bore," she said. "Just because you've never been in love—" She stopped abruptly, darting a look to Maggie, and gave him a secret smile, which made Edward want to not so secretly strangle his little sister.

"Let's get this over with. There's a door down the hall. It's only a short walk to where I have the carriage waiting. The only risk is that someone will see us in the hallway, but since everyone is still dining, we have a good chance of that not happening. Now, Maggie, you get on that side of your mother, I'll get on this side." Maggie got into position. "And lift."

As soon as they lifted the prone woman, she began to mumble protests. "What you doing?" she demanded groggily.

"It's time to go home, Mama."

"What? We just got here," she said, trying awkwardly to push Maggie and Edward away.

"My God, her breath could kill a cat," he said.

"Would you *please*."

"Mrs. Pierce, the ball is quite over. We must go to the carriage now."

"But I haven't eaten," she said. Then, "That's all right. I'm not feeling all tha' well, to be honeshed." She let out a loud and rather pungent burp.

"Let's get her outside before she gets ill."

"Oh, no," Maggie said, helping Lord Hollings to half drag her mother out the library and down the hall. Amelia stood as a sentinel to make certain no one saw their escape. When they reached the door, she hurried to open it for them, and it was just a few steps to the carriage.

"Can you make it up, Mrs. Pierce?"

"Of coursh I can, you idiot."

"Mother!"

"I'm not an invalid. Oh, goodness." She threw up then, all over her gown.

After a few body-racking heaves, she seemed to recover enough to be horrified by what had just happened.

"No worries," Edward said cheerfully. "Up you go now, and if you think you're going to be sick again, let us know, right?"

All the way to Hanover Square, her mother continually apologized until Maggie threatened to tie a gag across her mouth unless she stopped. Edward couldn't help himself—he laughed.

"It's not funny," Maggie said sternly, but after a few moments began laughing with him. It was either that, or cry.

After they got her mother safely in bed, Amelia, Maggie, and Edward went to his kitchen to forage for food. They were all famished, having missed the midnight dinner.

"Was Sir William awfully disappointed?" Maggie asked after they were seated around the large wooden table where the staff usually ate. In front of them was heated-up potato soup and cold beef. Nothing had ever tasted better to them.

"He was livid," Edward said blandly.

"Was he really?" Amelia asked.

"I would say he was irritated. I do believe he thought I conspired with Mrs. Pierce so that I would have to drag Miss Pierce away. I do not think he likes the fact that she is staying under my roof."

"It is quite proper," Maggie said, grinning, "especially with my mother's eagle eye watching me every moment."

"He seems to be the jealous sort."

"There's nothing improper about Maggie being here," Amelia said. "I'm here, and her mother's here, so to speak. And it's not as if you have designs on Miss Pierce yourself. No one could be more disinterested. Isn't that right, Edward?"

"That is true," he said, giving Maggie a little wink. She, in turn, gave her head an almost imperceptible shake.

"Actually, Amelia," she said with a wicked gleam, "your brother is madly in love with me. He has been since Newport." She shrugged. "But I'm completely uninterested in him. Poor fellow."

"I am madly in love," he said, and sounded entirely too serious.

"Yes. With his reflection," Amelia said, giggling.

"You have to admit I am a fine specimen."

The two girls were having fits.

"I don't expect my own sister to think so, but don't you, Miss Pierce?"

Maggie could hardly speak. "A fine specimen of what? Male conceit?"

"No. That category belongs to Amelia's cowboy."

Amelia gasped. "He is not conceited."

Maggie and Edward exchanged disbelieving glances.

"Well, perhaps he is a bit. But can you blame him? He's the most beautiful man in the world."

"The entire world?" Maggie asked.

Amelia gave a firm nod. "I do believe I'm going to marry him."

"Over my dead body," Edward said darkly.

"I shall mourn you at your funeral," Amelia quipped.

Maggie stifled a yawn. "As much as I enjoy your bickering, I am going to retire." She carried her dish to the sink.

"I'm following right behind you," Amelia said. "Though I do believe I'm far too excited to fall asleep right away."

The two women headed out the door.

"Miss Pierce. If you have a moment?"

Maggie stopped. She was afraid of what he might say, and even more afraid he wanted to kiss her again. For if he did, she wasn't certain she'd let him pull away, and she was very sure she could not. Nothing could be worse. She didn't know what was happening, why Lord Hollings seemed to suddenly take an interest in her. Was it simply that he didn't like to lose? If he did love her, then why had he left her behind all those months ago? Why hadn't he written? Why hadn't he said a single thing to her to indicate his feelings since she'd arrived in England? She wanted to tell him to let her be, let her go on with her life, to stop making her fall in love all over again. "I really am very tired. Can it wait 'til morning?"

He hesitated, then gave her a small bow. "Of course."

* * *

They stayed in London two more days, just so Amelia got a chance to see the Real Wild West Show, as well as let her spend a bit of time with her cowboy. During that time Maggie had successfully avoided being alone with Lord Hollings, and had seen Sir William only once; he'd come for supper the night after the ball. All conversation had been about Carson Kitteridge and how wonderful, amazing, handsome, intelligent, and charming he was.

Maggie wasn't certain just how old he was, but she was quite sure he wasn't old enough to have ridden with General Custer, who died at Little Big Horn nearly twenty years earlier. The more she learned about him, the more she thought he was a complete and utter fraud, but Amelia would have none of it. Maggie knew enough not to push too hard, for she knew Amelia would simply dig her heels in and become even more infatuated.

The afternoon before they left London to return to Bellewood, Amelia came back from an outing with Mr. Kitteridge with a much-repentant and very sober Harriet in tow, fairly glowing. Spying Maggie reading in the library, she practically floated in on a cloud of pure happiness, gushing about her day. She was filled with amazing stories of "Carson's" exploits. The more she said, the more suspicious Maggie became.

"You do know that General Custer died in 1876. That was nearly twenty years ago. Mr. Kitteridge doesn't strike me as being yet out of his twenties. Just how old is he?"

Amelia looked aghast. "I have no idea. And I can't say it would be at all polite to ask. He's been on his own most of his life, so he might have been quite young."

"Eight, perhaps?" Amelia actually stuck out her

tongue. "Yes, I can see you have a great need for politeness," she said dryly.

"If anyone should be worried about someone's age, Miss Pierce," she said, even though she'd been calling her "Maggie" for weeks, "it is you. Sir William is quite old enough to be your *grand*father."

"I simply want you to be careful," Maggie said. "I know Mr. Kitteridge can be charming, but charming men can lead you straight to a broken heart."

Amelia sighed. "Oh, I know he's full of himself, but I still like him. I think he *knows* that I know he's telling tales. It doesn't make it any less fun to listen to him."

"As long as you don't take all this too seriously. He is leaving in less than a month, you know. And we're returning to Bellewood tomorrow."

Amelia looked forlorn for perhaps a second before smiling again. "He is coming to visit."

"He is?"

"I have to ask the duchess, of course, but I'm sure she'll say yes." Maggie gave her a look that told the younger girl inviting Mr. Kitteridge was perhaps not a good idea. "Don't look at me like that. I didn't make any promises to him."

"Not yet?"

"Oh, Maggie," Amelia gushed suddenly. "I do believe he's going to ask me to marry him."

"No!"

"Yes!" she said, jumping up and down and clapping like a little girl who's just be presented a pony for her birthday. "I hope he does. You should see the way he looks at me." She fanned one hand in front of her face. "It does the most amazing things to me."

"Oh, goodness," Maggie muttered.

Amelia squeezed her arms around herself. "I'm so happy," she gushed.

Maggie gave the younger girl a sick smile. This was far worse than she had imagined. Amelia had only been with the man for two days and already she was getting ready to shop for her trousseau.

"Haven't you ever felt this way? Like you'd just die if you didn't see someone? Just die?" Amelia sobered. "Of course you have. You were engaged. I forgot, Maggie. I'm so sorry."

Maggie held out her hand and Amelia squeezed it. "I do understand," she said. "But I also know that falling in love can be one of the most painful things that can happen to you."

"That's so sad," Amelia said. "I wish you could feel the way I do now. I swear I don't care if I eat or sleep or anything."

Maggie smiled at her, feeling infinitely older even though she was only two years Amelia's senior. It was only a year ago that she'd felt as happy and care-free as Amelia. Since then, she'd lost the love of her life, prostituted herself, been engaged, jilted, and courted by a man she didn't love but planned to marry. She felt ancient and tired.

Amelia flounced from the room, her worries about Maggie's lack of love swept from her mind in an instant. Maggie was suddenly overwhelmed by a deep feeling of homesickness, which was only made worse by the fact that she had no home, no place to turn to, no soft place to lay her head where everything would be better. Amelia's happiness only served to underline how very unhappy she was.

Chapter 15

Dear Papa:

> *Everything is going wonderfully here in England.*
> *Mama and I almost feel guilty having so much fun*
> *when you are in that terrible place. We went to a ball*
> *in London—imagine us at a ball in London. I felt*
> *like a fairy princess! I danced all evening, for my*
> *dance card filled quite quickly. I have a feeling Sir*
> *William is about to make an offer for my hand and I*
> *cannot tell you how thrilled . . ."*

. . . Mother is. Maggie stopped writing, unable to
finish that sentence the way she knew she had to. She
had written her father several times since arriving
in England, letters all filled with happy news of
their grand adventure. Papa had enough to worry
about without wondering whether the family he had
brought to ruin was suffering. Likewise, her father had
written a letter filled only with comments about their
affairs, saying nothing of prison except to say he'd lost

a few pounds because he missed Cook's wonderful apple pies. That single sentence was enough to bring tears to her eyes. They were disillusioning each other; she only hoped her father didn't realize it and believed every word she wrote. She picked up the pen and completed the sentence the way she knew she had to: "I cannot tell you how thrilled I am."

Maggie and her mother had been back at Bellewood from London for three days and she was terribly behind on her correspondence. She never questioned whether or not her brothers and father cared what kind of dress she wore or the little observations she made, she simply wrote them down knowing it was the only way to be close to them. They didn't write nearly as frequently as she did, but it didn't bother her one bit. If she received one letter for every four she wrote, that was perfectly fine by her. Her latest letters were filled with amusing comments about Carson Kitteridge and the Real Wild West Show.

She had begun scribbling about the show to her father when a noise at the door distracted her.

"Oh, I'm sorry, I didn't know you were in here," Lord Hollings said, but Maggie had the distinct feeling he was being disingenuous. They had not been alone since the night of the ball, circling each other like skittish cats. Maggie wasn't sure who was avoiding whom, but the result had been the same.

"It's perfectly all right. I'm writing to my father." She looked around the room, at the carefully stacked piles of books. The duke's library was far more organized than a few weeks ago, but clearly Lord Hollings was not finished yet. "It looks as if you still have quite a bit of work to do. I don't want to disturb you," she said, and began gathering up her things.

"Yes. Of course."

Maggie looked at him a bit curiously, for his tone was curt and his expression stony. "Are you angry about something?"

"Angry? Not at all. I've nothing to be angry about. My life is complete bliss."

Maggie laughed. "Now I know you're angry. Do tell. Is your sister driving you batty about Mr. Kitteridge? Or is it the duke who will not let you escape this lair until your task is done?" She paused thoughtfully. "Or is it me?"

"Why on earth would I be angry with you?"

"Absolutely no reason I can think of," she said, capping her inkwell and placing it carefully in her little writing desk.

He stood in front her, his hands low on his hips, looking for all the world like he wanted to strangle her. "Would you please follow me? I'd like to show you something."

"Oh, dear, did I put a book on the wrong shelf?" she asked in mock concern, following him to the far corner of the library.

When he turned, his expression was almost frightening. "Do I mean nothing to you?"

Maggie felt her body flush. "How do you mean?"

"Do you care for me? At all?"

This was not at all what she had expected from him. "Of course I do. You are a friend. A lively dinner partner. And a very fine dancer." She smiled at him, pretending to not understand him, even as she felt her resolve weakening. If he crooked his finger, she would fall into his arms and never want to leave.

If anything, her words made him even more angry. "In Newport I fell a little bit in love with you. Did you know that?"

It was suddenly extremely difficult to breathe. "How could I? You never gave any indication that I was anything more than a flirtation. And if I recall, you told me specifically that you did not love me."

He closed his eyes briefly and shook his head. And he moved to her, so that her back was against the smooth paneled wall, until she could feel his heat, feel his breath on her forehead. "You torment me."

"I don't mean to," she said quietly.

"You cannot marry Sir William. You cannot."

Something inside Maggie's head began screaming, splitting her in two, so that she could not bear the pain of his words for a moment longer. Yet she still had the strength to ask, "Why?"

"Because I love you. Because you must marry *me*."

"I . . ." *can't. I can't.*

He bent his head and kissed her, possessing her in a way he never had before. He was claiming her, branding her, making her want him in a way she could not have imagined. With his hands on her hips, he drew her against him, against his hard length, all the while kissing her, making her whimper with raw need.

"Touch me," she said. *Make me forget.*

He let out a low moan and moved his hand to her breasts, kneading them gently, finding her erect nipples and teasing them with his thumbs. Even with the material separating his hands from her breasts, the feeling was exquisite. She moved her hips, unknowingly wanton, and he pulled her against his arousal, making her gasp in pleasure. He took her hand and pressed it against his erection, throwing back his head and letting out a soft oath, to God or the devil, Maggie wasn't certain.

"I want to see you," he said, and began unbuttoning her dress, one of the garments she'd bought when she lost her maid. It was easy to put on and just as easy to take off. She watched, mesmerized, as his strong fingers deftly undid the buttons, one by one, exposing her chest to the cool air of the library. She looked to the door realizing that where they stood was quite hidden. Someone could walk into the room and still not see them against the wall, for they were blocked by a stack of crates and she wondered if at that moment she even cared. His knuckles brushed against her skin and she hissed in a breath of pleasure.

"My God, Maggie, you are beautiful." He moved the fabric away, then peeled down her corset so that only the thin cotton of her chemise covered her. Her nipples were pebbled and clearly visible through the material, and he bent and kissed each one before bringing his mouth hungrily against hers. He left a trail of kisses from her mouth to her neck, leaving her weak-kneed and completely aroused. At that moment, she thought of nothing, only felt. When he started to unbutton her chemise she pushed his hands away, and with a smile, undid the buttons herself. That small gesture produced a deep groan of pleasure from him that only heightened her need. He pushed the fabric away from her breasts, staring in almost wonder before bending to kiss them, almost as if he were driven to, almost as if he could not have stopped if he wanted to.

She wanted this, wanted his hand on her breasts, wanted his mouth there. Oh, goodness, there, on her nipple.

"Lord Hollings," she breathed as he brought her nipple into his mouth.

"Edward."

"Edward. Don't stop."

He chuckled, then moved to the other breast, bathing it with his tongue, making her squirm at the sensations he was creating between her legs. She knew what her body wanted, as unbelievable as it seemed. She wanted him inside her. She didn't think she'd ever want that, ever. She moved against him, pushing against his arousal. It felt so wonderful, like nothing she'd ever experienced, and she wanted more.

"I knew you'd be like this," Edward said, kissing her. "I cannot wait to have you. Oh, God, it will be torture." He put his hand against her, at the junction of her legs, feeling her heat, and began slowly lifting up her skirts. "Let me touch you. Just touch you, I swear, I'll go no further. I just . . ." And then she felt his hand between her legs, and heard him let out a sound of pure male pleasure.

"Please, let me," he said, as if she'd stop him now, when she felt as if she were about to die from pleasure. He moved his hand against her, creating such an exquisite feeling, she could only cling to him. She let out a sound, she could not help herself, and he brought his mouth against her, frantic, his breathing as harsh as her own though she knew he could not be feeling the sort of intense pleasure she was. She was unaware of anything except his hand, his mouth, and the building sensation between her legs.

And then her world shattered and she collapsed in a heap of satisfied woman onto the library floor. He dropped down with her, continued to kiss her, even as she turned to a puddle. He kept his hand against her, and she could feel her pulse against his palm. It was a miracle.

"Did I just swear to go no further?" he asked with a small smile.

"You did."

"Damn." He was breathing heavily, his forehead covered with a fine sheen of sweat. He removed his hand from her skirts and pulled her into an embrace that seemed to Maggie to be more of a way to stop caressing her than to hug her. It made her smile. His breathing was still ragged, his arousal still large and hard against her. She sat on the floor, her legs slightly splayed, her skirt hiked up above her knees, her breasts still exposed to the cool air, and she felt absolutely wonderful. Edward knelt beside her, kissing her temple, her cheek.

"I don't want you to see Sir William again," he said, raggedly. "Not even to tell him good-bye. I cannot bear for him to even look at you."

"That's silly," Maggie said, kissing him lightly. She pushed her skirts down, then motioned for him to help her stand. Reality was slowly bringing her to her senses. "You cannot lock me away. And perhaps you noticed, but I didn't say yes to you yet," she said, buttoning her chemise and adjusting her corset.

He pulled back and gave her a fierce look. "You must say yes. I don't think I could bear it if you didn't. The thought of another man making you his wife, of touching you that way, I swear, I could not bear it. The thought of you in someone's bed. Unless you want to be an accomplice to murder," he said, smiling, "you must marry me."

He'd said it half jokingly, but Maggie's blood went cold. She'd forgotten what she was. How could she have forgotten? How? "Surely you are not the jealous type."

He shook his head hopelessly. "I find that I am. I drove myself crazy thinking about that Wright fellow kissing you. He didn't, did he?"

Maggie withdrew slightly. "Not the way you mean."

The relief he felt showed painfully clear. "Thank God. It is beyond bearing that another man touches you the way I have." He must have seen something in her expression, for he added quickly, "I know, I know. I'm not the sort of man to put stock in such things. But with you, it's different," he said fiercely, putting his hands on her shoulders and giving her a gentle shake. "To know you are mine alone, that you'll always be mine, that no one else has touched you or ever will, you cannot understand what that means to me. It is everything. You are everything. You are pure and good and I don't deserve you, but I know we'll be happy together. I just pray I make it to our wedding day. Please say you'll marry me."

You are pure and good. To know you are mine alone . . . In that moment, the strangest thing happened. Maggie's entire body, beginning with her heart, turned completely numb. She pressed her thumbnail into her wrist just to see if she could feel pain, and strangely, she could not.

"Maggie?"

She was staring blindly over his shoulder and she

slowly brought her tortured gaze to his. "I'm sorry. I cannot."

"Bend over, my dear, and grab the desk."

She saw the blood drain from his face, watched with her own eyes as his heart shattered, and felt nothing but blessed numbness.

"You cannot mean that," he said, stricken, his eyes filled with anguish. "I don't understand you. Make me understand."

"I'm sorry. It's impossible."

And then she watched as he got angry, and that felt better, so she smiled. Odd, that. "I have to go now," she said, and began walking away, buttoning her dress as she walked, her eyes blurring with unshed tears. Well, there, it looked as though she could still feel pain, after all.

"I'm not a virgin."

Maggie nearly laughed at the expression on Sir William's face. He'd just proposed and certainly that was not the response he was looking for.

"I beg pardon?"

"I'm not a virgin. So if that is important to you, perhaps you should withdraw your proposal." Maggie felt quite undone, like a fragile bit of glass knocking against a brick wall. Eventually, it would break, it was only a matter of time.

Sir William was clearly not pleased, but he was also thoughtful, his brow furrowed as he examined his feelings about the matter. He shifted uncomfortably in his chair, then looked up and smiled. "Honestly, my dear, I find it doesn't matter. I'm actually relieved.

Taking one's virginity is not particularly pleasant. For anyone."

Maggie smiled. "I was worried about it, you see." Even as she said the words, she realized she had not been worried at all, that she hadn't really cared one way or the other about his reaction to her news.

"No need, no need," he said, patting her hand. "But . . ."

"But?"

"Well, I can't help but wonder who," he said, and his tone became a bit flinty.

"It was someone in New York."

"Ah. The fiancé." He looked inordinately relieved and Maggie suspected he thought the deed had been done by Lord Hollings. How she wished that were so.

Maggie smiled, letting him believe what he would. This was good. Her mother would be so happy to find that all their financial worries were about to be resolved.

"You haven't given me an answer yet, my dear," he said with a small smile.

"Oh, I . . ." It felt as if suddenly something lodged in her throat, making it impossible to utter a sound. She couldn't do it. She couldn't tell him yes, not right now, not when just a day before she'd been making love to another man. "Can I think about it?" She hated to see the disappointment in his eyes, but she saw none of the anguish she'd seen in Edward's eyes. "It is only that I need to be certain. My home is in New York and marrying you would mean I would rarely see my family."

He looked slightly surprised by her response. "But I thought that is why you came to England, to secure a husband."

"Not entirely. Goodness, you must think me quite the opportunist. No, we of course hoped that I would meet someone, but I truly just wanted to escape New York. It had become quite intolerable, what with my father imprisoned. We became quite a tragic pair. But if you enjoy taking on the role of knight in shining armor, you may. I would never wish to take that from you."

He smiled at her. "You are quite the most charming woman I've met in years," he said. "I will be heartbroken if you reject me. I do love you, you know."

"I know."

He let out a sigh. "I'll give you two days to think it over?"

"That sounds fair." They were sitting together on a large couch in the one of the mansion's many sitting rooms. When he stood, she rose also, then embraced him warmly. "I'm sorry I couldn't give you an answer today. Are you very angry?"

He kissed her forehead. "I cannot be angry with you, my dear."

"That is a very nice thing to know," she said, smiling up at him. As soon as she saw a flare of lust in his eyes, she backed away and began chattering about Amelia and Mr. Kitteridge as she led him toward the door. She was looking at him, making certain she was entertaining him, when he paused.

"Good morning, Lord Hollings."

"Sir William."

He nodded toward Maggie without looking directly at her and continued down the long hallway in the opposite direction.

Just then, the fragile glass shattered into tiny little pieces.

Chapter 16

Maggie did not know where she found the strength to smile and hold out her hand to Sir William as he departed with a small kiss to her cheek. She turned and saw several servants going about their business; her mother was in their shared parlor. There was nowhere she could go to be alone, even in a house this large, and she so desperately wanted to be alone to cry and cry until she was completely drained. Two days of crying ought to be enough. She squeezed her eyes shut and briefly pressed her hands against her temples. She had a terrible headache and her stomach felt decidedly queasy.

"Miss Pierce, are you quite all right?"

Maggie looked to see the duke studying her with concern. "Oh, fine. Just a small headache," she said, embarrassed to be found so vulnerable.

"I've just been to see Elizabeth and she is going mad with boredom and complaining quite loudly that she hasn't seen you in a full day. If you are up to it, would you mind . . ."

"Of course, Your Grace. I'm certain Elizabeth's

grumbling will be wonderful for my aching head," she said, laughing. He smiled and Maggie silently congratulated herself for not dissolving into tears in front of the duke.

Maggie let out a sigh and forced herself to climb the stairs to the duke and duchess's private quarters, praying she met no one, particularly Lord Hollings, on the way.

Elizabeth *was* going insane with boredom. There were only so many booties and hats a person could crochet. She had a small chest filled with the things already. Now she was embroidering a duckling on a little white nightgown, holding the material to the light so that she could review her progress. The worst was she simply could not get comfortable, and turning this way and that to find comfort was nearly impossible. She'd had painful gas all morning and was finding it extremely difficult to expel it to get relief.

"I think it is time for you to come out," she said crossly to her baby, who at that moment gave her a nice kick.

"You still have two more weeks to go," Maggie said.

"Oh, thank God you're here. Talk to me. Tell me what's been happening. Rand can tell me nothing, for all he does is work and visit with me. Is Amelia still in love?" Elizabeth stopped her chatter abruptly, for never had she seen her friend so pale and forlorn. "Maggie, what is wrong?"

Tears instantly filled her eyes and Elizabeth held out her hand for Maggie to take. "What has happened?"

"Sir William asked me to marry him," she said, laughing and crying at the same time.

"So you are happy?" Elizabeth asked skeptically.

Maggie shook her head, her curls whipping around her.

"You are sad."

Maggie nodded, her face crumpling and fresh tears streamed down her face.

"Tell me," she said, wincing a bit as a particularly wretched bit of gas attacked her bowels. She patted her hand on the bed and Maggie sat facing her, her hands twisting the material of her skirt.

"Lord Hollings asked me to marry him, too."

"Goodness. You have been busy." Elizabeth searched her friend's face for a smile, but saw nothing but misery. She'd never before seen a girl so unhappy at receiving not one but two proposals. "I take it you don't want to marry either one?"

"Oh, Elizabeth," Maggie wailed, throwing herself onto her shoulder and sobbing uncontrollably. For several long minutes, all Elizabeth could do was hold her friend and murmur comforting words. Finally, Maggie pulled away, her face ravaged with tears and grief.

"I love him so much."

"Who?" Elizabeth asked cautiously.

"Lord Hollings," she said, as if Elizabeth had gone quite daft. "I've loved him since Newport. And he loves me."

"Why, that's wonderful. Is it not?"

Maggie shook her head, unable to speak as fresh tears rolled down her cheeks. She swallowed audibly. "I have to tell you something. I have to tell someone or else I will go mad. I feel as though I'm falling apart, Elizabeth. I cannot take any more. I cannot."

"Tell me," Elizabeth said, her concern increasing tenfold.

"It all started with my father's arrest, you see. It all started there." Maggie's eyes were glazed, as if she were no longer a part of herself, and Elizabeth grabbed her hand to bring her back. Her friend looked at her and Elizabeth had never in her life seen such abject despair. "We were told my father would likely be sentenced to five years. It was to be a lesson, you see, a way to point out the evils of greed. One of the men testifying against my father was an old friend, Charles Barnes."

Elizabeth wrinkled her nose. "I know him."

"I went to him and asked if there was anything that could be done to save my father, to reduce his sentence. And he told me he could help. He promised."

"I don't understand."

"I told him I would do anything. I knew what I was saying, I'm not that naive, but I was so desperate to help Papa. I thought it was such a small sacrifice to make for him."

It slowly dawned on Elizabeth what her friend was telling her. "Oh, Lord, Maggie. *Charles Barnes?*" Barnes was an odious man, completely unappealing. He'd always made Elizabeth exceedingly uncomfortable at their meetings. He had a way about him that made one's skin crawl.

Maggie covered her face with her hands and shuddered. "He promised me Papa would get just one year. If I let him . . ." She stopped and swallowed, and Elizabeth's horror grew. ". . . have me. And so I did," she finished, sounding almost calm but for the smallest trembling in her voice. "It was quite unpleasant."

"So now you think you are unworthy," Elizabeth said, guessing at what had made her friend so upset about the two proposals. "I should like to kill Charles Barnes. I should think you would want to as well."

Maggie lifted her head in surprise.

"Aren't you angry, Maggie?"

"With *him*?" It seemed as if she hadn't even considered the idea, which shocked Elizabeth. "I suppose I've been so ashamed and angry at myself, I didn't think to get angry with him."

"What he did is beyond despicable. He used you for his own sordid pleasure. He's the one who deserves to be in prison. I never did like the man and now I know why. He's the slimiest, dirtiest, most horrid man to walk the earth. He ought to be strung up in front of the entire New York Four Hundred and made to confess his sins."

Throughout Elizabeth's tirade, Maggie could only stare. She'd never considered how disgusting what Barnes had done was, only how disgusting what she had done was.

"He took advantage of a poor girl who wanted nothing more than to save her father. I cannot think of a more horrible crime than to do that. I think you should go to New York to kill him. I will gladly supply the gun."

Maggie burst out laughing. "No wonder I love you," she said, hugging Elizabeth fiercely. "I was so ashamed, so embarrassed. I still am. But I do believe I'm a bit angry, too."

"You should be angry. You should be murderously angry. How dare he do what he did! And not only that, he took you and didn't make good on his word."

Maggie looked down at her lap. "I was a bit angry about that part."

"The entire thing is unconscionable." Elizabeth winced. "I think I have to use the toilet," she said. "But first you have to promise to not let what that horrible Barnes did to you stop you from marrying the man you love."

"I can't do that. He could never get over it. I know it. He thinks I'm good and pure and a virgin. He wants to be the first, Elizabeth. He told me so. He would never look at me the same, it would always be there between us. I couldn't bear it if he looked at me in a different way." She twisted her hands painfully. "The truth is, I feel . . ." She took a long shaking breath. "Dirty. Unworthy of him."

"No!" Elizabeth said, grabbing her hands and squeezing gently. "You did nothing wrong. Well, practically nothing."

Maggie let out a watery laugh. "It was wrong. Very wrong. I still cannot believe I allowed that man to touch me. But I could only think that as horrible as it was, if it meant my father could go free after a year, it would be worth it."

"I don't understand why it would be fine to marry Sir William and not Lord Hollings. It doesn't make sense to me."

"I *love* Lord Hollings. And that makes all the difference, at least in my heart."

"I see," Elizabeth said slowly, and Maggie suspected she didn't understand at all. She hadn't heard what Edward had said, the joy in his voice. Better to hurt him once now than to have him pretend it didn't matter, to hurt over and over.

"And Sir William?"

"I told him only that I'm not a virgin. He doesn't seem to care, though he doesn't know the details. I could never tell him that."

Elizabeth made Maggie look at her. "I think if Lord Hollings truly loves you, it wouldn't matter."

Maggie shook her head.

"You should tell him what you told me."

"He would go to New York to kill him."

"Because he deserves it. Now, could you please help me to the toilet?" Elizabeth asked, wincing. She heaved her legs to the side of the bed and then with Maggie's help, stood up. And looked down, at the growing puddle at her feet.

"Where the hell do you think you're going?"

Edward watched as the maid closed the last of his trunks, then hurried out of the room as if her dress were on fire. "Home."

"To hell you are. Elizabeth's just gone into labor and I need you here."

Edward stared at his friend in disbelief. "I don't give a bloody damn if *you* are going into labor. I'm going home. I'm needed there. I need to leave." He grabbed a flask and took a long draught, grimacing as the heat of the alcohol seared its way down to his stomach. He wasn't drunk yet, but he sure as hell was on his way. He wanted to hit something, and right now his friend was standing in the way, blocking his escape, and he was damned convenient, so he took a swing.

Rand was almost shocked enough to let the blow hit its mark, but at the last moment he shied away, escaping the brunt of it. "What the bloody hell is wrong with you?" he asked, immediately taking a boxer's stance.

"Get out of my way," Edward said, his fists still clenched by his side.

Rand straightened, staring at his friend. "Edward?"

Rand was looking at him in disbelief, and Edward let out the most foul curse he knew as he realized why his friend was looking at him that way. He hadn't cried since his parents had died all those years ago, but damned if it didn't feel like he had tears in his eyes. He turned away from his friend, and with all his might, punched the wall. Then cursed again because it hurt like all hell.

"Who is she?"

Another curse as he looked at his bloodied knuckles.

"Edward, I've only hit a wall once and it was over a woman. Now, who is she?"

"Maggie." God, just saying her name hurt. "Miss Pierce."

"Ah."

Edward looked fiercely at his friend. "What does that mean?"

"Only that I suspected something between you two, but when Sir William came around I assumed nothing came of it. What happened?"

Edward walked to his window and stared stonily out, clenching his jaw painfully. "I offered for her and she rejected me." He shrugged, then turned to Rand. "The thing is, I love her so goddamn much." He shook his head angrily as he felt the sting of threatened tears. "I can't stay here and watch her with him. I can't."

"What is it about these American women who

drive us so insane?" Rand asked. He let out a long breath. "I understand you need to leave, but please stay until the baby is born. If something happens . . ." Rand, apparently, could not finish the thought, and so picked up Edward's flask and took a drink. "I need you here."

"Nothing's going to happen, Rand."

"Women die in childbirth all the time. Babies, too."

Edward felt his resolve to leave waning. He'd always come to Rand's rescue, always. And he wasn't going to stop now.

"I'll stay, but only until I know everything's all right. And then I'm gone. I'll finish the library later." *When Maggie has gone.*

"Thank you," Rand said, throwing his arm around his friend. "I owe you one."

"You owe me far more than one," Edward grumbled. "How is Elizabeth?"

Rand looked momentarily stunned, as if he'd forgotten why it was so important for Edward to stay. "Elizabeth. I told her I'd be right back." He ran through the door. "Go to the library, I'll be down presently after I make certain she's all right. And bring that flask."

Edward watched his friend disappear with a small smile. He tried to ignore the ache in his chest, but he sat down heavily on his bed and let the pain wash over him. It hurt so damn much. He picked up the flask, giving it a little shake to determine how much brandy was left, then took another sip. He'd stay drunk for a week, he thought idly. Maybe two. Once he was home and taking care of his estates, he'd be fine. He'd get over her. He just prayed she didn't marry Sir William, because no doubt in the years to come, they would see each other. She was the duchess's best friend, after all. He'd see her, see her children, watch her grow older with another man. Ah, God, he didn't know if he could endure it.

Chapter 17

Maggie stood at the entrance to Sir William's lovely country home feeling a bit of real regret. She loved his home, its warmth, the safety it represented. She could live out her days here content, mistress of her own home, perhaps the mother of a child or two. It would be so easy to marry him, to pretend everything was well in the world. She'd done that for so long, it was very tempting to do it again.

But not this time.

This time she was going to face her demons. She was going to New York to confront Charles Barnes. Perhaps she wouldn't kill him, though the dark part of her heart wanted to. The shame had been pushed aside and replaced by pure rage. Elizabeth was right. What Barnes had done was unconscionable and he should be made to pay. The only way to do that was to kill him. Or shoot his cock off. Maggie smiled at the thought, feeling strangely giddy at the thought of him writhing in pain. *Oh, goodness, I do believe I belong in Bedlam,* she thought happily. Maggie didn't understand where this rage she felt came from and could only conclude it had been there all the time, lurking inside her soul waiting for it to be sprung free.

The need to see Barnes, to tell him she wasn't destroyed, that she thought he was the most loathsome creature on earth for what he'd done, to make him beg for mercy right before she pulled the trigger, it was nearly overwhelming.

Then . . . Well, then she wasn't sure what she would do. Return to England, perhaps, escape before anyone knew what she'd done. No one would imagine she could be the culprit; no one knew what had happened. She would shoot him and drop the gun into the East River and hop on the first ship back to England. She wished she could be so callous. Perhaps by the time she arrived in New York that rage she felt would have festered long enough to turn her into a woman who could, indeed, commit murder. She hoped so.

In the most secret place in her heart, she imagined that when she returned, Edward would be waiting for her, that he'd forgive her everything. That he would hold her in his arms and tell her all was well and all the ugliness would simply disappear.

For now, she had to break the news to Sir William that she was leaving for New York and might not be coming back. With new resolve, Maggie turned the bell and waited, and was surprised when Sir William himself answered the door.

"I saw you walking up," he said rather sheepishly. "Please come in."

Maggie hesitated only a moment before crossing the threshold and following Sir William to a small sitting room. It was a lovely room, full of sunlight and potted plants, completely unexpected in a bachelor's home, and she felt another small twinge of regret.

"You've decided," he said, motioning for her sit across from him.

For a moment she thought he somehow knew of her murderous plan, before quickly realizing he was talking about his proposal. Her nerves were far more frayed than she realized, it seemed. "I have." She shook her head. "I am afraid I cannot marry you, Sir William."

Sir William nodded sadly, almost as if he expected this to be her answer. "May I inquire as to why?"

"I do like you. I think you are a wonderful, kind, good man. But I don't love you."

"I knew you did not," he said softly. "But I suppose I hoped you were desperate enough to accept my offer anyway."

Maggie looked at him fondly. "I don't believe I could marry anyone at the moment. I have some unresolved business back home and I must take care of that. And I . . ." She wasn't certain if she should be completely honest with him, for she didn't want to hurt him more. But he finished her sentence for her.

"You love him, don't you?"

They both knew he was referring to Lord Hollings, and she looked down at her hands. "I do. That's why I have to go to New York. I'd not make anyone a good wife now."

"What was this all about, then? A way to make him jealous?" His voice was tinged with anger and hurt.

"No. Never." She shook her head miserably. "I did love him, but I didn't think he cared at all. And then you came along and seemed so . . . safe."

"Safe." He all but snorted.

"I wanted to be safe. I haven't felt that way in a long time. Please don't be angry with me. I never intended anyone to get hurt."

"So you are marrying Lord Hollings. I suppose an earl is a better catch than a mere baronet."

Maggie bristled and stood. "I realize you are hurt, but you have no call to think such a thing of me. Titles have never mattered to me. Not one whit. Not that it is any of your concern, but Lord Hollings asked me to marry him and I told him no." Her eyes glittered with unshed angry tears.

Sir William's anger seemed to deflate before her eyes. "You told him no? Why?"

Her tears spilled over. "He thinks I am someone I am not. I cannot lie to him anymore. I am sick to death of lying." Maggie swallowed. "I have to go."

Sir William stopped her with a gentle hand. "My dear, whatever it is that is troubling you, please know that if you need help, I am here."

Maggie gave him a tremulous smile. "Thank you."

She walked out of the house and down the pretty lane that led to his property, tears streaming down her face. "I need something good to happen," she whispered. "I need something good."

Then she shook her head, and dashed away her tears fiercely. No one could save her, not Lord Hollings and not Sir William. She had to save herself. With renewed resolved she marched back to Bellewood, determination in every step, her anger growing. This time, though, it was not anger against herself, but at Charles Barnes.

He would pay for what he'd done if it was the last thing on earth she did.

* * *

The next Duke of Bellingham, Henry Randall Blackmore, was born twelve agonizing hours after the duchess's water broke, a lusty big baby who cried angrily to be pushed from his warm, watery world. As soon as Rand heard that cry, he was out of the library and up the stairs, taking two at a time.

Thank God, Edward thought. He didn't know if he could have taken another minute of his friend's stark fear that something would happen to his beloved wife. Edward had to give him some credit; he'd only banged on the birthing door half a dozen times before Dr. Walton threatened to tie him to a chair. Edward knew what he was going through, for there is nothing more agonizing than having someone you love in pain and being able to do nothing to help. If it had been him, he would have gone mad hearing his wife's screams.

By the sounds of it, the baby at least was healthy. He had only to wait for the news that the duchess came through the birth before he could leave. He settled down on a chair and halfheartedly grabbed up a book to catalog it for the duke's library.

"Lord Hollings."

He stilled for a moment at the sound of her voice, then continued writing as if he weren't being torn apart by her mere presence in the same room.

"I've come to say good-bye."

He looked up then, he couldn't help himself. She looked so damned sad he had to stop himself from going to her. What kind of fool was he?

"All right, then," he said, his eyes drifting back to

his work. If he ignored her, perhaps she'd go away. But she walked toward him instead.

"I'm going back to America."

"I can't see how that concerns me," he said, staring blindly at the book's binding.

She knelt beside him, placing her hands on his knee, and he turned his head away, unable to bear the pain of her touch. "Please look at me," she said softly. "Please."

Against his better judgment, he did look and wished he hadn't. She looked pale and as tormented as he felt, which made no sense. She'd broken his heart, not the other way around.

"I'm looking at you," he said coldly. "What do you want?"

"I'm going home, but I'm almost certainly coming back. I have to do something. And when I return . . ." Her throat closed as if she were fighting tears. He didn't care. He did *not* care. She took a deep and shaking breath. "I don't want you to hate me. Please don't hate me."

He tried to remain cool, but failed, and so he had to look away so she wouldn't see what was in his heart. She didn't deserve his love. "I don't hate you," he said, though his heart screamed for him to drag her into his arms, to beg her to love him. Ah, God, why couldn't she love him just a little?

"I've brought you something." She tried a smile, but failed miserably. "Here."

He couldn't bring himself to take whatever it was, so she simply put it on the table next to him.

"It's an early Christmas present."

He could feel her standing next to him silently, staring at him, but he didn't move to take the gift, he didn't look at her again. And when she bent and pressed a kiss to his cheek, he thought he might die from the anguish of it.

She straightened. "Well. Good-bye."

He could only nod, for he knew his throat was too tight to utter a word. It was only after he was certain she was gone that he buried his face in his hands and squeezed and squeezed, willing himself to forget her. After a long time, he looked over at the table and saw immediately that she had left him a book, tied in a bright red ribbon.

It was a copy of *All But Lost* by G. A. Henty, the first book his father had ever given to him. He picked it up, moving his index finger along the book's spine, wondering where she'd found such a fine copy. He smiled sadly down at it and held on to it, almost as a child holds on to a favorite toy. Suddenly he felt so damned tired. He meant only to rest his eyes, but he fell asleep, the book on his chest, giving him strange comfort.

Chapter 18

"You have to go find her," Elizabeth said frantically. "You have to stop her. Oh, my God, what have I done?"

"What the devil are you talking about?" Rand demanded.

"Maggie. Maggie's gone."

Rand's color slowly returned to his face as he realized Elizabeth was simply upset about Miss Pierce's departure. She had left before dawn. He'd chanced upon her as he was crossing from the kitchen to go back up and be with his wife. "Yes, I know. I saw her this morning. She said something about returning in a month's time and asked if I wouldn't mind having her mother as a guest in the meantime."

"And you let her go?" Elizabeth asked, clearly distraught.

"Elizabeth. What is going on?"

"She came in last night, to see the baby, to see me. And she was so calm. Far more calm than she's been. She told me she was going home, home to take care of . . ." She darted a look around the room. ". . . something important and I fear she's going to get into terrible trouble. It has to do with her father. I believe, oh, God, that she might do someone harm."

"What are you talking about?"

"You know Maggie's father is in prison for embezzlement. I believe she blames someone for her father's stiff sentence." She couldn't say more without completely breaking her friend's trust.

Rand furrowed his brow. "I can understand her being upset, but why return now? After all this time, why would she?" Rand asked calmly.

"Because I told her to," Elizabeth wailed. "I was trying to make her feel better and told her a certain someone should be murdered. I even told her I would supply the gun. I never believed she would take me seriously, but she came in last night. I was so tired, I didn't truly take in what she was saying until this morning when I realized she was gone. You have to stop her."

"Miss Pierce seemed very calm to me. I cannot imagine her harming anyone."

"She's under a lot of strain," Elizabeth said. "Oh, Rand, that poor girl has endured so much. I fear she might snap. I fear that I am the catalyst."

"If it will make you feel better, I'll send one of the footmen to search for her. She can't have gone far. And at this time of year it will be near impossible to find a ship. But I can hardly force her to return if she doesn't want to."

Elizabeth worried the sheets. She was still so exhausted from her ordeal. "Send Lord Hollings. He'll make her come back."

"I hardly think Edward would so much as blink to help her. He's rather devastated, you know."

"Not as devastated as Maggie."

Rand bristled. "I'd hardly say that rejecting a man's proposal is acting devastated."

"Oh, Rand, Maggie loves Edward. With all her heart. That's why she couldn't marry him. It's very complicated."

"She has a rather interesting way of showing her devotion," he said dryly.

"You don't know what she's gone through."

"Then, please, enlighten me."

Elizabeth swallowed miserably and shook her head. "If anything should happen to her I will always blame myself."

"You'll do nothing of the sort," Rand said, sounding very imperious.

Elizabeth laughed and held out her hand. "I do believe you think you could stop me. I love you, even when you are acting like a duke."

"That's good to know. I'll go tell a footman to try to find Miss Pierce and then I'm going to get my son and bring him to you."

"That would be very nice," she said, suddenly completely exhausted. "Very nice, indeed."

He bent and kissed her forehead. "The only thing I want you to worry about is your son. We'll find Miss Pierce and if we don't, she'll be fine. She seems to be a very levelheaded young woman."

"I'm sure you're right," Elizabeth said, slightly appeased. Most likely Maggie would be back by nightfall, feeling a bit guilty to have worried everyone.

Amelia had pouted for perhaps twenty seconds when her brother told her he was going home and she was going with him. She wanted to spend more time gazing at the baby, imagining what it would be like to have her own baby. With Carson, of course.

Now that she was nearly home and close to the general chaos of her nieces and nephews, she had to admit that coming back to Meremont was a good idea. She didn't realize how much she missed the smell of the sea until their carriage crested the hill overlooking the estate and the Irish Sea. She'd opened her window to let the cold blast of sea air buffet her face and breathed in deeply.

"You'll catch cold," her brother muttered darkly. It seemed lately he muttered everything darkly and she wondered if he'd gotten into some sort of disagreement with the duke. That would explain their abrupt departure. Amelia had asked if anything was wrong and got a grunt for an answer.

"Fresh air is good," she said, making a great show of breathing in deeply. "It cleanses the lungs and brightens the skin. You could use more of it, Edward. You look like death."

As usual, at least as of lately, he ignored her. But Amelia was truly worried about him. It seemed that for a time at Bellingham he seemed more like himself. She'd actually sneezed in front of him and he didn't lock her in her room. He'd done that more than once, fearing she was coming down with a sickness. Their poor doctor had been to their house numerous times when she was younger only to listen to Edward rail on and on that clearly his little sister was ill, for she had sneezed. Amelia gave him a bit of latitude, given what had happened to her parents and the fact that she'd been so very ill, but she was practically a grown woman now. A woman who would be setting up her own house, having her own children.

And they'd be tall and robust and have wavy hair just like their father.

Carson hadn't asked her to marry him yet, but she knew he would. They'd been sneaking kisses for days now, and the last time she'd let him touch her in what could only be described as carnal places. Just the thought of his hands on her breasts made her feel wonderfully alive. She never would have allowed such liberties if she didn't think a proposal was forthcoming.

Carson was such a physical man. She shivered deliciously just thinking about the way they'd been sedately walking down a hall together and he'd dragged her into an alcove and kissed her silly until a maid walked by. He'd pressed his large body against her, letting her feel all of him, even that strangely foreign hard male part of him that she was just dying to see.

All in good time. Carson just had to propose soon, he just had to. The company was leaving in January and he said he had to be back at the ranch to help his brother. Apparently his older brother was a bit of a simpleton and he didn't like to be away from him for too long. Poor man couldn't handle the large responsibility of running a ranch without help. She'd go with him to Texas, which seemed about as far away as could be. Imagine, America and being surrounded by cowboys and maybe even seeing an Indian. Texas was such a huge place. She hoped he lived near the sea, for she would miss the salty air.

"When you were in America, did you see Texas?" Amelia asked her brother.

"No."

"Because I might be going there soon, you know."

Edward just looked at her as if she were a child gushing about Santa Claus. He was clearly humoring her.

"I think Carson is going to ask me to marry him."

"It's Carson now. Not Mr. Kitteridge? Don't you think that's a bit informal?"

Amelia crossed her arms and stared out the window, letting the cold air cool her anger. "Not at all, given that we are in love."

Edward made absolutely no attempt to stop from laughing. "Is that what he told you?"

"Not in so many words," she admitted, and watched amazed as Edward straightened in his seat as if stuck by a needle.

"You are not to let him kiss you."

She blushed and hoped Edward would think her red cheeks were caused by the cold air. "Of course not," she said, acting affronted and feeling guilty.

"He's not a gentleman, Amelia." She began to protest and he stopped her. "He's not had the benefit of a gentleman's upbringing. I do not approve his courting you and certainly would not allow him to marry you."

"You are such a horrid man," Amelia said, feeling her entire body heat with anger. "He is the first man I care about. How could you say such a thing about him? He's far more the gentleman than you are, if you ask me."

"I did not."

"If he asks me to marry him, I am going to accept," she said, glaring at her hateful big brother.

"You will do nothing of the sort."

"We love each other," she shouted, feeling angry tears in her eyes.

"Love," Edward spat.

"Yes, love. You know, Edward, I feel sorry for you. You cannot imagine loving anyone enough to marry them, but I must tell you it can happen. Or perhaps you cannot find anyone who loves you enough. Now, *that* I can imagine. Who would want to marry such a domineering, controlling, hateful man as you?" She began sobbing in earnest now and slammed the window shut so no one outside their carriage could hear her.

It was silent in the carriage for a long time before her brother let out a heavy sigh. "You cannot help who you fall in love with," he said softly. "I know that. I simply want you to be careful. I don't want you hurt and I don't want you abandoned and carrying his child."

"I know. I'm sorry I said those awful things. You made me so angry."

"Yes. I know," he said with amusement, handing a handkerchief over to her. "I had no idea you could be so venomous."

Amelia giggled. "I know you think I'm naive, Edward. But I would never let Carson do anything that needs a wedding to do. Never." She blushed to be talking about such a thing with her brother. "If Carson does ask for my hand, what will you say?"

Edward shook his head. "I don't know. I'll have to speak with him, of course, and then think about it. You are an earl's sister, Amelia. We really know nothing about Mr. Kitteridge except what is in the newspapers."

"I know him," Amelia said feelingly. "He's coming to Meremont soon. I thought we could let him stay for Christmas."

"Doesn't he have shows to do?"

"They've had to reduce the number of shows," she admitted. The Real Wild West Show was not drawing the crowds it had, and with the colder weather, few people were willing to huddle in a drafty tent. "In fact, today is the last show. They'll be staying here for Christmas, then leaving after New Year's Day. Would it be all right if he were a guest until then?"

Edward gave his little sister a look of disbelief. "You've already invited him, haven't you?"

Amelia pulled in her lips and looked very much like a guilty child. "Perhaps."

"Or do you mean, 'yes, I invited him.'"

"I didn't think it would be a problem. And we have so much room at Meremont. And Lady Matilda could act as chaperone. And he's leaving in only two weeks. Edward, please." She thought she'd die if her brother didn't say yes. She hadn't seen Carson for two days and it was purely awful. Imagine if she never saw him again? It was unthinkable.

When Edward let out a heavy sigh, she knew she'd won and squealed with happiness. "Thank you, thank you, thank you," she said, launching herself at her brother and kissing his cheek.

"All right, all right," Edward said, much like a man who is pushing away an excited puppy. "But I'm not happy about it."

Amelia beamed at her brother, thinking he was the most wonderful man in the world.

Other than Carson, of course.

Chapter 19

Five days into her journey home, Maggie knew that she was going to die. She felt rather foolish to have thought that anything that had happened to her was important now that she stared death in its face.

She'd always loved the sea, the few times she'd been on it, and had a stomach of iron, unlike Elizabeth. She loved the salty spray, the frigid air, even the movement of the ship. Captain Sullivan had been duly impressed and joked at dinner one night that if she'd been a man he would have made her his first mate, for the other four brave passengers who had dared a December crossing rarely made it from their bunks. In fact, the only way Maggie knew there were others on board was the sound of retching coming from the cabin next to hers. Maggie felt at the time she'd booked passage it had been divine intervention that got her on a ship in December. The *White Star* was a passenger ship that was refitted each winter to handle cargo, so it was comfortable and fast—and because it was December, fares were low. It would take just seven days or perhaps even fewer to reach New York.

The first four days had been crystal blue with choppy seas and a brisk breeze. She was so glad to be heading home, still determined to murder—or at least hurt very badly—the man she blamed for all her troubles. But it was difficult to dwell on that when the sun beat down on your upturned face, when puffy white cotton clouds filled the horizon, when the heaving sea was so blue it was almost hard to imagine a sight more beautiful.

Then those puffy white clouds seemed to build and build, as if God were piling them up to a monstrous size. They became a frightening, roiling mass that seemed about to swallow up the ship as it trudged through waves that became higher by the hour. Maggie wasn't overly concerned, for no one else seemed to be worried about the weather they were clearly heading into. The crew, perhaps, moved a bit more quickly, seemed a tad more diligent about making certain everything was secure. At lunch on the fifth day, Captain Sullivan ate a hearty meal and joked about the other poor passengers, who were driven below sick with the increased waves. For the first time, Maggie's stomach felt a bit queasy, but she managed to eat a good meal. By two o'clock, Maggie was beginning to feel more than a niggling of fear as she clung to the railing, sea spray wetting her hair and stinging her cheeks. The sky had become menacingly dark, the waves shaved off by a fierce wind that sent a salty spray over the ship.

"I think you ought to ride this 'un out belowdecks, Miss Pierce," Captain Sullivan said, coming up beside her. He was smiling, but Maggie saw something in his eyes that frightened her more than those dark clouds—she saw fear.

"Is it a bad storm, Captain?"

"A fair-sized nor'easter churning up ahead. Now, you go below and don't come up until Donovan comes to get you. All right, miss?"

"Of course." That's when she looked about the deck and saw the crew members scrambling about the ship doing last-minute checks and reinforcing what they'd already done. *It'll be all right. It has to be.*

Two hours later, Maggie, black and blue from being tossed about her small cabin, sat up in her bunk, knocking her head hard against the railing. Bringing her hand up, she felt blood from a small gash. It was the noise that was perhaps the most frightening, even more than the feel of the ship being slammed again and again by what must be monster waves. The relentless, shocking bangs against the hull, the shrill scream of the wind, and the shouts of the other passengers who could barely be heard above the cacophony of the storm sent shards of icy fear down her spine. *I should go to the other passengers,* she thought, hearing a woman crying in the stateroom next to hers. It was an eerie sound, a whisper of despair, heard only during the infrequent lulls in the incessant noise. She heaved her feet onto the floor, and cried out. Swirling around her feet was at least three inches of ice-cold seawater.

"Oh, my God," she whispered.

Just then, a particularly large wave smashed into the ship's hull, driving Maggie to the floor, covering her with the water. Her skirts heavy with water, sticking to her legs already numb from the cold, Maggie made her way out the door and into the deserted hall. Moving drunkenly to the door next to hers, she let out a sound of frustration to find it locked.

"Miss Pierce, Miss Pierce!" She turned to see one of the young crewmen headed her way carrying a bundle of life jackets. "Jaysus, Mary, and Joseph, what are you doing out of your room?"

Maggie had to shout above the noise of the ship. "I was going to help Mrs. Fitzwilliam. She sounds terribly frightened." He shoved a life jacket at her and banged on Mrs. Fitzwilliam's door.

"Mrs. Fitzwilliam, it's Donovan. You must put on a life jacket." They both heard a wail of despair and looked at each other as if wondering what they should do.

"It's all right, Mrs. Fitzwilliam. The boat is built to take on a bit of water. It's supposed to," Maggie said, lying through her teeth. Donovan looked at her as if she'd gone mad.

"Put the jacket on, miss," Donovan said, dropping all but one jacket to the watery floor and helping her fasten the jacket. He banged on the door again. "Either you open the door, Mrs. Fitzwilliam, or I'm knocking it down." He winked at Maggie, just to let her know he likely wouldn't have to resort to such action. The door jiggled a bit before the panicked Mrs. Fitzwilliam realized it was locked; then it sprang open, a pale-faced, wild-eyed woman revealed.

"We're sinking," she shrieked, launching herself at Donovan, "Oh, my God. Oh, my God."

The ship seemed to climb, tipping so far Maggie feared it would stand on edge and flip over, and they all stumbled down the hall a bit, grabbing the railing, only to come crashing downward, leaving all three on the floor with water sloshing around them. Donovan starting whispering Hail Marys as he fumbled for the life jacket and put it on the now-docile Mrs. Fitzpatrick. His hands shook so hard the task was nearly impossible, and Maggie wondered if it was from the cold or from fear.

"Mr. Donovan, what should we do? Surely it's not safe to stay below." Maggie looked pointedly at her feet, where the water had risen halfway to her knees.

"The captain's doing his best. We'll be all right. Follow me," Donovan shouted. The two women slogged behind the seaman, lifting their skirts above the water as best they could while hanging on to the safety rail. He led them up to a small salon, which was thankfully dry and which already contained the other three passengers, all men.

The two women, shivering violently, were ushered to a couch and blankets were produced, which was somewhat of a miracle, Maggie thought.

"I don't want to die," Mrs. Fitzwilliam cried.

"We'll be fine."

"Fine! Did you not see that water? We are only two decks below. That means all the other decks are now underwater. The ship cannot take this kind of pounding. We are all doomed. Why did I ever agree—"

"Shut the hell up, will you?" one of the men shouted, and Maggie tried not to laugh, but she pulled the older woman into a reassuring embrace.

The five passengers spent the remainder of the hellish night praying as the ship listed farther and farther to one side. They expected to abandon ship at any moment even though they prayed that somehow the ship would make it into port. It was the longest night of her life, spent alternately praying and trying to soothe Mrs. Fitzwilliam, who finally became subdued as if accepting their fate.

Maggie didn't realize she had fallen asleep until a

bright light touched her eyelids. The sun had risen and they were still afloat, though listing frighteningly to port. In truth, Maggie never thought to see the sun again, and to have it shining on her warm and reassuring after the nightmare they'd all just endured was something of a miracle.

Just as she was sitting up, Captain Sullivan came into their little salon, his face grim. "Ladies, gentleman. It appears we will have to depart the *White Star* a bit prematurely. There's a fishing boat alongside us at the moment and if you'll follow me, we'll get you down to it promptly."

Maggie stood, her legs cramping from the cold, and with the blanket still wrapped tightly around her, moved toward the door to follow the captain out.

"By God, we survived," one of the gentleman said. "Well done, Captain. Well done."

The seas, so violent the night before, were nearly calm. To the north were the clouds, dark and menacing, on the horizon no doubt pummeling some other poor ship.

"Thank you for making it through, Captain," Maggie said.

The captain nodded. "It was a bit dicey, that, was it not?" he said, smiling.

"A bit more than dicey, I'd say."

The captain looked out at the horizon, an odd expression on his face. It was a mixture of relief, sadness and wonder. Maggie knew exactly how he felt, blinking away the sting of tears in her eyes to be gazing at the rising sun, so very beautiful on the horizon.

"Now, miss, you can start livin'. There's nothing

on earth better for your soul than to look death in the eye and laugh at it."

Maggie did laugh. "I'm afraid I wasn't laughing very much last night," she admitted.

"Nor was I, miss, nor was I."

One day later, Maggie stepped on solid ground in New Bedford, Massachusetts. Her funds were woefully low, so she was grateful that the ship owners had agreed to pay for a respectable hotel and train fare to New York.

Maggie was beyond exhausted by the time the train pulled into Grand Central Terminal. She stood in the train station, other passengers bustling about her, and wondered what in God's name she was doing in New York. Her great mission seemed ridiculous now. The loss of her virginity, even the circumstances surrounding it, was trivial suddenly. She was alive when she thought she'd be dead. Captain Sullivan had been right: now she could start living.

Standing among the mass of people streaming around her, Maggie knew she must see her father, despite his wishes that she not. She had to touch him, to look at his gentle brown eyes just to make certain he was all right. She'd heard terrible things about the prison where he'd been interned, a damp, crumbling building with little ventilation and even less light, and she prayed he was well.

But first she had to exorcise one last demon. She had to see Charles Barnes.

Chapter 20

Maggie knew she was a sight, but there was only so much one could do when nearly all of one's possessions were at the bottom of the Atlantic. At least she was clean, she thought, looking down at the simple dress she wore. She looked like a maid on her day off, a maid with not enough sense to put on her winter coat or muffler on a bitterly cold December day. Instead she wore a thin ready-made cloak that did little to shield her from the frigid Northeast winter. She needed the money she had left to pay for food and passage back to England. Clothes had suddenly become a luxury she could not afford. The small pistol she'd purchased in Liverpool before departing England had been in the same trunk as her clothes. Even if she could have afforded to buy another, she would not have. It was almost as if she'd been cleansed by the sea.

As she walked up two flights of gleaming marble stairs to the offices where her father used to work, she felt her determination grow with each step. Her father's offices had been rich and tasteful, with thick carpeting beneath her feet and well-polished carved wood paneling on the walls. It was a masculinely appointed office, for nearly all the people who walked these halls were men. The masculine oppulence made Maggie feel even more conspicuous.

With a fortifying breath, she opened the door to the outside office, spying a man she did not recognize sitting at her father's secretary's desk. The door to her father's office was opened, and appeared to be deserted.

"I'm here to see Mr. Barnes," she said, trying to sound imperious as she stood there in her cheap cotton gingham dress.

"Mr. Barnes is not in," he said, even though she could clearly hear him blustering behind the closed mahogany door. The secretary looked her up and down, a small but discernible sneer on his face. He was one of those men Maggie instantly disliked, but even that sneer could not tamper her resolve. She looked pointedly at the door.

"Please tell Mr. Barnes that Margaret Pierce is here to see him," she said, putting a slight emphasis on her last name.

The secretary's eyebrows rose in recognition and he seemed suddenly unsure what to do.

"I am not leaving until you tell Mr. Barnes I am here. And when he does come out of that office, I will inform him that you refused my entry."

Looking decidedly put out, the man stood and walked to the door, entering the office much like a snake slithers between two rocks. He returned shortly, standing at the open door and beckoning her to enter. Maggie hesitated, for she'd heard Barnes talking to someone, and the things she needed to say to him could not be said with company. When she entered the room, the secretary closed the door quietly behind her, and she had a stomach-churning memory of another time when Barnes himself had quietly shut the door to his office.

None of it mattered, Maggie told herself as she looked around the hated room. Other than Barnes's soft form, the room was empty. She was momentarily confused until she noticed the telephone on his desk.

"We are quite alone, dear," he said smoothly, apparently interpreting her confusion. "You are looking . . ." He paused, taking in her cheap dress, her simply adorned hair. ". . . well."

"I am anything but well, Mr. Barnes," Maggie said, coming forward into the room. She would not be afraid of him, she would not. But just then she wished she had her pistol, if only for the courage it gave her.

He offered her a seat, extending his strangely feminine hand to indicate a chair. "I will stand," she said, glad that her voice didn't shake. Lord knew her entire body did.

"I thought you were in England," he said, still smiling as if this were a casual social call.

"I was. But I returned to New York to kill you." Maggie almost laughed aloud at the alarm in his puttylike face. "Don't worry," she said with a smile. "I don't have the gun with me. I changed my mind."

"I think you should leave," Barnes said, starting to come round to the front of his desk.

"No," Maggie said, a sense of calm determination filling her. "I think I cannot possibly leave until I tell you what a despicable human being you are."

Something almost human flickered in his eyes before he returned to his luxurious leather chair, the same chair she'd stared at when he'd entered her from behind. "Do tell."

He was mocking her, but Maggie didn't care. "I was an innocent girl desperate to help her father. And you took terrible advantage of me. You cannot know how desperate I must have been to allow you to touch me," she said, feeling bile rise in her throat. "Did you feel flattered perhaps? That such a young girl was willing to have you? Let me tell you, I never would have allowed you to touch me if I had known you would not follow through on your promise. You make me literally sick, just being in the same room with you. I did what I thought I had to. And for the longest time, I was angry with myself. How could I have allowed such a vile creature as you to touch me, to take away the one thing I could give to my husband? Then I grew angry with you. Terribly so. I suppose planning your murder proves that. But now, looking at you, I realize you are pathetic, less than a man. Not worthy of my anger or hatred. I just wanted to tell you that. Good day, sir."

Maggie was vaguely aware of Barnes's face growing more and more red, but didn't care. When she finished, however, she became instantly aware of just how angry she'd made him. He stood so abruptly his chair flew across the floor and slammed into the bookcase behind him.

"I am a man of honor," he shouted.

Maggie laughed, further enraging him. "Honor. Do you call what you did to me honorable?"

He was breathing heavily, like an angry bull about to charge, his wide nostrils flaring, making him look rather piggish, and Maggie was glad they were separated by his large desk. He slowly got control of himself, though his face was still florid. "No," he said, surprising her. "No, it was not. But I have followed through on my promise."

"My father was sentenced to five years," Maggie said. "You promised me one."

He appeared taken aback. "You don't know, do you?"

"Know what?"

He smiled. "Your father is being released in seven months. One year to the date of his sentencing. Perhaps you'd like to thank me," he said, leering at her almost as if he was compelled to act like the evil man she knew him to be.

"I don't believe you."

"I told you he'd spend no more than one year in prison and he will not. Check with his attorney if you'd like," he said dismissively, as if he'd grown bored with their discussion. "I'm surprised no one has contacted you."

Maggie was stunned. "When did this happen?"

"One month ago, at least." He smiled again, making her skin crawl. "A very nice Christmas present for you, my dear."

"I am not your 'dear,'" Maggie said, regaining some of her ferocity. "And while I am grateful that my father is being released, if indeed that happens, what I've said about you still stands."

He gave her a mocking bow. "Of course. My dear. And Merry Christmas."

Maggie narrowed her eyes at him and smiled. "In the spirit of Christmas," she said sweetly, "I think I really should thank you for what you've done."

The idiot actually grinned at her, which only gave Maggie more courage. She stood directly in front of him, looking into his piggy eyes. From his perspective, he saw a beautiful woman with a bit of the devil hidden in the sparkle of her eyes.

"Merry Christmas, Mr. Barnes," she said, curling her fist just the way her brothers had taught her and slamming it as hard as she could into his soft belly. It sunk in perhaps four inches, knocking the wind from him, making him double over gasping for breath.

"Good day," she said, calming, and walked from the room, her face glowing with happiness at the sound of angry, helpless sputtering behind her.

Maggie Pierce, who had lost a bit of herself all those months ago, was back.

Chapter 21

"You are such a grump lately," Amelia said without preamble to her brother as she entered his study. As usual, she found Edward behind his desk, a pile of paper in front of him. The morning sunlight made his fair hair seem to glow about his head, a fallen angel, she thought whimsically. He looked tired lately, with dark smudges beneath his eyes. And his hair, usually meticulous, was a mess, as if he was constantly tunneling his fingers through it. Indeed, he looked like a man who'd been up all night in the clubs drinking. Yet Amelia knew this wasn't true, for he hadn't left the house in days and he rarely drank. "You're even more gloomy than normal."

"I have a lot on my mind," he said, and she noted he didn't even try to deny he'd been disagreeable. "I've a meeting with my property manager later today to discuss why nearly all my tenants are unable to pay full rent. And a sister who is convinced she's in love with a cowboy."

Amelia smiled. Anytime anyone mentioned Carson, good or bad, she smiled. She simply couldn't help it.

He was arriving at Meremont later today and Edward's scowl when she mentioned this fact was enough to set her off in fierce defense of her beloved. She knew she must be the envy of all her friends, because they'd all been as enthralled with Carson before he'd come to the Christmas ball. How in the world she'd ever gotten him to fall in love, she didn't know. She didn't understand why her brother was so against the only man she'd ever loved.

And he did love her. She just knew he did. Surely a man couldn't smile at her as he did, kiss her, touch her in the way Carson did, without loving her.

"I am in love with him," she said. "What do you think I should wear?"

"Why do you think I would care?" he asked, playing a rhyming game they'd often played when they were children.

"Because you are so fair," she quipped.

Edward smiled indulgently. "Fair as in handsome or fair as in I'm evenhanded?"

"That didn't rhyme," she said, but she smiled because she was so glad to see her brother acting more like himself. "You have seemed awfully busy," she said, coming around his desk to look at what he was working on. Spying a book he'd been carrying with him since they'd been at Bellewood, she laughed.

"Goodness, Edward, I've never seen you take so long to read a single book. You must be busy. Else the book is boring," she said, reaching for the familiar blue-bound book.

Edward made to move the book out of her reach, making her smile. "Is it naughty?" she asked, delighted. "Is it?"

He picked it up and showed it to her. Much to her

disappointment it was simply an ordinary adventure story. "I read this years ago," he said, slipping it into his desk. "I have been too busy to read it. Now, speaking of being busy, why are you interrupting me? Again."

Simply put, Amelia was bored and wanted a bit of company. Lady Matilda and the children were on a shopping expedition, one that she was not invited on as she suspected they were buying her Christmas presents. It was rather dreary and quiet and she was, frankly, bored.

"What are we planning for Christmas? Are we going back to the duke and duchess?"

"I hardly think they'll want us back given that we were there nearly two months. Besides, with the new baby, they have enough to think about without us invading their house again so soon."

"Perhaps after the holidays, then. When Miss Pierce returns. Or perhaps we can invite the Pierces here. It's so dreadfully boring round here in the winter, especially if Lady Matilda takes the children to visit her sister. I simply cannot wait until the season begins."

"About that."

Amelia felt panic grow in her. "You promised. And Mrs. Pierce will happily chaperone."

"I'm not certain she's an ideal chaperone," Edward said, recalling the drunken Mrs. Pierce.

"She's been fine since that one little incident. Besides, Miss Pierce can chaperone as well."

"Miss Pierce is a single woman not much older than you who needs her own chaperone. And not two minutes ago you were gushing on and on about Mr. Kitteridge and how much you were in love.

Why attend the season if you've already found the love of your life?"

"You are very unattractive when you are mocking," Amelia said.

"I'm sorry, Amelia, but be reasonable."

"Be reasonable! I have never had a season and you promised me that I would. Are you to tell me that the only purpose for attending all those parties and balls and operas is to find a husband? I daresay if that were true, then ninety percent of the people who attend those things are wasting their time. I'm hoping I can convince Carson to stay a few more months. Surely his brother can handle things at the ranch for a little while longer. That way we can experience the season together. Perhaps even as husband and wife."

Edward, who had been trying to work while he was talking, threw his pen into his inkwell. "Must we have this discussion now? The season doesn't even begin for months."

"And when it does, I am going. With Carson."

"This discussion is over," he said.

"I'll attend the season if I have to bring myself round," she said, then strode angrily away from her onerous brother. She could not believe that just moments before she'd thought him charming.

Edward watched his sister stomp from the room, knowing he was being unfair but not caring. There was no way in hell he would be able to endure a season with Maggie and her mother tagging along everywhere. How absolutely torturous to have her beneath his roof, attending parties, dancing with suitors, while he would have to pretend he wasn't being ripped in two. The only alternative, though, was to act as his sister's sole chaperone and Lord knew, he didn't want to escort his sister to every ball and soiree that London had to offer. And he had promised, not only Amelia, but Mrs. Pierce, who was probably as excited about attending a London season as his sister.

But he simply . . . could not.

When his parents had died, he'd been more than devastated. Their deaths had changed him forever. He'd been forced to grow up seemingly overnight, and he'd been forced to endure pain like he couldn't have imagined. Of course he knew logically that he wasn't to blame for their deaths. He hadn't known when he'd arrived home sick that it would result in the deaths of the two people he loved most in the world. He'd almost lost his sister, too. And when he'd sat by her bed, begging God to spare his sister, he realized that if she'd died, he would want to die as well.

"You feel too much," his mother would often say. Edward had seen it as a flaw, something that made him weaker than he ought to be. And from the way he'd reacted when he lost his parents, it was true. He lived, he breathed, he ate, he slept, but he wasn't alive for a very long time.

It frightened the hell out of him, loving someone that much. It hurt too much, the loss was far too painful. He hated it, hated the weakness, the loss of control.

Yet he'd allowed himself, finally, to fall in love. He'd let it happen. He could have avoided her, he could have married Maggie off to one of his friends and be damned with her. Instead, he'd thrown himself headlong in front of her, declared his love, asked her to marry him.

And she'd said no. God, how could she have said no? Edward let out a curse for allowing himself to get all maudlin yet again, and he picked up his pen with renewed vigor.

He'd just lost himself in his work again when Amelia walked into the room, white-faced, holding a copy of the *London Times* in her shaking hands.

"What is wrong, Amelia?"

"What ship did Miss Pierce sail on?" she asked, her eyes glued to the newspaper.

"I haven't any idea," he said. "Why?"

"Because a ship that sailed out of Liverpool soon after Miss Pierce left has sunk. The *White Star.*"

"Does it say anything about survivors?" he asked quietly.

His sister scanned the article. "No, only that it sank. Do you think the duchess would know?"

"I suppose I could ride over there to see," Edward said, feeling his panic grow. What were the chances that two passenger ships left Liverpool the same time in December? Edward started to leave his study, only to be stopped by Amelia, a bemused look on her face.

"Edward. The telephone. You can call the duke."

Edward looked momentarily startled, then smiled broadly. "You're right. I'd forgotten Rand had a phone installed a few months back. You, my dear, are a genius."

"Aren't I, though?"

Edward shuffled through the top drawer of his desk, looking for his phone directory. He lifted the receiver and gave the telephone a good crank before lifting it to his ear. Edward dragged his free hand through his hair while he waited for the operator to respond. "Yes. Operator," he fairly shouted. "Connect me to Bellingham 241, please."

He clutched the phone hard so Amelia would not see how badly he was shaking, saying silent prayers over and over. It seemed to take forever before the operator said, "Your party is available."

"Yes. This is Lord Hollings." He waited. "I said, this is Lord Hollings. I wonder if I could speak with His Grace, please. His Grace." He waited, his heart pounding in his chest painfully. The line had a loud crackling noise that made it nearly impossible for him to be understood or to understand the person on the other end. Finally Randall was at the telephone. "Randall," he said without preamble. "What was the name of the ship Miss Pierce sailed on?"

"Her what?"

"Her ship. The ship she sailed on."

"I don't remember. Why? You going off to chase her, are you?"

"Was it the *White Star*?"

"Yes. The *White Star*. She sent a postcard from Liverpool with a picture of it. We got it two days ago."

Edward felt his entire body go still. "Thank you."

"Edward, is something wrong?"

Edward couldn't talk, could hardly breathe.

"Edward. Is something wrong?" Randall repeated.

"No, no. Good-bye." He didn't want to frighten the duchess if all was well and he couldn't bring himself to say aloud what he was thinking.

He looked bleakly up at his sister. "It was the *White Star*."

"Are you quite certain? Because . . . because . . ." She couldn't finish her sentence.

She walked over to his desk and laid the newspaper down and pointed a shaking finger to the headline WHITE STAR SINKS. SURVIVORS UNKNOWN.

Edward read: "The *White Star*, one of Britain's premier passenger steamships, was reported sunk off the coast of New England. The ship and all its cargo were lost December twenty-second during a large coastal storm, according to the captain of the fishing vessel *Betsy May*, who witnessed the sinking. The fate of its crew and passengers is unknown at this time."

His eyes scanned desperately for more information, but there was none. "Today is the twenty-fourth. This is yesterday's edition. Did we not get today's edition?"

"We never get it the same day," Amelia said, and she began to cry. "It can't be true. It can't be. She was coming back. She was going to come back. She promised." Amelia began sobbing into her hands. "I can't take it if another person dies, Edward. I just won't be able to take it."

Edward's drew his sister into his arms and comforted her, even though his tortured mind was thinking exactly the same thing. If Maggie were dead, he wasn't entirely certain he could go on.

"I'll call the *Times*," he said, pushing Amelia gently away. He put his hands reassuringly on her shoulders and forced himself to smile. "No doubt they'll have more information. Why the hell they would put such a story in a newspaper without anything about survivors is beyond me. But we'll find out all is well and have an amusing story to tell Miss Pierce when she comes back."

Amelia gave him a watery smile. "I do hope so. She will be tickled, won't she?"

"We'll have a great laugh," he said, feeling an awful tightening in his chest.

He picked up his phone again, and asked to be connected to the *Times* in London. He began pacing and nearly pulled the telephone wire from the wall, and would have if Amelia hadn't lunged for the phone and stopped it from tumbling off the desk. Finally, he was connected. "Yes. I need to speak to someone about the *White Star* sinking. I say, I need to talk . . . Hello? Yes. I need to talk to someone about the . . . Hello? By God, these wretched things are useless," he shouted. "No, not you, sir. The *White Star*. I need information about the ship."

"It sank," he heard through a loud crackling. The person said something else, but he couldn't make it out.

"What? I cannot hear you, confound it. Were there survivors? Hello? Yes, survivors." He drew his brows together in concentration, trying to understand what the man was saying, but it was nearly impossible. Amelia hovered near him, pressing her ear near the receiver. No doubt she could hear even less than he could. "Bloody, bloody, bloody hell," he shouted in frustration. And then he heard the distinct sound of the connection being terminated. Edward slammed down the receiver, letting out a curse no doubt Amelia had never heard before, and her eyes went wide.

"My apologies," he said, "but I couldn't understand the bloke and he's hung up on me. I'm heading down to the wire office. Much more reliable service if you ask me."

"I want to come, too."

"No, I'll get there faster alone. I'll be home with news before you know it."

He was about to rush from the room, but he stopped, opened his drawer, and grabbed the blue-bound book. Amelia gave him a curious look, but he ignored it and began shouting orders that his horse be prepared.

Amelia sat down, feeling emotionally drained. She knew why she was so upset, but why was Edward? It was more than being troubled about an acquaintance. She hadn't seen him act this way since . . . her parents were dying. He'd looked tormented, which was quite astonishing since he claimed he held no special feelings toward Maggie. It made sense now. Maggie was the reason Edward had been so out of sorts when he'd returned from America, and she was the reason he'd seemed so briefly happy at Bellewood and why, of late, he seemed to have become the sort of man who hardly smiled.

"My God," she whispered. "He *is* in love with her." She began to pray in earnest that Maggie was safe, for she didn't know if her brother could take another blow to his heart.

Edward stayed at the telegraph office until he received a reply from the *Times*. His telegram had been cryptic and brief. "Request information on *White Star* survivors STOP Immediate response requested STOP."

While he waited, he paced until the telegraph

operator cleared his throat pointedly. He sat, holding the book and gazing at it, praying as he hadn't prayed since his mother and father died, since he sat by his sister's bed and watched her struggle to breathe. "You will not die," he'd whispered. "I will not allow it."

And now, clutching the precious book, he prayed again. Each time he heard the clatter of the telegraph machine, he raised his head only to have the clerk shake his. Even though he'd read it a hundred times, he opened the book to read her inscription: "Nothing is lost which is worth finding. Yours, Maggie." He still didn't know what the hell she meant, he thought, smiling.

The telegraph machine clattered, and he raised his head.

"This is it, sir," the clerk said, pulling the tape from the machine. He handed it over as soon as it stopped. Edward took the small slip of paper, thanked the man, and walked out of the office without reading it. It was a cold, blustery day and few people were walking about. It was Christmas Eve, after all. He slipped into an alley, pressing the paper against his lips. "Please, God, please," he whispered. He opened his eyes and read the message: "All survived."

"All survived," he whispered, his eyes filling with tears. He slid down the cold brick of the building because he found his legs could no longer hold him. And, despite the few passersby who looked at him curiously, he began to sob in relief so profound it unmanned him.

"You all right, mister?"

He looked up to see a small boy, only his eyes showing in his bundled up little body.

"I am exceedingly well," Edward said, laughing even though his face was wet with tears.

The boy gave him a baffled look, then went on his way, perhaps a bit frightened by the man who was crying but insisted he was "exceedingly well." Edward stood, dusted himself off, and pulled out a handkerchief to wipe his face.

It appeared, he thought grimly, looking at his tearstained cloth, that his efforts to get over Maggie had not entirely worked. That was not well done at all. Not at all.

Chapter 22

Really, Amelia thought, tilting her neck so that Carson could gain better access, Edward should take his responsibilities as chaperone much more seriously. Or perhaps he thought Lady Matilda was supposed to be making certain Carson wasn't taking liberties . . . or that she was happily giving him liberties. They were in a small alcove in the breakfast room, and as it was two o'clock in the afternoon it was quite deserted. Carson and Amelia had run to this room, laughing like children, knowing that they could kiss to their hearts' content without being discovered.

Had anything ever felt better than a man's lips on her neck? She was positively ready to melt to the floor, a puddle of lust. Yes, lust and desire and love. Love, love, love.

"I love you," she said, smiling when he moved his hand up to cup her breast through her dress.

"An' I love you, darling. I love everything about you. I just wish I could see more of you," he said, pulling her dress away and pretending to peek.

Amelia gasped, more in delight than shock. "Sir, you mustn't."

"I love the way you talk, too. Mmmm."

Amelia felt that *mmmm* right down to her toes.

"I think I'll die if I can't have you."

Amelia laughed. "You won't die, Carson."

"I'll expire right on the spot," he said, his breath coming harsh as he reached around her back and started unbuttoning her dress.

"What are you doing?" Amelia asked, feeling the first bit of panic hit her.

"I just want to see you. That's all. Just see you. I just know you're going to be the prettiest thing I've ever laid eyes on," he said. "It might be easier if you turned around."

"I don't think we should."

"I do," he said, kissing her neck and making her sigh. Then he started caressing her through her dress again, making her breast swell against his hand, making her nipple hard and aching. Until Carson, she'd had no idea, none at all, that a man would want to touch her this way or that she would so absolutely want him to.

"Oh, good Lord, Carson."

"Mmmm," he said, again, all the while his free hand worked those buttons, until she could feel the cool air on her back, delicious and naughty and wonderful. What would it hurt for him to simply look at her? She knew when to stop him. She knew she could never, ever let him take her virginity. Surely one look wouldn't hurt. She turned around saucily, presenting her back, and was rewarded by a sharp intake of his breath.

"Lordy, you are a beauty," he breathed. Then he

finished unbuttoning quickly, and returned to kissing her neck. He drew her against him, until she could feel his erection against her buttocks, a frightening and glorious feeling. He moved his hands to her front, to cup her breasts again, but this time he was bolder, moving his body against hers in a rhythm that was erotic and intoxicating. "I want you so bad, honey. So bad. Can you feel how bad I want you? You're drivin' me crazy, darlin'."

Then he slipped her dress from her shoulders and turned her gently around. In short work her corset was pushed down, her chemise unlaced, her breasts exposed to the cool air and his hot gaze.

"Holy God," he said. "I've been dreamin' of this from the first day I saw you, honey, and you're better than any dream I've had."

Amelia blushed, both from the compliment and from the embarrassment of having him stare at her so. She'd never thought of her breasts as beautiful or not. They were just part of her, a very feminine part to be sure, but nothing special. Now, as she looked down at her exposed breasts, she realized they were beautiful. He laid a hand on her bare breast and she closed her eyes. She felt him touch her nipple, twist it gently between his thumb and forefinger, and she nearly cried out at the exquisite feeling, a sharp, piercing sensation that went from her nipple to between her legs.

"Oh, Carson. Yes."

"Yes, darlin'. Oh, God, I have to taste you."

Amelia didn't know what he meant until she felt his mouth on her breast, sucking, tugging, licking. And nothing had ever felt so good as what he was doing to her now. Nothing.

"I have to have you, Amelia. You know I love you, right, honey? I want you in my bed. Now. No one will know. No one goes into my room during the day."

"Oh," Amelia said, groaning in pleasure as he lavished her other breast with the same wonderful attention. She began moving her hips, unknowingly trying to assuage the building pressure between her legs. "I can't," she gasped, wishing with all her being that she could. "You know that."

Carson muttered something beneath his breath. "You can't get me all riled up and then leave me hangin', darlin'," he said, smiling. "You just can't. Come on, darlin', just a little bit more. Just . . ." He picked up her skirts and felt her firm buttocks, pulling her against his erection. "Just a little more. God, you're killing me, darlin'." His hand had somehow made it between her legs when Amelia's sanity returned.

"No, Carson," she said, pushing his hands away. But he brought them right back.

"Please, darlin', you have to let me. I need you. I love you."

"I know, Carson, but it's not right. Not before we're . . ." She stopped herself, because even though Carson had said he loved her, he'd yet to mention marriage. "I mean, I could never do that with any man I wasn't married to."

He kissed her nipples again, losing himself in her, and she allowed it because it felt so good and because as long as he was caressing her breasts he was staying away from where he oughtn't to go.

"I'll marry you, Amelia. I'll marry you. Now, come on, darling," he said, tugging up her skirts again, stopping only when she squealed in happiness.

"Yes, yes, yes," Amelia said.

Carson pulled back looking momentarily confused. "Then let's find us a fine bed and we'll do this up proper."

"No, you silly. I'll marry you. Yes, of course I will. I love you. As to the other, we'll just have to wait until we're married. We'll have to be quick about it, because you're leaving so soon. Perhaps you could delay your departure? I was so hoping you could stay for the season. We must put the banns in the paper, find a church. Oh, and you have to ask Edward's permission."

"Permission," Carson repeated.

"I really think that's the proper thing to do. He is the head of the household, after all."

Carson rubbed his jaw. "Well, sure, honey. I'll do that. But . . ."

"But?"

"Well, I was just thinkin' that if we're getting married anyway, I sure don't know if I can wait all that long." He gently cupped her face in his hands. "You drive me crazy with wanting you, did you know that?"

Amelia smiled, his words making her entire body tingle. "You drive me quite crazy, too. I suppose if we are definitely getting married, it won't do much harm."

Carson let out a long breath. "Thank God, 'cause I'm about to bust here."

"Not *tonight.* You must talk to Edward first. You understand, don't you, Carson?"

He smiled. "Course I do. If anything was worth the wait, it's you. I'll talk to your brother tomorrow and we'll see if we can get you and me engaged before I head back to Texas."

Amelia squealed again and leaped into his arms. "Oh, Carson, I don't believe I've ever been so happy in my life."

Edward looked at Carson, dread in his heart. He knew, from the way the man was pacing, that he was here to ask for his sister's hand. He didn't want to give it.

"Lord Hollings," the American said, looking as if he were about to be ill. "I've come here to ask for your sister's hand in marriage."

"I see."

Carson Kitteridge was about the same age as Edward, and yet at that moment, the American looked far younger. "Well. Can I?"

Edward narrowed his eyes. "Do you love my sister?"

"Sure," he said affably.

"My sister is accustomed to a certain way of life. I don't know if she'd be suited to life on a farm in Texas."

He expected Carson to bristle as his use of the word "farm" but he didn't.

"I think Miss Hollings would do fine."

Edward gave him a grim smile. "Yes, I'm sure she would. My question, however, pertained to whether or not you can support my sister. I know nothing of your ranch, your home, your income."

"I do all right."

"I'm afraid I don't know what that means. What is your income, sir?"

Carson looked taken aback. "It's enough."

Edward let out a sigh of frustration. "My good man, you are coming to me to gain my permission to marry my sister. She is used to living like this," he said, making a sweeping motion with his hand. "She is used to having servants, buying the finest things. While I would never say she is spoiled, one does become accustomed to living a certain way. I simply want to be certain you can provide my sister with a good life."

"Sure I can."

Edward narrowed his eyes and wondered whether Mr. Kitteridge was not quite the brightest fellow. "What is your income, sir?"

"Money goes a lot further in Texas. My brother and I own one of the largest ranches in Texas. We have more than one thousand head of cattle. I don't know exactly what that's worth, 'cause the market fluctuates a bit every year. But it's enough to keep your sister wearing all the frewfaws she wants and then some. My house may not be as grand as this one, but it's the grandest house in Small Fork, that's for sure. Now, sir, can I marry your sister or what?"

Edward drummed his fingers on his desk, torn as to what to do. He knew his little sister would never forgive him if he forbade her to wed this man. He'd never seen her so consumed by anyone. Unfortunately, Edward knew all too well how love could make you act rather insane. Clearly, Amelia was engaged in an infatuation, one that most likely would run its course until Amelia came to her senses. The problem was, Kitteridge was leaving in less than two weeks. This was something he'd never thought to encounter. He always thought Amelia would meet someone in England, someone he perhaps knew or at least someone he could ask questions about. He leaned back into his chair and steepled his fingers against his mouth.

Standing abruptly, he said, "I'll give my permission, but I want my sister to have a season first, to make certain this is what she wants. If she still wants to travel to Texas in June, I'll happily let her go."

Kitteridge looked amazingly pleased with the plan. "That sounds right generous of you," he said. Then, apparently seeing Edward's confusion, he quickly added, "It's not that I don't want to get married right away, but I'm just glad you saw fit to say yes. You see, I have to get back to Texas. My older brother's been in charge, you see, and he's a bit dim-witted. Lord knows what he's been doing while I've been gallivanting around England. I can't stay here until June. Tell you what. I'll go back home and send for her."

Edward smiled. "If Amelia still wants to get married, I'll send her off." Edward was quite certain that once Amelia experienced her first season, the last thing she'd want to do would be to head to a strange land to marry a man she hardly knew. Chances were his fickle little sister would fall in love with someone far more appropriate than Carson Kitteridge. And if she didn't and still wanted to go to Texas, then he'd reluctantly let her go.

"In the meantime, we'd be more than happy if you would stay here through New Year's. It will get a bit chaotic with the children, but we've no other plans and Amelia would love to have you."

Kitteridge gave him a grin that fairly lit up the

room. "That sounds right nice," he said, clapping his hands together.

As he left, Edward wondered whether the man truly did love his sister. He was willing to wait for her, and he'd seemed sincerely happy that the meeting had gone well. And, Edward noted, he hadn't even asked about a dowry. That was perhaps the most interesting thing of all.

Chapter 23

Maggie stood on Centre Street outside the imposing the bleak facade of the Hall of Justice, known by New Yorkers as The Tombs. The building was designed to look like a Roman tomb, forbidding and unwelcoming. She pulled her cheap cloak around her tighter, trying in vain to stop the bitterly cold wind from penetrating the thin fabric. The sun shone weakly in a milky sky, giving off little light and even less heat. She wished she could visit her father wearing her old ermine-lined coat and muff. The last thing she wanted to do was to worry her father more by arriving looking like some sort of scullery maid. But it was Christmas Day and she was alone in New York and she wanted her father.

The Tombs, a huge granite building, took up an entire city block. Maggie hadn't known there were so many criminals in the city. It seemed as if all of New York could fit inside. Clutching a small parcel against her, she walked up the broad steps, fear touching her, almost as if she were to be locked up. At the top of the steps was a large portico with towering columns that seemed to block any light from penetrating the gloomy, frightening, cavernous entrance that was about as welcoming as the gaping opening of a grave. The portico was nearly deserted, but for a single uniformed guard leaning up against the dark granite lighting a cigar in his boredom. Maggie nodded to him, unsure where to go, until she spied a small sign directing visitors to a second building just beyond a courtyard.

She knew, suddenly, why her father had forbidden her mother and her to visit him. The Tombs was a frightening place. It smelled of damp and mildew, almost as if a fog of despair hung over the massive building. Men were killed here, sent to the gallows and hanged until they died. Maggie shuddered, more from that thought than the wind that swirled about the courtyard, kicking up long-dead leaves. She quickly walked to the door and opened it, finding herself in a small room where the smell of mold was almost overwhelming. Walking to a window where another guard sat, she informed him that she was here to visit her father.

"Reginald Pierce, you say?"

"Yes, sir."

"Fourth floor. Through that door and up. At the top is another guard, he'll bring you down to see him. What's that?" he asked, nodding at her parcel.

"A book," she said, suddenly afraid she wouldn't be allowed to give it to her father.

"Let's see," he said, holding out his hand. Then seeing her stricken face, he smiled. "It's for your protection and ours, miss." Maggie gave him the book, her heart breaking as he undid her ribbon and unwrapped the brightly colored paper.

"*The Strange Case of Dr. Jekyll and Mr. Hyde*," he read. "Never heard of it." He riffled through the pages. "You wouldn't believe what you can hide in books."

"People do that?" Maggie asked.

"Once found a pistol in a copy of *Moby Dick*." He handed the book and the paper and ribbon back to her. "Good day, miss. And Merry Christmas."

Maggie gave him a watery smile. Oh, this was just horrid. Her father should not be in this cold, damp, dark place. He should be at home in their beautiful town house, his feet up on his ottoman, his pipe in his hand, sitting before a cozy fire. He should be listening to her read to him or perhaps singing along as Maggie played Christmas carols on their piano. As she walked up the stone steps, she brushed a few tears away. She'd nearly cried that morning in church, her mind not on the birth of Jesus, but on her poor father who no doubt was unable to participate in any Christmas tradition. She pinched her pale cheeks and forced her mouth into a smile, just to test it. It would only make her father more upset if he saw that she was sad. She'd smile, pretend nothing was too horrid about the place, and let him know that all was well.

When she finally made it to the fourth floor, Maggie's thighs were burning from the exertion. She knocked on the door, which was almost immediately answered by a guard. "I'm here to see Mr. Pierce. I'm his daughter."

The man smiled at her, a genuinely happy-to-see-you kind of smile that seemed so out of place here, Maggie was completely taken aback. "So, you're Maggie," the guard said. "Reggie will be just tickled. And don't you worry that he'll be upset. I know he didn't want you to come here, but I just know he'll be pleased as punch."

"You certainly are a jolly guard," Maggie said, laughing.

"There's enough misery here without me adding to it," the guard said, becoming somber. "I'm Sergeant Fisk. Your father and I play chess every day at four o'clock. Haven't beaten him once but I've come awful close a couple of times."

Maggie smiled, so completely astonished to find such a nice man working as a prison guard. She followed the guard through another door and found herself high above the ground floor, walking along a long, open hallway with cells on either side connected by a bridge. Two stovepipes ran up the center of the building, connected to two large stoves on the ground floor, giving off dismal heat. Despite skylights on the ceiling, the prison was dark, as if light could not penetrate through the gloom. It was noisy with shouts from below, and the smell of unwashed bodies and human feces was almost overwhelming.

"Block your ears. And your nose," the guard said good-naturedly. "Lady coming through," he called out, a warning to the men in cells along the way.

"I need a lady," someone yelled from below. "Come here, lady." The prisoner proceeded to make obscene noises until another guard thankfully put a stop to it.

The guard ignored the catcalls and Maggie's flaming cheeks, concentrating only on his charges. "This fourth tier is the cream of the crop," he said. "We got a banker, a lawyer, and . . ." As he passed by one cell. "What are you again, Vonner?"

"A falsely accused schoolmaster," came the disembodied answer from one of the cells.

They skirted around a woman sitting on a small bench outside one of the cells, clutching the hands of the inmate inside, and continued on to the last cell.

"Yeah, a schoolmaster. And, of course, your father. Reggie," he called. "You got yourself a visitor and a mighty pretty one, too," he said, winking at her. "You sit yourself right here." He pulled a small bench closer to the cell, then turned and left, good-naturedly returning all the gibes the prisoners threw at him.

"Oh, Maggie, what are you doing here?"

Maggie clutched at the thick, cold iron bars and gazed into the gloomy cell. "Papa, come here and let me see you," she said, her eyes filling with tears. She simply couldn't take it in, that her father was living in this tiny cell in this horrid place. It was worse than her imagination, far worse. Two cots were crammed into the tiny cell, and another man lay on another cot, apparently sleeping.

As her father came to the bars, she got an even greater shock. He looked . . . wonderful.

"I hate to say this, Papa, but prison seems to agree with you."

Her father, his blue eyes glittering with tears, smiled. He'd lost weight, and his eyes had lost that fear, the worry that had etched so many lines on his dear, dear face. She put the book down on the bench, then reached through the bars and grabbed one of his hands, holding it against her. "Oh, Papa, it's so good to see you," she said. "I should have come sooner. I should have ignored your order. Shame on you for making us stay away."

"I didn't want to worry you, my dear. Oh, Maggie,

please don't cry," he said, laying a trembling hand on her head. "How are you? How is your mother?"

"We're both fine. Mother is still in England, but I had to come back. I'm so glad I did. I can't believe you're spending Christmas here. But it's your last, isn't it? Why didn't you write to us that you were being released? It's wonderful news."

"I did write. Perhaps you haven't received it yet. I could hardly believe it myself. Apparently Charles Barnes worked on my behalf to have the sentence reduced. I'll be in his debt for a very long time."

Maggie remained silent, not wanting to talk about Charles Barnes or even think of him. She certainly didn't want to feel grateful toward him. She couldn't stop looking at her father, taking in all the changes in him. "I imagine the food here is terrible."

"It's edible," he said. Reginald had always been a man who overindulged in everything—food, wine, spending. "I do miss Cook's *tarte a l'oignon*. Sometimes I dream about it," he said wistfully. "And how is your Sir William? Is there a wedding to look forward to?"

"Well, perhaps," she said. "But not to Sir William. He did propose, but I said no. He was a very nice gentleman, but I don't think I would have made him a good wife."

"Of course you would have," her father insisted loyally.

"I didn't love him, Papa."

"I take it there is someone else, then?"

Maggie swallowed a knot in her throat and nodded. "Do you remember Lord Hollings?"

His eyes widened. "The earl from Newport?"

"I haven't said so in my letters, but I've seen quite

a lot of him in England. He is best friends with the Duke of Bellingham and spent a lot of time at Belle-wood. It seems as though he loves me. At least he did. When I return to England I have to sort things out. And if I don't, I'll always have you, Papa. Oh, here," she said, spinning around to gather up her present. "Merry Christmas."

"*The Strange Case of Dr. Jekyll and Mr. Hyde,*" her father read.

"It's supposed to be quite entertaining. I haven't read it yet, myself."

"Stevenson is one of my favorite authors," her father said, smiling. "Thank you." He went back to his cot and laid the book upon it. The task seemed to take an inordinate amount of time and Maggie suspected he was trying to compose himself before returning to her.

"How is your friend?" Maggie asked, nodding toward the sleeping man.

"Quite diverting. He's only in for six months. Seems he was skimming off the parish books."

"From a church?" Maggie whispered, aghast.

"My dear, people will do just about anything when they are in desperate need of money," he said sadly.

During the rest of the visit, Maggie entertained her father with stories of England and her mother, omitting anything that might be upsetting to her father. She did tell him about her harrowing experience on the ship, making him laugh at Mrs. Fitz-william's hysterics. She painted a wonderful picture of Bellewood and Lady Matilda and her brood. All he needed to know was that they were happy and being well cared for. He had enough worries on his mind.

"Here comes Sarge. Looks like you'll have to go, Maggie-mine."

Maggie grasped his hand. "I'm so glad I came, Papa. You've made this a wonderful Christmas."

Reginald let out a disbelieving laugh.

"Really. Seeing you is the best Christmas present I could have asked for. And before you know it, you'll be free and we'll all be together. It hasn't been too horrid, has it?" she asked.

"I just thank God every day it's almost over. It's hard to believe only seven more months. Send your mother my love. Tell her . . ." His throat closed and he shook his head. "Tell her I miss her more than I thought possible."

"I will. She will be so happy to hear you'll be coming home soon."

"Home." He said the word with such sadness.

"Home is where the heart is," Maggie said, repeating the old platitude just to make her father smile.

But her father didn't smile. "You know, I've never given that old saying much thought, but it's true. I'd live in a tent if I could be with my family."

"Have the boys been writing?"

"Oh, yes. Not as much as you, but I do receive a letter now and then. This is hard on them."

"It's hard on everyone. Most especially you."

Her father's expression grew fierce. "I don't care about myself. I deserve to suffer. But none of you do. While I've been in here I've had a lot of time to think about what I did. I'm ashamed, Maggie. Ashamed of what I did to my friends, ashamed of what has happened to my family. I'm sorry, more sorry than you can know."

Maggie held out her hand. "I know, Papa. But if

this hadn't happened, I'd be married to Arthur. So I do believe all this was quite worth it."

Her father laughed, just as she intended.

"I've missed you," he said. "My little bit of sunshine." Maggie's eyes immediately filled with tears. "Now, don't you go crying on me."

She sniffed and wiped her face. "I won't. I've cried enough in these last months. I'm done with all that." She gave her father one last embrace. "I'll write and let you know what's happening. Oh, Papa, I cannot wait until you are free. Good-bye."

Later that night, Maggie sat in her hotel room feeling lonely, but strangely happy, as if the dark cloud that had smothered her for months had drifted entirely away. For the first time in a long while, she was glad to be Margaret Pierce. She looked up toward heaven, knowing that even though she hadn't received a single thing this Christmas Day, she'd been given the most wonderful gift: her life back.

"Thank you," she said. "And merry Christmas."

Chapter 24

Amelia loved the pretty scarf Carson had given her for Christmas. Truly she did. It was the loveliest blue wool, soft and warm, and Carson said he bought it because it matched her eyes. That was wonderful, even if the scarf did not match her eyes—it was far too dark for that. But she couldn't help being a bit disappointed that he hadn't presented her with a ring.

"I know you were expecting something else," he said. "But I want my wife to have my mother's ring. Can't say I expected to be gettin' engaged while I was in England and that ring is back home. Unless my brother got hitched while I've been gone."

Amelia was immediately worried, and Carson chuckled. "Don't you go worryin' about that. Boone isn't one to go skirt chasin'. Fact is, the girls don't much fancy him." He flashed a grin. "Not when they've got me around."

She giggled. "Perhaps they'll find Boone more interesting once you've got a wife. And I completely understand about the ring. Is Boone really your brother's name? It's quite unusual."

"Yeah. My parents named me after Kit Carson and him after Daniel Boone, the frontiersman. Guess they hoped we'd be heroes or something."

"You are a hero," Amelia gushed, making Carson laugh.

"If you aren't the sweetest thing this side of the Rio Grande, I don't know what is."

"I love the way you talk," she said. She loved everything about him, his eyes, his long hair, his towering frame, the way he looked at her as if he wanted to take her to his bed.

If there was one thing that dampened her Christmas spirit, it was her brother's insistence that she have her season and then marry. She didn't know why they couldn't get a special license and marry right away before Carson had to leave. And he did have to go; it was something he was adamant about. Poor Boone just wasn't capable of handling things on his own any longer and Carson was truly worried about his brother. That was another thing she loved about him.

All this meant that Carson would leave and she would follow after the season and they would be married in Texas instead of England. Amelia knew exactly what her brother was up to. He was hoping she'd forget about Carson or perhaps meet someone else in London. She knew that wouldn't happen. At least she would get to enjoy the season, though it wouldn't be the same if Carson wasn't by her side.

"You know we only have two days before I have to go back to London, and then I'm gone."

"I don't want to think about it," Amelia said, feeling tears threaten. "I'll miss you so much. I can't wait until June so I can go to Small Fork. You've told me all about your ranch and the house, but you've said nothing about Small Fork. What's it like? Is it a city or a village?"

"Well, it's the prettiest little town you ever saw. The main street has a church with a white steeple that stretches to the sky, pointing up to heaven. There's roses everywhere and houses with white picket fences, children playing everywhere you look. And in the center of town is a park with a whitewashed gazebo where the local band plays concerts every Saturday night. All the townspeople gather 'round and there's dancing."

Amelia sighed. "It sounds lovely."

"Don't it, though? Now, back to what I was talkin' about."

"What was that?"

Carson drew her away from the rest of the family, who was gathered around the piano singing carols. "I want to come to your room tonight."

"My room?" She knew what he meant, but she couldn't hide her shock that he'd suggest such a thing. And on Christmas night.

"I'm going in two days, honey. This could be our last chance."

"But . . . But we're not married," she whispered, her face turning beet red. "We can't. What if, you know, something *unfortunate* happens? I won't see you for four months!"

"I know what to do to stop you from gettin' in the family way."

"You can do that?"

"Sure, sure."

Amelia smiled. "It's only six months. We'll have a lifetime together."

Carson took a bracing breath. "I need you, darlin'. I don't think you understand what it's like to be a man needin' a woman. I'm crazy with wantin' you. Crazy."

"I'm crazy, too. But it's wrong."

For a moment, Carson actually looked angry, and Amelia was slightly alarmed. Then he smiled, putting her at ease. "Tell you what. We'll just kiss. How's that?"

"Just kiss?" Amelia asked skeptically.

"Maybe a little bit more. Come on, darlin'."

Amelia grinned. "All right. But you have to promise not to go any further than that."

"I sure will try," he said, the devil in his eyes.

Amelia gave him a friendly swat on his arm. "You better, sir, or I shall be forced to drastic measures."

"Now, that sounds interesting."

She laughed, delighted with his flirting. Carson made her feel like a sophisticated, desirable woman. She only prayed she had the willpower to stop their "kissing" before it was too late. Lord knew it was getting more and more difficult to resist temptation even though she knew she must. No matter what he said, Amelia would not get married with a rounded belly. Not only that, but it was a sin to be with a man before marriage—especially on Christmas, for goodness' sake! She could just picture God looking down at her with a fierce frown for even thinking such a thing. She would never shame herself or her family in that way. She only hoped Carson could understand.

* * *

"I don't understand," Carson said, his forehead wet with a fine sheen of perspiration. "We're gettin' married. Now, come on, honey, let me touch you . . ."

"No," Amelia said, pushing his hand away from between her legs. "I said no and I mean it. I want you to leave, Carson."

Amelia had foolishly agreed to let Carson visit her in her bedroom, believing they would be able to resist temptation. She never would have believed it would be so difficult.

Carson moved his hand to her breasts and continued to kiss her, long drugging kisses that had her moving her hips against him if only to feel that delicious sensation more. "See, honey? You want it, too. There's nothing wrong with wanting to be with the man you love. Nothing wrong." He pulled at one nipple, and she let out a sound of pure pleasure. "Don't you love me, darlin'?" He moved his hand down again and applied the most exquisite pressure between her legs. "There, that feels good, doesn't it?"

"Hmmmm."

He moved his hand in time with her hips and Amelia let out a gasp. She had to resist. She had to, had to . . . *Oh, Lord, please give me the strength* . . . "Oh, God, Carson, yes."

"I know, honey, I know," he said, moving his mouth to her erect nipple, gently biting through the fabric of her cotton nightgown. "Let me, darlin'. Oh, please let me. I need you so bad. Can you feel how much? Let me show you. Let me."

He worked the buttons on his trousers and brought out his erection for her to see.

"Touch me. Please."

Amelia looked from his . . . *thing* . . . to his face,

and let out a small mewling sound, something between despair and yearning. She swallowed, then shook her head. "I think you should go."

"Christ!" he growled, then shoved his erection inside his pants. "If you ain't the biggest tease I've ever met."

"I'm sorry," she said in a small voice, and started to silently cry.

Her tears did him in, because he gathered her against him, murmuring his own apologies, kissing her hair. "It's all right. Don't you turn into a watering pot on me. You're different than other girls an' I should have known that. You're a proper lady. I guess that's why I want you so much, darlin'. No harm done, right?" He pulled away and looked into her tearstained face, smiling gently down at her. It was the nicest smile Amelia had ever seen, for it wasn't full of bravado or flash, it was real.

"Thank you for understanding," she said against his chest. "Once we're married, I'll do it every day."

Carson let out a deep chuckle. "I'm sure you will, honey. I shouldn't have pressured you like that. No more tears, right?"

She shook her head. "No more."

He stood up and tucked in his shirt. "Do I look presentable?"

Amelia smiled. "You're the handsomest man I've ever seen, Carson Kitteridge."

This time when he smiled, it was one of regret and sadness. "I really think I'm going to miss you," he said, as if that was a foreign concept.

"Of course you will," Amelia said happily. "But it won't be for long. We'll have forever once I'm in Texas. I'm so excited."

"Yeah, me, too," Carson said, buttoning up his pants.

"We still have one more day together. And then, come June, I'll be Small Fork's newest resident. Do you think people there will like me?"

"Sure," he said, almost absently. "I'll see you in the morning."

"I love you," Amelia said, feeling suddenly unsure of her decision. Carson was being kind, yes, but it was as if something had changed, a slight shifting, and it made her feel uneasy and unsure.

Then he bent over and gave her a long, wonderful kiss, and all her doubts melted away, just like that. "Good night," he said, and winked at her, making her heart expand with love.

After he'd gone, she closed her eyes and tried to imagine the pretty town he described. White picket fences. A gazebo in the center of town. Roses everywhere. It sounded so beautiful, so wonderful and idyllic. Amelia wished she was already there, already walking around her house with its wooden floors and windows looking out onto the bubbling brook that Carson told her about. She wondered if she'd be able to hear the cows at night, or what the sounds would be way out in the Texas countryside.

Amelia hugged herself with pure happiness. Small Fork was where she would get married, raise a family, and forever be with the man she loved. She knew she must be the luckiest girl in England.

Edward closed the book and smiled. For a while, he'd been transported back in time, when he was a boy reading a grand adventure. He used to sit with his father in their cozy parlor reading by the fire. His father was a great reader and not one to collect books simply for their beauty or worth. In fact, he was quite certain his father would have been appalled by the idea of collecting books one had no intention of reading.

But books had held a bit of magic for Edward. They were something that brought him and his father together, the only thing they shared. He loved the feel of them, their smell, their ability to bring you to another time, another place, where boys could be heroes, where no one you loved ever died, ever left you.

Books had lost some of their magic after his parents had died, but none of their fascination. But for a while, sitting in his own library, he was nine years old, praying his father wouldn't notice how late it had grown, praying he would get in at least another chapter before being sent to bed.

Like so many other times, Edward pressed the book against his heart and closed his eyes, allowing himself to think of her, to hold something she held. It was foolish, of course. As foolish as holding on to her letters, as foolish as being content just to touch the small bundle in his desk.

You feel too much.

His mother had been right, of course. For all his flirting and cavalier attitude, he'd merely been trying to protect his heart. He knew that. Just look what happened when he finally gave it away. He was reduced to the kind of man who drew comfort holding a book merely because she'd once held it. He really should stick it on a shelf and forget about it. Forget about her.

Instead, he tucked it into his pocket, feeling its weight there, a constant reminder that he was a fool and weak. And so much in love it hurt.

Two days after Christmas, Meremont had finally returned to something like normal. The servants, feeling merry and well rested after Boxing Day, were back at work, humming beneath their breaths. The tree would remain standing until Twelfth Night, January sixth, but Amelia felt like taking down all the decorations the minute Carson walked out the door. He couldn't even give her a proper kiss because her brother was standing right there with the strangest expression. It was almost as if he didn't like Carson, which couldn't be true because how could anyone not like Carson?

"I cannot wait until June. I will miss you," Amelia said, on the brink of tears.

"An' I'll miss you," he said, holding her hands in his larger ones.

And then he'd gone, without saying he loved her, without holding her like she wanted him to. It was all so disgustingly proper because her brother had insisted he be there when Carson said his good-byes.

Thank goodness they'd been able to have a more improper good-bye the night before. Amelia smiled just thinking about it. Carson had been well into his cups, celebrating his return to America, he'd said. He'd come to her room again, swaying on his feet, a silly grin on his face.

"I'm jush here to say good-bye, darlin'."

Amelia drew him into her room before anyone saw her or heard him. He was being overly loud and completely imprudent and Amelia loved every minute of it. He held her and kissed her, a bit more ardently than before, but when she told him he had to leave, he was good-natured about it, muttering something about it being no good tonight anyway.

"I wish I could have had you, though. It will be my life's regret," he'd said. "Give me one more kiss good night."

Amelia had obliged indulgently and led him to the door. "You are the sweetest thing. I'm gonna miss you sorely. Don't you go forgettin' me, now, darlin'."

"How could I forget you? You're my fiancé, you silly man. And I'll be seeing you in just a few months."

"An' then I'll have you?" he asked, grinning and swaying. Lord, he was drunk, Amelia thought. He obviously was a man not used to spirits.

"You'll have me. Forever."

"A lady with Carson Kitteridge. That would be somethin'. Back home, they wouldn't believe it. Not one word. Too bad, too bad," he said morosely.

"Yes. Too bad. That's why we have to be married first."

"Yup." He grinned again. "Now give me that kiss."

"I already did."

"Then give me another. My last one. Ah, girl, I am gonna miss you. You smell so good," he said, burying his face against her neck. "I almost wish . . ."

"What?" she asked, giggling because he was nuzzling her.

"Nothin', darlin'. Wishin' don't mean shit."

"Carson!"

"Well, it's true." He kissed her then, holding her

against him in an almost desperate way, and if Amelia had any doubts that he loved her, they were assuaged at that moment.

Amelia chose to think of that, rather than the almost formal good-byes they'd had at the door. And when he had disappeared from view down that long, tree-lined road that led to Meremont, Amelia threw herself into her brother's arms and sobbed.

"I already miss him," she said, making Edward laugh. She glared at him. "I would never laugh at you if you had a broken heart."

"I know. I'm sorry. It's just that you can hardly miss a man who most likely is still on our property."

"It's just that I won't see him for six months," she wailed.

Edward held his little sister, felt her body shake, felt her tears seep through his shirt, and wondered just how devastated she was going to be when Kitteridge did not send for her. Perhaps he was wrong about the man. Why would he request his sister's hand in marriage if he had no intention of marrying her? It didn't make sense. And yet he simply could not bring himself to believe he'd be putting Amelia on a steamship come June. Maybe he didn't want to believe it.

"I'm going to write to him right now," Amelia said fiercely, and Edward laughed again. This time, his sister joined him.

"I know I'm being silly, but I don't care. Just think how happy he'll be when he returns to the ranch and finds a letter there waiting for him."

Then his sister, her mercurial mood swinging back like a great pendulum to the side of happiness, hurried from the room to find her writing instruments.

The season wouldn't begin in earnest until after Easter, which came April 2. That gave him weeks and weeks to knock some sense into his sister's head. If she was anything like him when it came to love, he should admit he'd taken on an impossible task. For once the Hollings heart was given, it was almost impossible for it to be taken back.

Chapter 25

Maggie was greeted at Bellewood like the prodigal daughter returning after a lengthy absence. When she'd left, she'd given little thought to the people she'd left behind and how they would worry about her. She'd been in such a state of despair and uncertainty, it was truly the first time in her life she'd acted so completely selfishly. And Maggie refused to feel one bit of guilt.

Her mother, looking younger and fresher than she had in months, embraced her warmly, tears streaming down her face. Then she immediately launched into a fierce talk about how worried everyone had been, especially after it was discovered that the ship she'd been on had sunk.

"And not a word from you. Not one word," her mother said, then pulled her daughter in for yet another hug. Maggie gave the footman who was standing nearby an embarrassed smile.

"I'm sorry, Mama. You have every right to be angry with me."

Harriet's face went from frown to beaming smile.

"Oh, Maggie, we've received the most wonderful news." Harriet, as if suddenly aware they were standing in the public part of the palace, linked arms with her daughter and led her to their private quarters. "I'll let you visit with Her Grace in a moment, but I'd like to speak to you first."

"Oh?"

Once they were in their rooms, Harriet turned to Maggie, fairly brimming with happiness. "Your father is to be set free in August. His letter arrived the day before Christmas, can you believe it? It was the best gift that man has ever given me."

Maggie smiled, so happy to see her mother acting more like herself. "I know," she said. "I saw Papa."

"How was he?" Harriet asked, as if afraid to hear the answer.

"Actually, quite well. He's lost weight, but not too much. The prison is awful, but he's with men who are like him. No hardened criminals. The guards seemed polite and even kind. One plays chess with Papa every day. He told me to tell you he misses you."

"Your poor father," Harriet said, her eyes filling with tears once again. "He'll never be the same."

"None of us will. And perhaps that's not such a bad thing."

The two women sat down together on the sofa of their shared sitting room. "You never told me why you had to leave."

"No, I didn't," Maggie said without embellishment.

"I wish you would."

"I'm sure you do."

Harriet gave her daughter a look of exasperation. "Maggie, you haven't been yourself for weeks. And now . . ." Her mother studied her so closely, Maggie began to feel self-conscious. "What happened?"

"I think when that ship sank, I realized that life was very precious. Of course I already knew it was, but there is something so jarringly eye-opening about facing death. I simply let everything go."

"Let what go?"

Maggie shrugged. It was difficult for herself to wrap her mind around how different she felt, and far more difficult to explain to her mother. She could not tell her about Charles Barnes; it would only hurt her mother to know such a sordid thing. "I let go of all my troubles," she said finally. "I think I got a little lost and now here I am."

"I do believe the same thing happened to me. What doesn't kill you—"

"Makes you stronger," Maggie finished, laughing. "I never realized how true that statement was. Now, tell me everything that's been happening here"

Harriet let her daughter change the subject, and in quick measure Maggie was brought up to date. Bellewood had been quiet over the Christmas holidays, the usual visits and dinners canceled because of the new baby. "It was lovely," Harriet said. "But you were missed. And it's been so quiet here, with Lady Amelia and Lord Hollings gone as well. I did hope they'd come for the New Year, but it looks as though we won't be seeing them until we all go to Town. Oh, goodness, you must not know about the engagement."

"Not Amelia and Mr. Kitteridge."

Harriet nodded. "How could Lord Hollings have allowed such a thing?"

"That's what we've been asking ourselves. I could

not think of a less fortunate marriage for that
lovely girl."

Maggie shook her head. "No doubt he completely
charmed her. And Lord Hollings," she added skeptically. "Honestly, what do we really know of the
man? I never heard of him until I came here. For all
we know, he's simply an actor with an unusual show.
Unless . . ."

"Unless?"

Maggie blushed. "Are they to be married, um,
quickly?"

"Oh, no. And shame on you for thinking such a
thing. According to Amelia's letter—that one does
like to write—he's gone back to Texas and she's supposed to follow him in June."

"But the season is hardly started by then."

"Apparently, we're all going to Town immediately
after Easter. That will give us all two months to enjoy
the season."

"There isn't much point to the season if Amelia is
already engaged," Maggie grumbled, still trying to
figure out how Kitteridge could have managed to
convince Lord Hollings he would be a fit husband.

"Apparently, Lord Hollings is adamant about
her having her season. Adamant," her mother said
pointedly.

"You think he's trying to dissuade Amelia from
marrying Kitteridge?"

"That would be my guess. After all, what brother
in his right mind would foist a character like Kitteridge on his sister?"

Maggie found the entire thing rather baffling. "I
suppose we'll find out in April."

"And speaking of the season."

Maggie resisted the urge to run from the room. She knew that look in her mother's eyes, for she'd seen it every year at least once since her coming-out when she was eighteen. "Yes?" she asked, bracing herself.

"I was simply wondering what our plans are, now that you've thrown away not one, but two chances at a good marriage."

"Isn't it obvious, Mama? I plan to win Lord Hollings's heart once and for all."

Elizabeth looked down at her sleeping baby wondering how on earth she'd done such a wonderful thing as giving birth to this bit of perfection. Rand came up behind her, putting his arms around a waist that was already beginning to slim.

"He's always sleeping," he said.

Elizabeth looked at him as if he were quite insane. "He's wide awake at two o'clock in the morning," she pointed out.

"I told you to get a wet nurse if you wanted."

Elizabeth looked down at her little boy and shook her head. "I really don't mind."

Both Graces turned at the sound of a quiet knock on the nursery door.

"Maggie!" Elizabeth said, rushing over to her friend. "Oh, it's so good to see you. You must tell me everything, and not leave out a single detail. I was worried sick about you. And then Lord Hollings telephoned to ask what ship you were on and that's when I saw the article in the *Times* that the ship had sunk. Of course by then Lord Hollings already had word that everyone had survived. And it's a good thing, too, because now that you're here I quite want to thrash you for making us all so worried."

Maggie laughed. "That's about what my mother had to say as well. And I am sorry. I simply had other things on my mind."

Elizabeth looked up at her husband, who was watching the two women with an indulgent look on his face. "Rand, might Maggie and I catch up without you hovering about?"

"Was I hovering?" he asked, raising one brow.

"Yes. Now shoo."

Rand gave his wife a kiss on the cheek and left the room. "So. Are the authorities after you?"

"No. At least not for murder. Perhaps assault."

Elizabeth widened her eyes and grinned. "What did you do to him?"

"I punched him in his great soft belly. I must say it felt rather good."

"You didn't."

"I did. After the ship sank, I lost any desire to kill him," Maggie said, as casually as if she'd been talking about a hat she'd decided not to buy. "I don't know if I could have done it, but I did buy a pistol in Liverpool. It sank with the ship."

Elizabeth looked at her friend in disbelief. She was being so completely nonchalant about relating her plans to commit murder. "What did he say?"

Maggie walked over to the ornate bassinette where Henry lay sleeping, his sweet mouth making little sucking noises. "He's beautiful, Elizabeth," she said, her eyes growing misty.

"Oh, bother that. Tell me what happened with Barnes."

Maggie turned to Elizabeth in surprise. "He was

obnoxious. I told him what I thought of him, and then I punched him. That's all there really was to it. And I visited my father on Christmas Day. That was wonderful."

Maggie filled Elizabeth in on the visit with her father, giving her details about the prison she couldn't bring herself to tell her mother.

Elizabeth listened as her friend told her various stories of her adventure, the ship's sinking, her taking a train from New Bedford to New York all by herself. And during their visit, something occurred to Elizabeth. Maggie had changed. She was more like her old self yet more confident, as if she'd lived ten years in the last month.

"I didn't realize how much you were suffering until now," Elizabeth said, grasping her friend's hand. "You hide it so well. Or rather you try to."

"I quite literally was falling apart," Maggie said. "I feel as if the black cloud that was following me about is gone. I didn't know how awful I felt until I felt normal. I have you to thank. I never would have gone to New York if you hadn't pushed me."

Elizabeth look horrified. "Please don't blame me."

"It's not blame, it's giving you credit." Maggie took a bracing breath.

"Christmas must have been terribly lonely. Here I was with Rand and a new baby, probably happier than I've ever been, but I couldn't help thinking about you alone and likely frightened in New York."

"I've never had a more wonderful Christmas," Maggie said, surprising Elizabeth. "I'd just survived a horrible ordeal, punched a man I loathed in the gut, and found out my father was going to be released early. It was the first time in a long while I felt completely at peace. For a long while now, I've thought God was conspiring against me and my family. But this Christmas, it was as if He was saying, 'See? Now you appreciate what I've given you.' It was a wonderful gift."

Elizabeth's eyes misted over, amazed at her friend's resilience.

"Now I need you to help me with something else," Maggie said with a mischievous smile.

"Anything."

"I need to win Lord Hollings back. Do you think it's possible?"

"I don't know," she said truthfully. "To propose to a girl and have her reject you. I don't know how a man like Edward can get over that." Seeing Maggie's expression, Elizabeth said, "I want to be honest with you."

"Thank you," she said, looking down at her hands. When she looked up, she had a sparkle in her eye. "Oh, pish. I'll have that man wrapped around my little finger in a week. You'll see."

"Do you really think so?"

"He doesn't have a chance."

Chapter 26

Edward knew the minute he saw her standing outside his Hanover Square town house that he didn't have a chance in hell. He hadn't seen her in four months and in that time, she'd gotten even more beautiful. Damnation.

Every day, he told himself he was over her. He'd stopped carrying around the book like a lovesick puppy. He hadn't even opened that drawer where her letters lay in weeks. He hadn't thrown those letters away, that was true, but he sometimes went days without even the temptation to look at them, touch them.

Of course, he knew she was back in England, for she'd written to his sister. She hadn't written to him, which was fine. Why should she? Amelia had shared the letters, of course, the delightfully detailed missives that had his sister in stitches over her description of the shipwreck, which must have been harrowing. In her letter, she made it sound more like a great adventure than a near tragedy.

He stood in his library on the second floor looking down at her and felt his entire body react to her mere presence. She wore a large hat with an ostrich plumb curving back that hid all of her face but the fine line of her jaw. When she looked up at the town house, he saw her face and damned if his heart didn't start beating painfully in his chest. She looked . . . happy and for some reason that made his heart ache even more. Couldn't she be suffering just a bit of what he felt? What was it about her that left him so completely unmanned?

Other than paying for a hotel for his sister and the Pierces to stay in for the duration of the season, he didn't know how to avoid having them in his home. When he'd suggested such a thing to his sister, she'd acted baffled.

"Why would we stay in a hotel when we have more than enough room here?" she'd asked. "The only people who stay in hotels are the ones who cannot afford a house in Town."

And because he had no good answer, he was standing on his second floor gazing down at Maggie with a yearning that bordered on obsession.

"They're here," Amelia said, rushing into the room and grabbing her brother's arm. "Come on, Edward." She tugged on him until he walked with her, feeling like a man headed to the hangman. "Honestly, it won't be that tedious bringing us about. You might think we were dragging you to a funeral for all the enthusiasm you're showing. We don't want to hurt their feelings."

"Since when are you looking forward to the season? All you've done for the past three months is complain incessantly that I've forced you to stay here when you could be with Kitteridge. By the way, has he written to you lately?"

"You know how long the post takes from the States, never mind Texas. He's probably written a dozen times and I just haven't received the letters. And the one letter I have received was wonderful."

Edward grunted in response. His sister had read the letter to him, and he nearly laughed aloud at the pap it contained.

"And don't change the subject. The only reason you are dreading the season is that you're still in love with Miss Pierce."

He stopped dead.

"You are mistaken," he said in a deceivingly calm tone.

"For goodness' sake, Edward, I'm not as stupid as you seem to think I am. It's obvious to me that you love her. I think being in love gives one greater insight into others. I cannot think of any other reason why you have so suddenly become reasonable about Carson. Clearly you are in love."

"If you say one more word about love, I shall tell the Pierces to turn around at this moment and return to Bellewood."

Amelia tsked. "So dramatic. And you'll do no such thing."

"When did you become so annoying?" he asked.

His sister laughed. "I've been annoying you since I learned to talk. You know that."

"All too well," he grumbled as they began down the stairs.

By the time they made it to the ground floor, Maggie and her mother were handing off their coats, gloves, and hats to his butler, Wilson.

Edward had expected Maggie to be a bit reserved in her greeting. After all, the last time they had seen each other, she'd been about to leave after rejecting his marriage proposal. He should have expected her to act completely the opposite of what a normal girl would act.

"Amelia, Lord Hollings. It's so good to see you both," Maggie said, rushing over to give Amelia a hug. Then she turned to Edward and grasped his hands. "You look wonderful, Edward," she said, smiling up at him.

He didn't want to look at her, didn't want to smile back at her, wanted to drop her hands in disgust. But he made the mistake of meeting her eyes, and it was like a blow to the gut. She was smiling, as he had seen her do a hundred times since she'd arrived in England, but this time was different. He couldn't say what it was, but it was the kind of smile that made men want to climb the highest mountain just to get a glimpse of it. It was as if her smile had been broken and was now fixed.

"I cannot wait for the season to begin. I'm so excited, I feel like a girl at her first coming-out. Amelia!" She turned to his sister. "Wait until you see the dresses I've had remade from Elizabeth's old gowns. I cannot wait until I can wear them. And you, Edward, must promise me at least one dance for every ball we attend."

It would have been extremely impolite to publicly decline such an offer, so Edward was forced to nod in agreement.

"I'm so glad to be back in London. Elizabeth has secured several invitations for me already. Of course I wouldn't think of attending anything without you, Amelia. I'd be too lost. And I need you to help me navigate through this world of yours."

Edward narrowed his eyes. This was the Maggie he remembered, that effervescent chatterbox that had captured his heart. Something had happened in the past few months that had changed her; he prayed fervently it wasn't another man, for he didn't know if he could take another such blow.

"Only if you promise to tell me everything you know about Texas."

Maggie laughed. "I fear I know far more about British society than I do about Texas. Why, that feels like a foreign country to me." Maggie and her mother turned at a commotion at the door. "Our bags have arrived."

"Wilson, could you please show the ladies to their rooms."

It was on the tip of Edward's tongue to ask this vivacious woman standing in front of him if she was aware she had a twin living hereabouts, and one that wasn't nearly as charming. He studied her, looked for something that told him she was putting on an act, but saw nothing but the girl he'd fallen in love with. And all he could think was *No wonder I fell for her. No wonder.* And then, tumbling after that thought was the real bafflement that she'd felt none of the reluctance or awkwardness that he had. Because, he had to admit, he still had feelings for her and perhaps she had none. Perhaps she felt as if she were seeing an old friend after a long separation, and there he'd been foolishly trying to calm his beating heart, to stop himself from falling to his knees.

"How is your little cousin, Lord Hollings?" Maggie asked. "I hope she is doing better."

"Lady Matilda has brought the entire brood to

Scarborough to the spa there. Janice's doctor believes the mineral waters there may do her good."

"And you doubt that?"

"She vomits nearly every time she eats. But not every time. I think it's more likely she keeps eating something that disagrees with her. Matilda agrees, but she hasn't discovered what that something is. Regardless, the resort is lovely and the children should enjoy themselves."

"Mama," Maggie said, turning to Harriet, "perhaps before you return to New York we can visit Scarborough. Or perhaps Brighton. I've heard that's very nice as well."

"Oh, no, Miss Pierce. It's very passé. Quite the place for the middle class nowadays," Amelia said.

"Well, I certainly wouldn't want to go there," Maggie said in mock horror.

As the women discussed where they would visit, and whether it was worth it to travel to Italy for the thermal baths there, Edward became rather stuck on a single sentence Maggie had uttered, seemingly without thinking. She'd said to her mother "before *you* return to New York" not "before *we* return to New York." What did that mean? Surely she had not secured yet another fiancé since her return to England. He'd pictured her safely ensconced at Bellewood cooing over the duchess's newborn, not gallivanting about the countryside batting her eyes at the gentry. Before he could ask what she'd meant, the two women departed, following Wilson to their rooms.

"You are frowning again, Edward," Amelia said.

"Am I?"

"It is a very unfortunate look for you. Otherwise you are quite handsome."

"Thank you," he said dryly, as if being handsome was the last on his list of important things.

That night at dinner, Maggie entertained them all with her harrowing stories of the shipwreck, though she gave no clue at all as to what had brought her to the States in the first place. It seemed a glaring omission, one they seemed, by tacit agreement, not to broach. Edward decided to be a cad and ask her point-blank.

"Miss Pierce, what brought you to New York in the first place? You never did say."

Maggie's expression was almost comical. It seemed to Edward to be a logical enough question, but one might have thought he'd just asked her what kind of underclothes she was wearing. Instead of answering him, she looked to her mother, who gave her daughter a pained look.

"I don't see the point in hiding it any longer," Maggie said.

"Hiding what?" Amelia said, leaning forward as if she sensed a great secret were about to be imparted.

Maggie's mother gave an imperceptible nod, apparently giving her permission.

"I went to visit my father," Maggie said, and winked at her mother.

"Oh?" Her bland answer made him even more confused.

"He's in prison. He's been in prison since last August, right about the time His Grace issued the invitation for us to visit."

"Prison!" Amelia gasped, delighted that the secret was so exciting. "Did he murder someone?"

Maggie laughed. "It's not quite as sordid as all that. He embezzled money from his friends. It was all very humiliating for the entire family. He was supposed to be imprisoned for five years, but he's being released in August. I don't see the point in hiding it anymore."

"It's still not something we like to talk about," Harriet interjected, apparently displeased with her daughter's forthrightness.

"Of course not," Edward said, frowning. This explained a great deal, he realized. It must have been the reason Maggie seemed a bit changed when he saw her. Now he understood why she was wearing remade dresses, why she'd seemed in such a hurry to get married . . .

Only not to him.

His face flushed with humiliation and he took a long drink of his wine, holding up his empty glass to the footman for a refill. God, he was such a fool.

"We were left quite destitute," Maggie said lightly. "We truly have only the clothes on our backs." She said it as if it were of no consequence. Or as if it were something she'd already resolved by securing a new fiancé. *That* simply did not bear thinking about.

"You certainly seem to be in high spirits considering," Edward pointed out. "Certainly you can't be that destitute if you are planning trips to Scarborough or Italy."

Maggie simply beamed him a smile. "I think we'll manage, at least I hope so," she said vaguely.

But her mother blurted, "My Maggie's getting married."

"Mother! Nothing is finalized yet. You know that.

You shouldn't have said anything," Maggie said, her tone livid.

Harriet appeared to be trying not to laugh, so giddy was she over the prospects of her daughter's upcoming nuptials. She was quite unaware of the fury in her daughter's eyes.

"Married! Oh, how wonderful," Amelia gushed. Then she quickly cast her brother a look and instantly sobered, which Edward found exceedingly annoying. He did not like to be pitied by his little sister. "I am very happy for you," she added in a much more subdued tone. "Who is the gentleman?"

"I'm not at liberty to say. And neither is my mother," Maggie said pointedly.

Edward lifted his glass in a toast. "Congratulations, Miss Pierce." It was happening all over again, that sick feeling of falling, of his heart being trampled on. Again.

Maggie looked at Edward and wanted to murder her mother. Though she hadn't been drinking lately, this night Harriet had had three glasses of wine and they'd obviously gone straight to her head. Imagine announcing Maggie was getting married to the very man she planned to wed. Now Edward believed her to be engaged to another man and really, other than proposing to him on the spot, there was nothing she could do. She hadn't had a chance to truly gauge whether or not he still loved her.

"No banns have been read," she said sickly. "This really is all quite premature."

"But you have an understanding?" Amelia asked, looking confused.

"Most definitely," Harriet gushed.

"Not yet," Maggie said at the same time. Then, "Mother, please."

Harriet looked quite happy with herself. "Would you like a hint?" she asked.

Oh, goodness, Maggie thought, perhaps her mother had more than the three glasses she'd seen her drink. "I think my mother needs to . . . go," Maggie said, standing abruptly and grabbing her mother's arm.

"Maggie, let go of me," Harriet said crossly.

"Let her have her fun," Edward said, his tone hard. Maggie stopped and gave Edward a look that was meant to tell him to leave off.

"See?" Harriet said, pulling her arm away from her daughter. "They don't mind a bit of fun. You are being a very poor sport, Margaret."

"Edward, perhaps—" Amelia started, but was immediately interrupted by her brother.

"I enjoy games. Do give us a hint, Mrs. Pierce."

"Mother," Maggie pleaded, on the verge of tears.

Finally, Harriet recognized the stress she was causing her daughter. "The only hint I'll give you—"

"Mother, *please.*"

Harriet smiled triumphantly. "—is that he is taller than I."

There was complete silence in the room for two beats; then Maggie laughed, so completely relieved that her mother hadn't exposed her she nearly collapsed. She would put off murdering her for later.

"That isn't much of a hint," Amelia said, laughing.

"Because there isn't much of an engagement," Maggie said, sitting down and rubbing her temples with her index fingers. She was beginning to get a rather hideous headache.

The small dinner party was interrupted by the footmen presenting a lemon sponge cake with honey drizzled over it as a light dessert. Maggie took a small forkful even though she was feeling slightly ill.

"I have business to attend to," Lord Hollings said, standing abruptly. "If you ladies will pardon me."

Maggie watched him go, feeling the temptation to throttle her mother grow tenfold. "Mother, how could you say such a thing?" she hissed.

Her mother looked at her like a puppy who's been caught ripping up a cherished item. "I spoke out of turn, didn't I?"

"That is quite the understatement," Maggie muttered, pushing her plate away. The cake was delicious, but her stomach simply couldn't take another bite.

"Who is your intended?" Amelia said, her eyes going to the door where Lord Hollings had just disappeared.

"There is no intended," Maggie said, more harshly than she intended. "The only thing engaged in this room is my mother's imagination."

"And me," Amelia said, grinning.

Maggie smiled. "And you."

Lord Hollings was quite good at not being seen. Over the next four days, no one saw hide nor hair of the man who was supposed to be accompanying the women to all sorts of entertainments. He'd missed a small private concert in Lord Wakefield's home, a luncheon at Lady Spindleton's, and a supper at Mr. Randolph's massive mansion in Mayfair. His obvious absence put a damper on the events, for all three women, if not especially Maggie. She had wandered the house at all hours hoping to see Lord Hollings, but either he was not actually living in the town house or he kept such late hours he managed to avoid all contact.

In a bit of desperation, Maggie decided to write to him and ask for a meeting.

> *Dear Lord Hollings:*
> *I have something of importance to discuss with you regarding my upcoming engagement.*
>
> > *Yours,*
> > *Miss Pierce*

Maggie smiled down at the brief note knowing he would likely crumple the thing into a ball and toss it into the fire. But he would no doubt schedule a meeting.

Edward did precisely what Maggie had predicted, except for the part about him scheduling a meeting. God, did the woman have absolutely no heart in that ice chest of hers? Did she not recall him begging her to marry him, telling her he loved her, making a complete and utter ass of himself over her? To think he had carried that damned book around with him like a child carrying a favorite toy. Never in his life had he been so disgusted with his behavior. She wanted to meet with him? Too damned bad.

Thus far in what he knew would be a torturous season, Edward had managed to avoid attending the events with his sister and her two chaperones. But he could not avoid attending Lord Wethering's ball. Wethering had been one of those cash-poor peers who was genuinely interested in making money by working for it. Edward counted the viscount as a friend and they had muddled through a few business dealings together. Edward was a bit more knowledgeable having had an uncle who was a genius at business. Wethering was celebrating a good year, having made more money in the past twelve months than his father had in the past twelve years.

So it was an irritated Lord Hollings who tugged at his cuffs in impatience while he awaited the grand entrance of the females. He had not seen anyone in nearly five days, for he found, for some reason, any female living beneath his roof highly annoying. His sister could only gush on and on about Carson, even though he deeply suspected the letter she waited for on tenterhooks would never arrive. Maggie was far too pleased with herself, far too oblivious of the knife she was twisting delightedly into his back. And her mother was . . . well, she was simply irritating for no particular reason other than she was related to Maggie.

He could not wait until this evening was over.

When the three of them finally made their entrance, he scowled and muttered, "Of course." Of course she would look stunning. Why wouldn't she? No doubt she would attract a herd of men to her side this night. No doubt she would delight them with her effervescent personality and that dress that hardly covered her. He fought the strong urge to throw a blanket about her. The dress, a deep copper with some sort of gold lacy underskirt, exposed her chest to an alarming degree. He could clearly see the plump mounds of her breasts and wondered if she would be totally exposed if she simply bounced a bit.

His sister, on the other hand, wore an extremely modest off-white creation that fit her like a sack compared to the form-fitted dress Maggie wore. She might as well have hung a sign around her neck saying "Unavailable."

"You are all lovely," he said in an obligatory way.

Amelia smiled at him. "Really?"

The brat knew she looked plain, not an easy task for a girl as lovely as his sister. She certainly wasn't dressed the way she had been the night she'd met Carson.

"I do believe Cook has an old potato sack in the kitchen you could wear at the next ball," he said dryly.

"Oh? I do hope she can spare it," Amelia said with a smug smile. "And there is absolutely nothing wrong with this dress, is there, Maggie?"

"Perfectly appropriate for a single girl."

"Who wants to remain single," Lord Hollings added.

Amelia simply laughed. "You know, Edward, I could have had my feelings hurt."

"But you didn't, did you?"

"No." Amelia looked entirely too pleased with herself and Harriet simply shook her head, completely confused by the entire exchange. "You must not have had any brothers growing up, did you, Mrs. Pierce?"

"No, and I'm beginning to thank goodness I didn't," she said.

Edward helped the women into his coach, keeping his touch as brief as possible as he handed Maggie up. He did not meet her eyes, even though he sensed she was staring at him, almost willing him to look at her. The ride in the carriage was brief, but necessary; one simply did not walk to a ball. Waiting in the queue took longer than actually reaching it, and by the time they stopped in front of the manse, it was all Edward could do but run from the chattering magpies that filled his coach. They had not stopped talking for a moment but to breathe, and while one was breathing, the others were talking. He longed to do nothing more than head to the Wetherings' billiard room, but knew he had to do his duty first by hanging about his sister.

"I know someone will ask me to dance, and I will of course, but I certainly will not enjoy it," Amelia vowed.

Maggie laughed. "But what if the most handsome, richest, kindest man in England comes up to you? What shall you do?"

"That man has already left," Amelia said, and Edward barely suppressed a grown.

As he'd predicted, the men could not keep their eyes from Maggie. He ignored them and tried his best to ignore her. It was the first time he'd attended a ball and not asked her to dance. Too raw was the memory of the last ball, when they'd gone out to the terrace and he'd kissed her. He'd not repeat that mistake again.

Instead, he made an effort to dance with every other beautiful woman in the room and hardly noticed the bevy of admirers constantly surrounding Maggie. All he could think of was that she certainly was not acting like an engaged girl. At least his sister, as disillusioned as she was, was trying not to attract attention to herself. He was rather proud of her loyalty and hoped Mr. Kitteridge warranted it. Unfortunately, if Amelia continued to act the wallflower, she would have little hope of attracting a man to replace the one occupying her heart. Edward suspected his entire plan was doomed to fail. He had underestimated his sister's complete devotion to Kitteridge. Just as he had woefully overestimated Maggie's attraction to himself.

Just as he was about to leave the ballroom, Amelia came up to him looking miserable. "I wish to leave," she said.

"Has something happened?"

"I simply cannot enjoy myself without Carson here."

"Try. I'm going to the billiard room to discuss business. I shouldn't be more than an hour. Can you at least endure that much?"

"I suppose."

"You know, Amelia, you might find yourself having fun if you would allow yourself to."

"I could say the same to you. I've noticed you haven't had a single dance with Miss Pierce."

His eyes found her on the dance floor as she looked up, smiling, into the face of a viscount who was heir to a dukedom. The young man looked completely entranced. "She seems to be having a fine time without me. If you will excuse me, Amelia, I'll try not to be too long."

Though Maggie tried not to let it show, she was disappointed Lord Hollings hadn't asked her to dance, though she understood why. No doubt her mother's "announcement" was not well received. She was relieved when Amelia found her, just after one in the morning, and told her they were leaving.

Tonight, she would not let him escape her.

Chapter 27

When the four walked through the door, they were a subdued bunch, all lost in their own thoughts.

"Good evening, ladies," Edward said, removing his coat and handing it off to a footman.

"If I could have a moment, Lord Hollings," Maggie said. Everyone in the room stopped still for a moment, before the other two women continued up the stairs even though they were no doubt dying with curiosity.

"It is quite late, Miss Pierce. If you don't mind . . ."

"I do. I need to talk to you about my engagement."

"I don't see why I need to know the details of your love life," he said succinctly.

Maggie closed her eyes briefly. "Edward, please. This is very difficult for me."

He gave her a mocking bow, then led her to his second-floor library, where a fire had been lit by servants who apparently knew well their lord's habits. He walked to a side table as if to pour himself a brandy, then turned to her instead.

"Go on, Miss Pierce. I'm waiting with bated breath."

"Could we please sit?" Maggie asked, nodding toward a small couch. She wasn't certain her shaking knees could hold her much longer.

Edward hesitated a moment before walking over to the couch and sitting down. Maggie sat, perched on the edge, and clutched her hands together in her lap.

"I need to tell you some things." She steepled shaking hands in front of her face, pressing the bridge of her nose, before forcing them back to her lap. She couldn't look at Edward, was so afraid that he would never look at her the same again. If he did, if he looked at her with disgust, if he turned away, she wasn't certain she could bear it.

"When you asked me to marry you, I could not. It wasn't because I was in love with Sir William. And it certainly wasn't because I didn't love you." Her throat closed and she swallowed. Edward let out a small sound, of anger, disbelief, pain, she wasn't certain. But she forged ahead, letting out a small, shaky laugh. "This is so difficult. I knew it would be. I . . . I . . ."

"Good God, Miss Pierce, just say it."

She finally looked at him. He looked angry and impatient and she almost lost her nerve then and there. "It is not easy for me to say what I have to say." Her eyes filled with tears and her throat burned.

When he saw her tears, his expression softened slowly, almost reluctantly. "Go on," he said softly.

"When my father was arrested, everyone told us he would likely be sentenced to five years. He was very much a pariah in New York. We lost all our friends. My brother lost his job. It was as if overnight we had become outcasts. That was bad enough. But one night I overheard him with my mother and he was crying, my father was *crying*, and he was telling my mother that he couldn't bear five years. One, perhaps. But not five. It tore at my heart to hear him so."

"I'm sorry, Maggie."

She continued on as if he hadn't spoken. "I thought I could help, you see. I went to his partner to see if anything could be done. If perhaps he had any influence or knew of a way to have the sentence reduced. He laughed, and told me I had no money, nothing to give him to convince him to help me. I was desperate to help my father. I would have done anything." She let that last sentence hang there, gathering its sordid meaning.

"You don't have to tell me this," Edward said harshly, but with an underlying kindness that gave Maggie courage.

"I do. I do, because you have to understand why a woman so desperately in love would say no to a marriage proposal from the only man she has ever loved."

Edward shook his head, as if trying to deflect the words that battered him.

"That man, he agreed with the bargain and so I let him," she said, nearly whispering as tears spilled over. "And then when my father was sentenced, it was for five years. Five."

"Oh, God, Maggie."

"And then Arthur broke it off and we came here. I was so ashamed and I loved you so much, but I wasn't the girl I'd been in Newport. I knew that even if you did not. Then you said you loved me and wanted to marry me and . . ."

Edward closed his eyes. "And I told you I was so glad to be your first." When he opened his eyes, they were filled with a profound remorse.

She nodded, so overwhelmed she could hardly speak. "I couldn't tell you. I was afraid if I did, you wouldn't love me anymore."

Edward smiled. "You do know how foolish that is, don't you? God knows I've tried to stop loving you. I hardly think this will work."

Maggie let out a watery laugh. "I so wanted you to be the first. The only."

His eyes became suspiciously wet. "You will be, Maggie-mine. That other hardly counts, does it."

"I don't want it to. It wasn't very pleasant. Not like with you, when you . . ." She blushed. "Lord Hollings, will you marry me?"

He let out a laugh, and looked at her as if she'd gone quite mad. "Marry you?" he asked, sounding incredulous, and Maggie's heart sank like a stone. "My God, Maggie, of course I'll marry you."

She threw herself into his arms, but he pushed her gently away.

"I must say, it's quite improper and rather unmanning for you to have proposed to me. I'm afraid, just for that reason, I must insist we do this properly."

Maggie, suppressing a smile in an attempt to be serious, nodded enthusiastically. Edward leaped up, looking excited and boyish, his blue eyes sparkling with something almost mischievous. "Stay here," he said, and ran from the room, leaving Maggie alone with only her grin.

She could hear him bounding up the stairs, most

likely taking them two at a time. He was back in less than two minutes and came directly to her, getting down on one knee. Then with a dramatic flourish, he pulled out a spectacular diamond and ruby ring.

"Margaret Pierce, will you make me the happiest of men for the rest of my life?"

For once, Maggie was speechless. She simply nodded her head and threw herself into his arms, crying happy tears.

"I'm quite lost without you, you know," he said.

"I know," she said on a watery laugh. "I could tell. You are not very good at hiding your feelings."

Edward drew her to him and kissed her, deepening that kiss until she was melting against him. Kissing him, holding him, was so right, so good.

"And you are too good at hiding your feelings. I had no idea how much you were suffering. You must have been working very hard at that. I have to blame it on the fact that I was out of my mind in love with you and you didn't seem to care a bit for me. You are never to do that again," he admonished.

"It was the hardest thing I've ever had to do," Maggie said. "There's only one more thing I need for you to do. And this is perhaps the most difficult thing for me to say."

His brows furrowed in concern. "Anything."

She pressed her lips together. "Make me forget. Make me forget everything but you and me and this." She leaned over and kissed him softly, then pulled away to look into his eyes silently telling him what she wanted, needed.

"You mean, now?"

Maggie blushed and giggled. "If you don't mind."

"If I don't mind, she says. My God, Maggie, I've

dreamed of making love to you from the moment I saw you in Newport."

"Truly?"

"Yes. Truly."

"Then if you don't mind."

He let out a laugh. "I don't mind if you don't mind getting married as soon as possible and be damned the gossip. Unless you want to wait until your father is released?"

Maggie shook her head slowly. "He'll understand. I've already told him all about you." She tilted her head, smiling. "My room or yours?"

"Maggie," he said, pulling her in for a quick kiss, "you are too good to be true."

They agreed to meet in his room in twenty minutes. Maggie silently entered her room, and once a sleepy maid helped her remove her dress, she dismissed her, her nerves jangled and raw. Suddenly, everything she touched seemed impossibly sensual. Her cotton gown, which she'd worn a hundred times, brushed against her nipples, which had become incredibly sensitive. She brushed her curling black hair, her eyes gazing at her reflection, and she smiled in happy anticipation.

She was going to make love this night and it would be for the first time. That thing she'd done with Barnes was simple mating, and was somehow so distant from the woman she was now, it seemed like a different person altogether.

When twenty minutes had passed, she tiptoed down the hall, past the library, to Edward's suite, which she had never laid eyes on, never mind entered. The door had been left open a crack, and instead of knocking, she simply pushed it open, feeling a welcoming cool breeze from the opened French doors at the other end of the room. She closed the door and looked about the room, lit only by a single gas sconce. The room appeared empty, but Maggie heard what sounded like running water from behind a door. She stood at the entrance, uncertain what to do, whether she should wait for him to finish whatever he was doing, or climb upon his bed. For an instant, she had the particularly naughty idea of removing her cotton nightgown.

It was rather warm and humid, this night. That breeze would feel far better caressing her naked skin. Maggie smiled, wondering what his reaction would be if he came out of his bathing room to find her naked on his bed, wearing nothing but a smile. It was quite a singular way to make this planned event a bit spontaneous, and she bit her lower lip trying to garner the courage to do something so completely outrageous. The old Maggie would have done it, she realized, feeling a surge of bravery.

Quickly, before she could change her mind, she pulled the nightgown over her head and made a beeline for his bed, lying down on her back. No. This would never do. She felt far too exposed. Then she lay on her stomach with only her backside exposed, facing the bathing room, her knees bent and her feet in the air and crossed, as if she were doing nothing more risqué than reading a book. Somehow it seemed more proper and less bare. Propping her chin on her hands, she waited for him to come out.

* * *

Edward put his hand in the water to test it and smiled. It was perfect. She would be here any moment, and he wanted this bath to be a surprise. Wiping his hands on a soft Turkish towel, he walked out of his bathing room and stopped dead.

There before his eyes was a vision he would never forget. Maggie lay naked on his bed, smiling up at him, her hair a frothy black tangle around her head and down her back. Her very smooth, silky, lovely *naked* back. The soft gaslight seemed to make her skin glow, and it was all he could do not to rush to her and hold her against him. He was instantly and painfully hard. The wind was literally knocked from his lungs and he nearly sank to his knees and thanked God for this gift.

"Hello," said the little imp on his bed.

"Hello." Barefoot, he padded over to the foot of the bed where she lay waiting for him, and knelt down so their heads were even. Then he kissed her, letting out a groan of love and need, placing his hands on either side of her head to deepen the kiss. She let out a sound of pleasure that drove him mad, and he thrust his tongue against hers, moving in an erotic rhythm. After several long, drugging moments, he pulled back. "I have a surprise for you."

She smiled. "I adore surprises."

He stood, holding out his hand, and for a moment he thought she would be too shy to take it and stand. But she did, a playful smile on her face, as if she knew perfectly well he knew she was only pretending to be so bold. He led her into his secret place, his one real indulgence. A bathing room so elegant and sinful he'd almost felt guilty when he ordered it built. It was a room filled with marble and gilt, warm fluffy towels, soft gas lighting, with fingers of steam coming from a bathtub large enough to hold five people, though it had only ever held one.

"This is my secret lair," he said, a bit sheepish.

Maggie stared open mouthed and he could tell she'd never seen anything like it in her life. It was a room made for sin and decadence. One almost expected nymphs to come dancing into the room holding out plump, juicy grapes to nibble on. With a little squeal, she let go of his hand and ran for the huge tub, a glorious sight of happy naked female. Amused and delighted, he followed in her wake and was somehow not surprised that she not only climbed right in without testing the water, but sank in past her head, letting out bubbles like a child.

Slowly she raised her head out of the surface, her face shiny and wet, laughing as her hair tangled about her like an exotic mermaid. "This is wonderful," she said, moving her hands through the water and obscuring her naked form beneath the surface. She suddenly, unexpectedly, got shy as if realizing for the first time she was naked in a tub with a man standing over her. She put her hands over her breasts and bit her lip.

"Oh, no, you don't," he said, drawing her hands away. He shook his head in wonder looking down at her, knowing without a doubt he was the luckiest man on earth. How many times had he fantasized about such a moment, tortured himself with visions of Maggie looking up at him like this? And now she was here, in this room, wet and warm and smiling shyly up at him. "Tell me this is not a dream, Maggie."

She shook her head. "I'm sorry, Edward. I cannot. This is a dream. A wonderful, magical dream where anything can happen. Anything good."

He nearly wept right then, for gratitude, for love, for just having her finally, finally, with him.

"Will you be . . ." She pressed her lips together in that way of hers, exposing her charming uncertainty. ". . . joining me?"

"I think I shall." He made short work of his clothes, and stood before her, smiling when she averted her eyes from him, a shyness that tugged at his heart. He let her be shy. For now. "Here I come," he said, and climbed into the tub on the opposite side. He touched one of her feet with his knee and she pulled it away, then slowly brought it back. Then, moving deliberately, he went to her, and without laying a hand on her, kissed her gently, savored her softness, the small sounds she made when she liked what he did to her. He sat next to her, and then, in one fluid moment, pulled her onto his lap and laughed aloud at her expression. She might not have been a virgin, but she was exceedingly innocent nonetheless.

"You can feel me," he said, his hands on her waist, and she nodded. His erection lay between the heat of her legs, throbbing and hard beyond anything he'd ever felt. "I sure as hell can feel you. My God, Maggie, you are the most beautiful woman. Look at you." He raised his hands and laid them on her breasts, wet and round, uplifted and glowing softly in the light. He swallowed hard, then brought his mouth to one nipple, letting out a groan of pure need. She gasped when he tugged and suckled, and let out a small sound when he flicked her with his tongue.

"That feels delightful," she whispered.

He moved to the other breast, and she put her hand behind his head, guiding him, pushing him against her. And then, as he loved her, she began moving against him in the subtle rhythm that began to drive him quite mad. He had to stop himself from lifting her up and driving hard into her, for more than anything he wanted this to be good for her.

He moved back to her mouth, ravished her with a kiss, which she returned. Their skin, slippery with water and the scented oils he'd placed in the tub, made every nerve ending in his body feel electrified. Her hands moved restlessly on his shoulders, his neck, his chest. Every touch sent shards of pure pleasure down his body and he knew he would not be able to take much more.

Maggie was lost in a world where nothing existed but exquisite sensation. Never in all her imaginings did she think of how wonderful a man's naked wet body would feel against hers. His erection pressed against her, his hands touched her everywhere, his mouth moved on her hot skin, and she could only squirm and try to relieve the building pressure between her legs. He was beautiful, like a perfect statue come to life, turned into warm flesh. She wanted to touch him, taste him, take him into her. It became an urge and a strange undeniable need, to mate, to have him become part of her. Any shyness she'd felt had disappeared the moment she'd felt his mouth on her nipple suckling her, driving that wonderful feeling growing between her legs. She needed to do something, anything, to make it go away or make it better, she didn't know which.

When he reached down between her legs, she pushed against him, her relief nearly profound. "Yes," she whispered. He moved his thumb against her, back and forth, until she was moving with him, until she was letting out little sounds of pleasure with every stroke.

"Maggie?" It was a question, a plea.

"Yes."

He moved her up and she clung to him, kissed his neck, felt his strong hands on her hips as he guided her down, opened her, filled her the way her body was craving. Her breath came out in short bursts, and he let out one long groan.

"Oh, God, Maggie."

He brought his mouth to her breasts and laved her nipples, and he brought his hand between her legs. She let out a small mewling sound and began moving against him, until she could feel his arousal moving in and out of her in a rhythm so erotic she nearly cried out with the joy of it. That wonderful sensation was happening again, something wonderful, building, building, until she was moving against him, not caring about anything but the way he was making her feel. She was mindless of her cries and to the warm water sloshing around them, until finally, oh, God, finally, it hit her with such a delicious intense wave of pleasure, she thought she might die of it. She cried out, pressing herself against him, against his hand, and he thrust over and over until he pulled her to him and let out a deep cry of satisfaction.

For several long moments, they clung together, feeling their tremors, the wonderful warmth of their bodies. Finally, she lifted her head from his shoulder and kissed him.

"You look happy," she said. His face was flushed and damp from the steamy bath, making him look even younger than his twenty-eight years.

"I am. How could I not be?"

"Thank you," she said, kissing him lightly.

"The pleasure was mine."

"And mine," she said rather saucily. Then she let out a shiver.

"Let's go to bed," he said, rising up, completely comfortable to be naked in front of her. She stood, too, feeling almost as if he was daring her to, and he laughed.

"You delight me," he said, and pulled her to him, kissing her loudly.

After they were dried and safely in bed, she lay curled up in his arms, loving his warmth and strength. She leaned up on one elbow, and brushed a kiss on his smiling lips. "There's one more thing I need to tell you," she said, laughing at his mock look of horror.

"I didn't go to New York to see my father. I went to New York to kill that man."

"You *what?*"

"I bought a pistol in Liverpool and planned to shoot him when I got to New York. Then the storm hit and we nearly died. I know I've made light of it, but it truly was the most terrifying experience of my life. And after it was over and we made it safely ashore, I realized that life was too precious to allow myself to be miserable about something that hardly seemed important anymore. I knew if I told you the truth and you rejected me, then it would be a flaw in you, not me. And you, sir, are perfect."

"Maggie-mine, I am completely imperfect. And I'm afraid I have my own confession."

He seemed entirely too serious, and Maggie was instantly worried. "What? You are actually married and have a mad wife somewhere in Scotland."

"You read too many books. No, nothing as dramatic as that." He smiled at her, then stared at the ceiling, his beautiful blue eyes filled with a sadness that tugged at Maggie's heart. "It's just that when I learned of your ship sinking, there was a time when I didn't know whether there were any survivors or not. I did not take it . . , well."

He turned to her, his head resting on his hand, his eyes sweeping her face. "I'm afraid I love you a bit more than is prudent. I did try not to. So you must promise me you'll never do anything foolish, and if I insist you see a doctor for the sniffles, you will see a doctor. And if you carry our child, you are to do nothing more strenuous than, say, read a book."

Maggie couldn't help herself, she giggled. "I can see you are going to be a very difficult husband. A tyrant, even."

"Yes. I am sorry, but I cannot help myself."

Maggie leaned over and kissed his lips, little pecks until he was chuckling. "I suppose I could live with such a tyrant. But you must promise me one thing," she said solemnly.

"Anything."

"You must promise we'll always be this happy."

"I promise."

"And you'll love me forever?"

"Forever."

"And you'll never get angry with me?"

"I promise to love you forever."

They both laughed, for that is what they did best together.

Epilogue

Amelia looked at her calendar, a surging desperation making her feel quite ill. It was the first of June and still Carson had not sent for her. She'd begun to doubt their plans. Had he said specifically that he would send for her, or was she supposed to go to him whether or not she received word? The fact that she must rely on the not always reliable post was maddening.

Suppose he sent for her and she never got the missive? Suppose he was already waiting for her in Texas and she was here in England ridiculously waiting for a letter that would never come? And then he'd come to the conclusion she didn't love him any more, which couldn't be further from the truth. She loved him more now than when he'd said good-bye and one of her greatest regrets was being so ridiculously adamant about keeping her virginity for her wedding day. Now it seemed so petty and shortsighted and wrong to have denied him that.

So she waited for him, and he was likely waiting for her, and they would never see each other again simply because some inept person lost her letter. It was beyond bearing.

Oh, why hadn't the letter arrived?

Even though Edward wasn't being mean about it, he did ask quite often whether anything interesting had arrived in the post. As if she wouldn't have gone straight to him if the letter had arrived. Edward, stubborn, besotted man, refused to let her make any travel arrangements until the letter arrived. Just to thwart him, she'd been packed for weeks and would be ready to depart within hours of receiving news from Carson.

"What if the letter got lost?" she'd said two weeks ago, when her gut was twisting after yet another post came with nothing but silly invitations to silly season events.

"I'm sure that is a possibility," Edward said, rather indulgently, like an adult telling her the same about Santa Claus.

"If the letter was lost, Carson would be waiting in Small Fork for me right now thinking I have spurned him."

"Or perhaps there is no letter," Edward said, saying aloud what Amelia was certain he believed all along.

"How can you say that? He is my intended. He loves me. He asked me to marry him. Would you ask a girl to marry you that you did not want?"

"Of course not," he said, "but I am not Carson."

"No. You are not. Carson is a much better man than you. I'm quite certain he would never cast aspersions at your character the way you are casting them at his."

Edward had given her a withering look, but otherwise did not respond.

Oh, how she hated not knowing. She knew in her heart that Carson had sent a letter and was awaiting word of her arrival.

Amelia sat at her desk, the morning sun streaming through her window, making her uncomfortably warm. It was unusually warm for this early in the summer. She'd heard Texas was warm, but she didn't know how warm. She hoped it wasn't as hot as London in July, for that was nearly unbearable. It was probably lovely there, and green, with flowers blooming and streams bubbling over with cool water. She smiled wistfully, tapping her pen against her mouth.

She had no idea how long it took to travel from London to Texas. No more than three weeks, certainly, with train travel so advanced in America. Maggie told her one could take a train nearly everywhere. If only the letter would arrive. It had to, it just had to.

She just knew they would be even more happy than Edward and Maggie, if that were possible. Seeing them get married only made Amelia want it more for herself. She was dreadfully lonely and feeling very much out of sorts with Maggie as the new mistress of the Hanover Square home. Not that Amelia had ever acted the mistress, but servants did often come to her with questions about the household. Now they went to Maggie. It was a small thing, really, and not that bothersome, but it did make Amelia realize that she wanted her own home to manage.

In two weeks, her brother and his new bride would be taking an extensive honeymoon to the Continent and she would travel back to Meremont quite alone but for the servants. Lady Matilda and the children would not be back at Meremont until August and it would be terribly lonely there.

Edward was finishing up final details of his travel arrangements for his honeymoon. Maggie pressed up against him as they discussed where they would stay and which countries they would visit. They were leaving in one week and still did not know precisely where they were going. Every time he mentioned a country as a possibility, she would say, "Oh, yes, let's go there." At present they had a list of ten countries to visit and would be gone four years.

"We have to whittle this down a bit, Maggie-mine, else by the time we return, we'll be old and doddering."

"All right, then, Italy, France, and . . . Switzerland."

"Switzerland?"

"Don't they have glorious mountains there? I want to see that."

He smiled indulgently. "Italy, France, and Switzerland it is."

She kissed him soundly. "Perhaps one day we can go to more exotic places."

"Next year. We'll go to a new place each summer. Until we have too many babies to carry with us."

Maggie looked at him in mock horror, but Edward knew she was getting used to the idea of having children running about. "I suppose I will like them if they are mine. Mother says that's what happened to her."

"You will be a wonderful mother," he said, looking up at her. He put his hand behind her head and drew her down for a long, drugging kiss. They broke apart when they heard an ear-shattering squeal from the hall.

Seconds later, Amelia burst into the room waving a piece of paper in her hand. Edward knew, from the large black wax seal, who it was from. "It's come! It's come! He's sent for me."

"How wonderful," Maggie said, and Edward looked at her sharply, because damned if she didn't sound sincere. He thanked God every day that the post came and didn't have a letter from Carson. Even though he knew his little sister's heart was breaking, he felt in his bones that a letter would never come. Now he'd been proved wrong.

Amelia hugged the letter to her chest. "I told you he'd write," she said fiercely to Edward. "You didn't believe it."

"I did have my doubts. I still don't know if you should go."

"What?" Amelia said, nearly hysterically. "I'm going. I'm leaving tomorrow, in fact. Or as soon as I can book passage. That shouldn't be a problem, should it?" She looked almost about to cry at the prospect that she couldn't leave immediately.

"You don't have to leave as quickly as all that. It will take a while to pack your things. Especially if you are leaving forever. . . ." Edward let his voice drift off. Forever. He might never see his little sister again, he realized. Texas seemed so very far away; the other side of the earth practically.

"I'm not leaving forever. Texas isn't China, for goodness' sake," Amelia said, so excited to have her letter she couldn't begin to feel sad about leaving everything behind. She was simply insanely in love, and unfortunately, Edward could sympathize. But Texas. And Carson Kitteridge.

"Could you have your secretary book me passage as soon as possible? It took forever for the letter to arrive and I fear Carson is already expecting me. Oh, I should write to him immediately and tell him of my departure."

She flew from the room, still clutching the letter to her breast, happy beyond measure.

Two days later, she was gone.

The house seemed empty without his little sister grumbling and complaining and shrieking her excitement about something.

"I shall miss her," Edward said, pausing as he handed a maid his favorite pair of cuff links to be packed. "She was all I had of family for a long time."

Maggie came up behind her husband and hugged him, and he placed a strong hand on hers. Thank God he had Maggie, for he would have been quite a bit more despondent this day without her.

"She is well out to sea now and probably so excited she'll probably want to jump off the ship before it safely docks," Maggie said, laughing. "I do hope she's done the right thing."

Edward let out a breath. "I couldn't forbid her to go. I wanted to." He turned so that he was embracing Maggie. "Did I do the right thing? Damn, I just don't trust the man. But he did ask to marry her."

"I think if you had forbidden her to go to him, she would have found a way on that ship despite you. And instead of having a maid and extra funds with her, she'd be quite alone and nearly destitute. It's better this way. You did the right thing, Edward. She's a grown woman." When he gave her a disbelieving look, she continued. "She'll be twenty years old in a few months. She's only two years younger than I."

"But you seem ancient compared to her," he lamented.

Maggie gave him a swat. "I'm ancient, am I?"

Edward chuckled and kissed his beautiful wife. "I love every ancient inch of you."

"Beggin' your pardon, sir."

They turned to see a maid standing nervously in the doorway, holding what looked like the letter Carson had written to his sister.

Edward took the folded paper, looked at the bold black seal, one that Amelia had noted, all misty-eyed, proclaiming even that black wax blob something wonderful. The address was written in a rather feminine hand, something Edward hadn't noted with the first letter, which Amelia carried about with her for days and forced him to read. Twice.

He looked at the maid, who worried her hands in the apron covering her dress.

"There ain't no writing, sir. It's blank."

**Did you miss Elizabeth's and Randall's story?
Then pick up and enjoy
MARRY CHRISTMAS.**

A Christmas wedding to the Duke of Bellingham. Any other socialite in Newport, Rhode Island, would be overjoyed at the prospect, but Elizabeth Cummings finds her mother's announcement as appealing as a prison sentence. Elizabeth has not the slightest desire to meet Randall Blackmore, let alone be bartered for an English title. Her heart belongs to another, and the duke's prestige, arrogance, and rugged charm will make no difference to her plans of elopement.

Against his expectations and desires, Randall Blackmore has inherited a dukedom and a vast estate that only marriage to an heiress can save. Selling his title to the highest bidder is a wretched obligation, but to Randall's surprise his intended bride is pretty, courageous, delightfully impertinent—and completely uninterested in becoming a Duchess. Yet suddenly, no other woman will do, and a marriage in name only will never be enough for a husband determined to win his wife in body, heart, and soul . . .

"Miss Cummings. Is that you?"

She jerked her head up and took an extraordinarily short time to compose herself before walking toward him. From the tree.

"Would you care to stroll with me?" Rand asked.

"Actually, I'm getting a bit chilled and was going back inside," she said, and continued walking by him toward the house. He grabbed her arm firmly, ignoring her small cry of outrage, and steered her away from the house. Some girls might have screamed, but Elizabeth it seemed had been well-schooled on the art of not creating a scene.

"I'm so glad you've decided to join me." He looked down at her and she stared straight ahead. She was such a stalwart little thing, he nearly smiled.

"We had a beech tree like that in our garden growing up. Much larger, though. It was a wonderful place to hide. I imagine they were imported from Europe."

"I believe so," she said, her voice sounding strange.

"A perfect place for a tryst."

She stiffened next to him. "I wouldn't know."

"Wouldn't you," he said blandly.

"I want to go back inside now."

"That is too bad."

Her arm felt slim beneath his hand and he thought he felt the slightest trembling. Good. He wanted her afraid at this moment, he wanted her to feel as much discomfort as he had when he realized she was beneath that damned tree with Henry Ellsworth.

Finally, they reached the end of the lawn and stopped. She crossed her arms in front of her as if she were the affronted one.

"I do not want you seeing him again," he said, before he even realized what he was going to say.

"I don't know what you mean." Ah, she was getting her fire back. He smiled at her, which only made her frown more fiercely.

"Henry Ellsworth. The man you think you love."

She gasped and his smile widened.

"You are rude," she said, "How dare you imply—" She stopped and let out a breath, and he watched as myriad emotions crossed her features. Then, lifting her chin, the effect of which was ruined by the slight quivering there, she said, "Yes, we love each other. And you are keeping us apart."

"You cannot love him. You cannot love anyone you have not been with for more than ten minutes at a time. I am always amazed how quickly foolish girls fall in love."

"I am not foolish and I am not a girl. You cannot know what is in my heart, or his."

He stepped to her, their bodies only inches apart. They were so close, he could feel her panicked breath, coming out in short puffs, hitting his throat. "Have you been kissed?"

His question seemed to startle her. "I don't know how you mean."

"Tonight. Have you been kissed?" he ground out.

"Henry would never take such liberties. He is a gentleman," she said, lifting her head imperiously.

The relief he felt was staggering, and extremely disconcerting. "I'm very glad to hear it," he said. "Because I daresay I wouldn't want my mouth touching yours if you had."

With one quick motion, he pulled her to him, giving her perhaps two seconds to scream her protest before pressing his lips against hers. She kept her mouth shut tight, her body stiff against his as he moved his mouth gently against hers even as he held her relentlessly in his arms. "It doesn't matter whether you enjoy this or not," he said against her lips, feeling angry and perverse and jealous beyond measure. "Your friend beneath the tree is likely watching and cannot know you hate me. He did not steal a kiss and now he must watch you willingly kiss me." She gasped and he chuckled lightly.

"I do hate you," she said. "I will never willingly touch you. I will never willingly kiss you. You make my skin crawl."

Rand lifted a hand to her face, holding her so loosely she could easily have wrenched free. He moved a thumb along her full bottom lip and felt her tremble beneath him. "You're trembling," he said softly, mesmerized by the way her mouth felt beneath his thumb.

"I'm cold. And frightened."

He smiled, his eyes looking into hers. "Yes, you are," he said. "But not for the reasons you think." He stepped back, releasing her and thought for just a moment she might actually rear back and slap him, but she restrained herself. Frankly, he thought he deserved a good slap.

"You are cruel beyond measure," she said, her eyes darting to the beech tree and for a fleeting moment he actually felt sorry for her. Anger overcame that softer emotion almost immediately.

"You would be well to remember that should you ever think to speak to Mr. Ellsworth again I will make your life a living hell. I will not be made a fool. I will not." Rand forced a smile that wasn't truly a smile at all. "Shall we go back to the ball?"

Rand hated the way she looked at him but didn't know what else he could have done. Certainly he was not going to allow her to continue this fantasy that she could be with Mr. Ellsworth. He'd best secure her as his bride as soon as possible. This entire trip was not going at all like he expected, most surprising being his own reactions to her. He had never in his life threatened a woman and had anyone told him he would, he would have laughed. Even now, his words still ringing in his ears, he was slightly ashamed that he had sounded so cruel for he was not a cruel man. Make her life a living hell. Indeed. Other than marry her, he was unsure what he could do to make her more unhappy. He didn't know why the thought of her being kissed by another man drove him nearly mad, but it did. He wanted to force such weak thoughts from his head, he wanted to feel nothing for this girl.

And be sure to catch up with your favorite
characters from
A CHRISTMAS SCANDAL
and meet a sexy new couple in
Jane's next book,
coming in 2010!

Romantic Suspense from
Lisa Jackson

See How She Dies	0-8217-7605-3	$6.99US/$9.99CAN
Final Scream	0-8217-7712-2	$7.99US/$10.99CAN
Wishes	0-8217-6309-1	$5.99US/$7.99CAN
Whispers	0-8217-7603-7	$6.99US/$9.99CAN
Twice Kissed	0-8217-6038-6	$5.99US/$7.99CAN
Unspoken	0-8217-6402-0	$6.50US/$8.50CAN
If She Only Knew	0-8217-6708-9	$6.50US/$8.50CAN
Hot Blooded	0-8217-6841-7	$6.99US/$9.99CAN
Cold Blooded	0-8217-6934-0	$6.99US/$9.99CAN
The Night Before	0-8217-6936-7	$6.99US/$9.99CAN
The Morning After	0-8217-7295-3	$6.99US/$9.99CAN
Deep Freeze	0-8217-7296-1	$7.99US/$10.99CAN
Fatal Burn	0-8217-7577-4	$7.99US/$10.99CAN
Shiver	0-8217-7578-2	$7.99US/$10.99CAN
Most Likely to Die	0-8217-7576-6	$7.99US/$10.99CAN
Absolute Fear	0-8217-7936-2	$7.99US/$9.49CAN
Almost Dead	0-8217-7579-0	$7.99US/$10.99CAN
Lost Souls	0-8217-7938-9	$7.99US/$10.99CAN
Left to Die	1-4201-0276-1	$7.99US/$10.99CAN
Wicked Game	1-4201-0338-5	$7.99US/$9.99CAN
Malice	0-8217-7940-0	$7.99US/$9.49CAN

Available Wherever Books Are Sold!
Visit our website at **www.kensingtonbooks.com**

Thrilling Suspense from
Beverly Barton